THE COWBOY

and

The Bombshell

By
Dove Cavanaugh King

Pam

For the nights we
Can't Remember

Thanks
DCKing

KC.

Copyright

The Cowboy and The Bombshell

Cover Design: Haelah Rice Covers

Proofreaders: Eve R. Hart & Lighthand Proofreading

Dedication

To my husband and son,
who cheered for me every step of the way

To Emily,
who didn't complain when I
yammered on and on

To Shawn & Sandra,
the original Cowboy and Bombshell

And to every person who thinks that they could
someday maybe do that thing they have always wanted
to do.
Trust me.
You can.

The Cowboy and The Bombshell

CHAPTER ONE
Penelope

This was it. This was the day I had been working toward for the last seven years. Everything I had done, everything I had sacrificed, had been for this.

Everything I ever wanted was hanging in the balance of this one meeting. Nothing could go wrong today.

Nothing.

I studied myself in the polished steel doors of the elevator, checking again to make sure my outfit was perfect.

Pencil skirt just the right length to entice but not distract? Check.

Silk blouse in a beautiful royal blue to perfectly accentuate my eyes and just enough cleavage to hint at what remains hidden? Check.

Sky-high stilettos that were tall enough to ensure I would be crippled by the time I was fifty? Double check.

And last but not least, my blonde hair was pulled into a neat bun at the back of my neck, looking tidy but not matronly. I smiled at my reflection and

4

applied one last coat of shimmery rose-colored lip gloss. Today was my day. I could hardly contain my heart as it beat excitedly in my chest.

Watching the numbers on the digital display climb higher and higher, I thought back on everything I went through, every obstacle I faced to get here.

I started college straight after high school, jumping right in for the summer semester so I didn't waste any time. After struggling my way through the four year's worth of curriculum it normally takes to earn a Bachelors of Marketing at NYU and completing it all in only three, I immediately started my internship here at Pennington Hotels. Even though the one-year internship was unpaid, it was worth it to be able to secure a spot on the marketing team when my term was up.

For as long as I could remember, my one goal in life had been to work at a Pennington hotel. When I was a little girl, my parents both worked regular blue-collar jobs. My mother was a nurse and my father had been a dedicated member of the New York City Police Department. Growing up in Queens, it was easy to see the difference between the haves and the have-nots; all I had to do was look across the East River at the shining towers of Manhattan to see that, while I didn't want for much in my life, there were definitely people who wanted for absolutely nothing.

I didn't resent them; far from it. I simply noted the differences between us. While some people rode around in a shiny black town car driven by a man in a neatly pressed suit, my family didn't own a car at all, relying on New York transit to get wherever we needed to go. Some kids went shopping on Fifth Avenue for back to school clothes and left with more than they could ever wear, while my mother taught me how to bargain hunt at thrift shops and update and alter the clothes to make them cool again. Well, cooler anyway.

And while some families traveled to distant beaches or exotic cities for their vacations, my parents saved up every year so they could take me across the Queensboro Bridge on my birthday, where we would stay in a beautiful room at the Pennington Hotel.

It always felt magical, walking into that incredible lobby, with its high ceilings, gleaming marble floors, and gigantic chandeliers dripping with crystals. Like I was finally the princess I always dreamed I would be when I binge-watched Disney movies and drove my parents nuts by singing along at the top of my lungs. My parents would splurge on a park view room, allowing me to see all the way across Fifth Avenue, watching the sun glinting off the waters of The Lake. I would beg every year to go the Central Park Zoo where my parents would follow along patiently as I raced from exhibit to exhibit, loving the different animals that were housed there, always feeling like we were in the center of an enchanted forest. Then we would wander the park, eating from food trucks and taking in the street performers and families out enjoying the last few days of their summer vacation. In the evening, we would go out to dinner, wearing the nicest dresses my mother and I could find and alter, eating at the best restaurant we could afford. We tried a different place every year, but always got our dessert from a little shop that we swore only we knew about (ridiculous, I know, because there was no way our three slices of cheesecake a year were enough to support a business, but we liked to think we were special, if only for a day).

At night, I would stay up as late as I could, wrapped in a blanket and sitting at the window to watch as the late August sun would dip below the horizon across the park, painting the tree tops in liquid gold, the sky on fire with reds and yellows.

Needless to say, some of my best memories involved the Pennington Hotel.

I frowned slightly, remembering how long it had been since I had a birthday in Central Park. My heart clenched painfully as I thought of the reason those special trips had stopped.

I shook off the memories, both good and bad, as the elevator pinged my arrival at the penthouse level of the hotel, the very same hotel I spent all those birthdays in. The owner of the company, Mr. Harold Pennington himself, lived here permanently. After his divorce ten years ago, he had renovated the entire top floor, tucked away behind the copper topped towers that ringed the roof of the hotel, turning half into a private residence, the other half into the corporate headquarters. In my time at Pennington Hotels, I had never been called to this floor, but I had never been up for promotion to Vice President of Marketing before, either.

Stepping off the elevator, my heels clicking on the imported tiles, I walked into the foyer, noticing a small reception desk in the middle with two closed doors behind it, one on each side. Seeing the woman sitting at the desk cast a bored glance my way, I headed in her direction.

"Penelope Lund here to meet with Mr. Pennington," I said politely.

The woman arched a single well plucked eyebrow as she ran her gaze over my outfit. I could sense her silent disgust as she pursed her lips. The clothing I was so proud of just moments ago now felt like dirty rags under her scrutiny.

Looking down again, I noticed things I hadn't before. The buttons I'd sewn on multiple times because the blouse was too expensive to just replace. The skirt which I had hemmed by hand last night after finding it in the clearance section at the Bloomingdale's outlet; it had been marked way, way down, because it was two seasons old. And while my shoes *were* Kate Spade, upon closer inspection I could see the scuff marks I had tried to cover with felt marker when I picked them up at a charity shop in Brooklyn.

Not wanting to let her know that her judgment stung, I brightened my smile and dared her to actually say something.

She didn't.

She did, however, tilt her head ever so slightly, indicating a row of uncomfortable looking chairs. I assumed she wanted me to sit there, so I did, crossing my legs and bouncing the top one rapidly, as I tended to do when I was nervous. My confidence was a bit shook, thanks to the silent fashionista over there, but I took a few centering breaths, remembering all the reasons why I was the best choice for VP.

My grades at NYU were impeccable, the reference letters from my professors glowing. My time at Pennington Hotels had been well spent, quickly rising from a junior consultant, to project leader, to department head. My specialties were social media and digital marketing, as well as brand expansion. I was a key player last year when Pennington Hotels added a line of boutique rental cottages along the Jersey Shore.

There was no way they could turn me down. I had this position in the freaking bag!

At least I thought I did. That was until the door to the private residence across the foyer opened and out walked a man and a woman I knew all too well.

Constance Pennington-Grover and her husband, Toddrick. Constance detested when anyone referred to him as just plain old Todd.

Constance was Harold Pennington's oldest daughter, and while not an official employee of Pennington Hotels, she was a face I saw on an almost daily basis. Firstly, because of her father, and secondly because her husband, Toddrick, also worked in the marketing department.

Toddrick was the bane of my existence. He was a pale, doughy man with no chin and watery blue eyes. He felt, as the son-in-law of the CEO, that it was his place to tell everyone in the department what to do, even though he had the worst track record of any employee. His ideas were all either completely idiotic, not financially feasible, or a blatant copy of another company's work. He did nothing but drag the department down, then tried to blame anyone but himself when his projects failed miserably.

I also suspected he had a bit of a coke habit, if his constant sniffing was anything to go by.

Constance, on the other hand, was the quintessential picture of uptown New York elegance. She was tall and slender and she never had a single item of this season's most sought after clothing out of place; no clearance racks for Constance Pennington-Grover. Her brown hair, so dark it almost looked black, was cut into a severe bob so that it angled perfectly with her sharp cheekbones. Her nose was slender, but not naturally so, and the same plastic surgeon who had reduced it had also given her a pair of obviously fake breasts that would defy gravity until the end of time. She was thirty-two but continued to tell people she was twenty-nine.

And she was an absolute bitch.

Walking over to the woman at the desk, Constance leaned down and delivered air kisses to both her cheeks. "Lovely to see you, darling," she simpered, sounding about as genuine as a used car salesman. "We should get lunch later this week." The woman smiled thinly, then turned her attention to me, causing Constance to turn my way as well.

Her gaze found me almost immediately, her eyes narrowing when she saw me sitting there, bouncing my foot. There was a second where I thought she was going to say something, as her eyes took on an evil glint, but before she could open her mouth, Harold Pennington himself appeared, opening the boardroom door with a flourish. Constance immediately dropped the calculating look on her face and replaced it with a fake smile.

Toddrick never even looked up from his phone. He trailed after Constance as she moved quickly to intercept her father before he could address me.

"Hello, father," she said, all sugar-sweet and giggly, like she was still eight years old. Gag me.

"Connie, I didn't expect to see you here. I have a meeting-"

She didn't let him finish. "I know, father, but I thought it would be best to come now, with Toddrick, and just get the whole thing over with, don't you agree?" She attempted to pout, but her over filled lips barely moved.

"Well, Connie, I don't really think it's appropriate to-" he looked at me, worry lining his already wrinkled face.

Harold Pennington was an old man. At seventy-four years old, he was still overseeing all the aspects pertaining to being CEO of the company he inherited from his own father. The word around the water cooler was that he was hoping to pass the Pennington Hotels to one of his children. But while Constance excelled at being a manipulative trophy wife, she had yet to convince her father that Toddrick would be a suitable replacement. Her younger sister, Daphne, was only twenty-one, and still in school out in Nevada. She was a bit of a wild child, or so I'd heard, and it was unlikely that she would choose to take on such a huge responsibility any time soon.

There were rumors that Harold had fathered a son before he married Constance's mother, but no one had ever laid eyes on him, so it was all just speculation.

"Oh, father, don't you think it's best if she finds out now? You know, like taking off a band-aid." That malicious glint was back in Constance's eye as she turned her head to level me with a glare. Her eyebrows would have furrowed if they hadn't been so full of Botox.

Wait. What was she saying? The conniving look on her face brought me up short. She couldn't be talking about me, cold she? What could Constance possibly have to do with my meeting for VP?

But as my gaze moved past her to the fleshy lump in a wrinkled suit she was married to, I knew exactly what made her so supremely happy.

Toddrick was going to be taking my promotion away from me.

I could feel the sweat beading on my back, starting to make my silk blouse stick to my shoulder blades. This could not be happening. I had worked too damn hard to lose this opportunity to a trust fund baby whose only goal was to unite his nostrils. I refused to go out like this.

But as Harold stood there, glancing uneasily between his daughter and me, I knew there was no hope for me. Toddrick was in, and I was out.

"Miss Lund, please, won't you come in?" Harold gestured to the door he had just come through, and I started toward the conference room. Just before I reached the door, Constance stepped forward and cut me off, determined to enter the room before me, juvenile thing that she was. As Harold followed us into the room, he placed himself at the head of the long table, Constance taking the seat to his right, gritting her teeth at her husband as he plodded in last. She pointed to the seat on Harold's left, which Toddrick eventually slouched himself into, still more interested in his phone than the nuclear bomb he and his wife had just dropped on my life plan.

With the three seats at that end going to Harold and his minions, I was left with no choice but to find myself a seat farther along the table. I chose to sit on the same side as Constance, but three chairs away so that I wouldn't be forced to look at her face and see her reveling in my misery.

"Now then," Harold began, still looking uncomfortable. "Miss Lund, as you know, a position has recently opened up for Vice President of Marketing for Pennington Hotels. This position would oversee all departments for all regions in our North American branch of the company. Your track record has been stellar in the short time you have worked for us. I must say, the board and I are all very impressed with your work."

"Thank you, Mr. Pennington," I said, trying to keep my heart under control. No matter how high his praise, I wouldn't allow myself to get my hopes up, not with the Wicked Witch of Central Park West sitting here, sniffing the waters for my blood like a shark. "I take great pride in working for Pennington Hotels." Such few words to convey the depth of what this company actually meant to me, but I choked on any words I may have used to elaborate.

"And we appreciate that," Harold said with a smile that reminded me of my grandfather, warm and friendly. It was cut short, however, when Constance not-so-discreetly cleared her throat. Harold glanced at her, then at Toddrick, releasing a deep sigh before continuing. "However, at this time you are not the only candidate vying for the Vice President position." Harold leveled a pointed glance at Toddrick, who was still ignoring the entire conversation in favor of whatever he was doing on his phone. "It is very important that we make the right choice." He swung his gaze to Constance, but she simply scoffed at him. "The company can't afford to gamble on..." he said, trailing off to look at the wall over my head. I was worried he was having a senior moment, drifting off into his own world, but then his eyes snapped back to mine. "Yes, exactly."

Constance glanced at me, then at the wall behind us, trying to see what her father was looking at. Toddrick sniffed, not looking at anything.

"What, exactly, father?" she asked, losing a bit of her own calm, as if she sensed that things may not completely go her way for once.

"Gamble. Casinos. That's what we'll do." He clapped his hands, suddenly very excited. I bit my tongue, waiting to see what had made him so very happy about the situation that would literally ruin my life. "Miss Lund, how do you feel about a little friendly competition?"

"Um," I said, caught off guard when he addressed me so suddenly. "I, uh, welcome the challenge." I didn't quite make it sound like a question, but it was close.

"Excellent. This is what we will do then. Pennington Hotels is getting ready to launch into the casino business. Namely, we are opening two casino hotels, one in Las Vegas and one in Atlantic City. Since it has become so...difficult to choose between you and Toddrick for the Vice President position, we will have a little contest, a duel of sorts. Both you and Toddrick will spearhead a launch for one of the new locations. I'm talking entirely new campaigns, from the ground up. We want social media, grand opening parties, galas, celebrity appearances, the whole thing."

Was this really happening? I had led my own campaigns before, but nothing of this scale. I was already compiling ideas in my head. Sleek and classy, The Pennington Hotel would showcase the very best that Las Vegas could offer. It would be like Sex and the City meets Vegas Showgirl. This could work. I could still earn this position, and it would have nothing to do with nepotism.

"Father, do you really think this is the way to go?" Constance was clasping her hands on the table in front of her, knuckles white, likely to keep herself from clawing my eyes out. I smiled at her, my grin stretching from ear to ear.

There was no way Toddrick would run a better

campaign than I would. The man was two cards short of a full deck. I huffed out a laugh at my own casino reference.

"Yes, Connie, I absolutely do."

"Father, the board will never go for this."

"You let me handle the board. Now, do you have any reason why you can't participate, Toddrick?"

We all looked at him, waiting for a full fifteen seconds before he finally finished what he was looking at and raised his head. His red rimmed eyes blinked at his wife, then he slowly turned to look at Harold. "You said Vegas, right?" He actually looked excited about the prospect, though likely not for the same reasons I was.

"No," Constance cut in. "You can't go to Las Vegas. I need you closer to home. You will run the Atlantic City campaign. I am chairing the gala fundraiser for the animal shelter in a few weeks, and another for the Save the Seas Fund shortly after that. I won't have you halfway across the country and unable to attend my benefits. The animals need our support, Toddrick."

Please. The only animals Constance cared about were the ones used to make her shoes.

Toddrick deflated a little, then shrugged and went back to his phone with another sniff. I could practically hear Constance grinding her teeth.

"Well, then," Harold said, standing and moving toward the door. "I will have the packages and guidelines drawn up by the legal department by the end of the week. You will each have four months to complete your campaign. Whoever has the best launch will become the new Vice President of Marketing for Pennington Hotels." I beamed at him, matching his warm smile with one of my own this time.

"Pack your bags, Miss Lund. You're going to Las Vegas."

CHAPTER TWO

Penelope

"You're going to Las Vegas?"

My mother stared at me in shock. Really, she had every right to be surprised. I hadn't ever been away from the east coast, barely venturing farther west than the Pennsylvania border. Honestly, it was as shocking to me as it was to her. Not to mention a little bit overwhelming.

I sat at the kitchen table in our small townhouse in Woodside, Queens, the same one we had lived in for my entire life. My parents purchased it shortly after they were married, because of its close proximity to the Woodside Community School, and they had never left. My mom hadn't even considered moving when we lost dad. Even now, after everything, my mother was still happier living here, saying that it was the place that held her best memories.

That was one of the reasons I still lived with her. Aside from the fact that real estate in New York was astronomically out of reach for just about everyone, mom and I shared the bills on this place. It was only a twenty-minute ride on the train to get to work, and a

18

thirty-minute walk for mom to get to her job at Mount Sinai hospital. If the weather was bad, she took the bus, but she tried to walk as often as she could because she said it was good for her heart.

"It's only going to be for four months, Mom, and I'll still pay my share of the bills while I'm gone."

She waved me off. "You know that's not what I'm worried about."

But she was, even though she'd never admit it.

When dad got sick, the bills were coming in fast. They piled up and before we knew it, mom was taking a second mortgage out on the house. It kept on that way and when dad died just after I turned eleven, we were drowning. Mom had taken so much time off her own job to care for him that we were barely able to keep the lights on. I had no idea at the time because I wasn't old enough to understand the true significance of what was happening; I just knew that mom spent her nights crying in her room, and that we were eating more and more ramen noodles.

By the time I graduated high school I was working an after-school job and a weekend job. I somehow still managed to pull down excellent grades, likely due to my complete lack of social life, and I earned a full ride scholarship to NYU. Mom was elated and told me how proud she was of me, but I could see the relief flood her system when that acceptance letter came in the mail.

Again, I didn't mind. Mom and I were a team. She would never have left me to fight on my own, so there was no way I was ever going to leave her. That was why I still lived at home. Even if I could afford a place of my own, I knew my mom needed me, and I would never let her down.

"It will be worth it in the end, Mom. I'll earn the VP position and start making enough money to really make a dent in things." The amount of medical bills we were still trying to pay off was insane. Fifteen years after his death, and we still hadn't gotten very far. There were over one hundred million people in this country in the same boat we were, paying bills for a person who had long since passed away, or avoiding seeking medical treatment because they simply couldn't afford it. It was criminal, really.

That was why I couldn't let Toddrick and Constance mess this up for me. We needed the money to get out from under the black cloud that had been following us for the last fifteen years. I wanted to be able to help my mom retire, or at least reduce her hours. She deserved a break and I wanted to give one to her, Toddrick be damned.

"When do you have to leave?" she asked, already moving from worry mode to planning mode. She would work with me to get packed, ensuring I had everything I would need to make a good impression and do my job well.

"The contracts were presented and signed today," I said. "My flight is Monday morning." I had waited to tell her what was going on until I could be certain that it was really happening. Harold had again called me up to his private penthouse boardroom this afternoon, along with Toddrick and his ever-present shadow, Constance. We had gone over the terms and conditions of the challenge, reviewing budget constraints and staffing. Both hotels were currently under construction, their designs were each different, but top secret and awaiting the new marketing campaigns for the big reveals. We wouldn't even know what we were working with until we arrived on site.

After the contracts had all been signed and everything was official, Harold pulled me aside and informed me that he would like me to stay at his personal home in a community on the far west side of Las Vegas called Summerlin South.

"Really, Mr. Pennington, that's a very generous offer, but not necessary. I'd be happy to stay in one of the rooms at the hotel."

"Please, Miss Lund. I insist. None of the rooms at the Las Vegas property are ready to be lived in, and I just can't stomach the thought of giving money to any of our competitors until they are." He wiggled his eyebrows at me.

"Well," I said laughing. *"In the name of supporting Pennington Hotels, then I guess I accept."*

"Good. Good," he replied, then paused. *"There is one more thing. You will have a roommate in Summerlin, if that's not too much trouble."*

"Oh," I said cautiously. *"Who?"*

"Oh, just my kid," he said with a wave. *"Nothing to worry about, truly. The house is quite large. Eight bedrooms. You two probably won't even notice each other."*

It made sense, I guessed, with Daphne going to school in Nevada, that she would be making use of her family home in the area.   I remembered seeing what the dorm rooms looked like on campus when I was in school.   I would have spent as much time in a mansion as I could have, too.

Plus, it might be nice to not be alone.   If Daphne was familiar with the area, perhaps she and I could hang out a time or two.

"That will be no problem, Mr. Pennington.   No problem at all."

So now I sat, looking into my mother's watery eyes as she processed the fact that we had just over forty-eight hours left together before I would be traveling half way across the country.   It would be my first time on a plane, and the first time I had been away from my mother for longer than a sleepover in my entire life.

Some may have seen that as pathetic, but mom and I shared such a close bond that it was completely natural for us.   We had needed to lean on each other so heavily in the past that it almost seemed like we were joined at the hip.

"Okay.   Monday.   Of course," she said, putting on a brave face.   "Then I guess we had better get started."

We spent all of Friday night doing laundry, washing what meager work clothes I owned, and then most of Saturday was spent on our mending and alterations.   Mom and I almost always had a pile of clothes waiting for a bit of inspiration.   We were chronic thrift shop junkies, stopping in at our favorites on a regular basis to scour the bins for treasures.   I liked to stop at a few in the city when I could as well.

There were often designer pieces to be found if you looked hard enough. Some rich lady who couldn't imagine wearing a blazer for longer than a single season, or some boots that were must-haves last year, but were quickly forgotten in the whirlwind that was the New York Fashion scene. It benefited me well enough.

Mom made my favorite dish for dinner, lasagna, and we sat side by side on the couch, stuffing our faces and watching The Bachelor while we added embellishments to a power suit mom had brought home after Christmas. We guessed someone had gotten a new one from Santa, so this one, practically new, was up for grabs. Mom was patiently stitching some delicate lace around the hem of the skirt, trying to add a little modesty for my overly-long legs.

At a commercial break, I worked up the nerve to say the thing that had been on my mind since Friday afternoon.

"I'm going to see Dad tomorrow," I said quietly, watching my mother's breath stall in her chest. "I want to make sure I say goodbye."

Putting down her sewing, she reached over and squeezed my hand. "I think he'd like that very much."

Sunday morning mom went to church as usual. I hadn't joined her in a very long time, and while at first she was upset by that, she now understood that I couldn't bring myself to talk to a god who had let the things that happened to my dad, and so many others, continue.

Wearing an over-sized hoodie, my hands stuffed

deep in the front pockets, and a knit hat to protect against the biting winter wind, I walked slowly between the rows of headstones at St. Michael's Cemetery, taking my time, savoring the quiet. The snow had been cleared from the roadways but was still several inches deep at the grave sites. Making my way to where I knew my father was laid to rest, my eyes ran over the names on the other grave-markers, familiar to me after so many days spent here since dad had died. As I walked the same road the funeral procession had followed that day, dozens of my father's uniformed colleagues from the NYPD following behind my mother and me, I could see it all again in my head. Row upon row of men and women, their dress uniforms pressed to perfection, the white gloves on their hands standing out in stark relief against the dark blue they each wore. The flag draped coffin being carried by six of my dad's closest friends from the department. The flag they folded so very carefully before handing it to my mom. But most of all I remember the silence. The absolute and soul crushing silence that hung over the cemetery as they lowered my father into the ground.

That same silence hung over me now, the low gray sky of winter hovering like an oppressive blanket, pressing against the snow covered ground, making me feel as if that pressure was a physical thing, constricting my lungs and making it hard to breathe. I clutched my hands into fists in my hoodie pockets, feeling my nails pressing crescents into my palms, the slight pain grounding me and bringing me back to the moment.

When I reached the appropriate row, I stepped

off the road and into the snow, lifting my booted feet high over the drifts as I made my way to my father. Stopping in front of his grave, the dark granite looking harsh against the fresh white show, I closed my eyes as my heart squeezed in my chest. Taking a deep breath, I opened my eyes again and smiled down at his name, Frederick Lund.

"Hi, Daddy," I said, swiping at the single tear that moved down my cheek. "How are things? Mom and I are good, but you probably already know that." I knelt down in the snow, heedless of the cold that started soaking into my jeans, and used my hands to clear some of the snow away from his marker. I dug down until I could see the engraved shield with his badge number on it in the lower left corner. "I've got some big things happening right now work wise," I continued, carrying on a one-sided conversation as I always did, talking to him as if he was right here with me. I liked to think he might be. I went on for some time, talking about the competition, the position, and how Toddrick and Constance were standing in my way. "Oh, Dad, she is simply awful. Exactly how you'd expect her to be. I know. I know," I said, already hearing my father's voice in my head, telling me not to be so judgmental, that everyone had their own obstacles to face, and that maybe Constance was struggling just like the rest of us. "But she makes it so hard to try to be understanding, dad. She's like a lemon in a basket of peaches. Sour for the sake of being sour."

I laughed, thinking of how my dad would have made a face, pretending he was sucking a lemon, and how, in my head, it looked a lot like the pinched look Constance had given me the other day. Taking a breath, I continued. "I really want this, Daddy. I want this so bad. For Mom, of course, but for myself, too. I want to prove that I can, you know? That all my hard work, all my studying and sacrificing and effort actually means something. That my struggle can count for something against people like Toddrick, who get ahead, not because they earned it, but because they are related to the right people. It has to count, Daddy. Other wise, what were all our sacrifices for?"

I was quiet for a time, thinking of all the hours mom and I worked, all the pennies we saved, trying to keep our heads above water. There was absolutely no way I could let someone like Constance, who had never had to go without a day in her life, take this from me simply because she felt she could.

"Anyway," I continued, shaking off my heavy thoughts. "I have to leave town for a bit, so I won't be by to visit. But look after Mom while I'm away, okay? Don't let her feel lonely. I think, I mean I hope, that she will use this time to do some things for herself for a change. She deserves it."

Standing, I brushed the snow off my now very damp knees. Running my fingers along the top of the gravestone one more time, I kissed their tips and pressed them to his name. "Love you, Daddy. Always."

*   *   *   *

26

Monday morning arrived in a flurry of chaos. I was supposed to be at the hotel in Las Vegas for a project meeting at two, Nevada time. Harold's silent receptionist, who I had learned went by the predictably insufferable name of Angelique, had emailed me my flight information. I was on a six a.m. flight out of JFK, which meant that my alarm was set to go off at three a.m. So when my door flew open at a quarter to four, my mother flying in wearing her house coat and shrieking about me being late, I was in complete panic mode.

Skipping my preferred scalding hot morning shower in favor of a quick face wash and an extra swipe of deodorant, I slid into my best skinny jeans and a white button-up blouse, hurrying through my usual routine at warp speed. Forgoing make up and slapping on a layer of chap stick, I tossed my hair back into my usual bun and raced out of my room to find my mother near the door where she was arranging my suitcase and carry-on bag for me.

"I had hoped we would have time for a coffee before you had to go, but when has our life ever gone how we planned, hey my girl?" she said with a wry smile. I reached out and wrapped my arms around her, squeezing for all I was worth. "You go kick some serious butt, okay, Penelope? You got this in the bag!"

"Thanks, Mom. I'll call you every day, I promise."

"Oh, pish posh," she said, surreptitiously wiping her eyes. "You will do no such thing. This is an incredible opportunity for you, Penelope. I want you to live it up out there in Sin City! Go to a club. See a show. Maybe even meet a man."

"Mom, no," I said, rolling my eyes. I had spent next to no time worried about boys in school, and even less since I had started working. I'd had boyfriends, of course, but nothing that I would qualify as a serious relationship. When your whole life was spent with a single goal in mind, namely staying out of bankruptcy, there was no space left to think of things as trivial as dating. "I will not be wasting any time on…that!"

"*That* is love, Penelope. *That* is something you won't even realize you are missing until you find it. Don't be so quick to dismiss its importance."

I watched as her eyes lightened, getting a far away look I recognized as the one she wore when she thought of my dad. Blinking, she looked back at me with a soft smile. "Just do me a favor and keep your eyes and your heart open, okay? For me?"

I hugged her again. "I will, Mom. I promise." I stepped back, moving to pick up my carry-on bag, when my mom gasped.

"Oh, shoot! I almost forgot. Wait. Just wait one minute." She dashed off back to her bedroom, leaving me standing at the open front door at four-thirty in the morning. She was back only moments later with a wrapped box in her hands.

"Mom, what is this? You shouldn't have done this." We didn't have the extra funds for gifts.

"I didn't do it alone. All the nurses from the hospital pitched in. You know how much those gals love you."

My mom had worked as a pediatric nurse at Mount Sinai hospital for almost thirty years. Her friends and coworkers there had been instrumental in our lives when things got rough. They were over almost every day while dad was sick, bringing food, helping with the chores and washing so mom and I could spend as much time focused on dad as possible. When he passed, they circled around us, lifting us up and helping us through. They were all like aunts and uncles to me, and I loved them very much. "Now, hurry, you don't have much time."

Grinning like a loon, I peeled back the paper, revealing a box with words on it that I couldn't bring myself to comprehend. Looking up at mom with huge eyes, she was smiling for all she was worth as tears poured down her face.

Removing the lid, I carefully withdrew the most glorious pair of magenta pink suede Jimmy Choo pumps I had ever seen. I remembered the day mom and I had first spotted them in the window of the Jimmy Choo store on Madison Avenue. We were window shopping, our favorite pastime, when the gorgeous shoes had caught my eye. I stared like a kid at a pet store, my face pressed up against the glass, admiring the stunning works of art that were those shoes, until mom tugged me away by my elbow. The fact that I was now holding these shoes was beyond belief.

"Mom, this is too much," I said, now remembering the price tag that came with the beautiful shoes. "Really. I can't."

"You can and you will. All the ladies helped. Bernice had her daughter go over and pick them up yesterday. They said the first rule of getting a promotion is dressing the part. These shoes will help you get there in style. You will do the rest."

My heart felt like it was going to explode. How could I possibly be away from Queens for four months? How could I leave my mom, my biggest cheerleader, here while I went to partake in this ridiculous contest? Not to mention the countless people around us who showered us with love. My whole life was here in Queens. I wasn't prepared to give them up. Any of them.

"Penelope," my mom said, rubbing my arms as my heart fluttered out of control. "You are going to be fine. I am going to be fine. This is just another adventure for our memory books. I will see you in four months. You will be the Vice President of Marketing for Pennington Hotels, and everything is going to be great. Believe me. I'm a mom. I know these things, you know?"

So, for hopefully the last time today, I wiped my tears, tucked my incredible shoes into my suitcase, hugged my mother - again - and set off on my first big adventure.

I mean, how bad could it possibly be, right?

CHAPTER THREE

Stone

The sun had barely crested the horizon and I was already returning to the barn at the end of a ride. My horse, McNally, was being extra surly because I had hauled him out of his warm stall and made him drag my ass around in the dark.

Rising early was a way of life for me here on the ranch, but today I was up even earlier. Hell, I had hardly slept to begin with. I was too damned pissed off to get much rest. Ever since that phone call from Harold, I had been a pressure cooker of anger, just waiting for someone to snap at. I figured a ride out to the back quarter all alone might take some of the edge off before I had to catch my flight. I certainly didn't need some TSA agent getting in my face. I'd be liable to end up in cuffs at this rate.

As I walked McNally back to his stall and began the process of unsaddling him and rubbing him down, I thought about why I was so damn angry in the first place.

A phone call from Harold Pennington was never a pleasant experience. They were even less pleasant when he was calling to ask things of me. Three days ago he called with the biggest ask yet. I had wanted to turn him down. I really did. His motivations were always suspect, and I didn't trust the man as far as I could throw him.

Which was saying something, because Harold Pennington was my father.

At least, biologically.

As far as the rest of being a father went, the man was sorely lacking.

Harold Pennington had come to Austin almost thirty-four years ago to open a new Pennington Hotels property, a luxury spa retreat on the outskirts of town. He was looking to cater to all the newly wealthy oilman's wives. You know, the type that will spend hundreds of dollars to paint their faces in some exotic mud flown in from a riverbed in north Africa. As a part of the launch, he was overseeing the hiring and training of all the new staff, which included a beautiful young woman in housekeeping, Eleanor Montgomery. My mother.

She was twenty-one years younger than him, but that didn't matter to him in the least. She was taken with his big city ways, I guess, and she fell for all his lines.

When the launch was complete he left her behind. Took off back to New York City like a thief in the night and didn't look back for over four years. Needless to say, he was shocked to come back to the hotel and see three-year-old me wandering around the staff room. I did spend a lot of time there with my mother, and when I wasn't at the Spa, I was with my grandparents on their ranch, riding and climbing trees, and scraping my knees. It was great. A perfect Texas childhood.

My mother had never gotten over Harold, never moved on with another man, always holding out hope that Harold would come back for us. So, when he showed back up in Austin, she got her heart broken again when she learned that in the intervening time, Harold had gone and gotten himself married. Some fancy rich lady from Manhattan who would never lower herself to looking after her own child, which she proved with the army of nannies and maids she kept in their penthouse apartment to take care of her own new infant.

When Harold learned about me, he immediately tried to throw money at the situation. He offered to put mom and me up in a fancy house so she didn't have to work anymore. Mom turned him down, saying she liked living at her parent's ranch, and that she was proud of her work at the spa. She had worked her way up from chambermaid to housekeeping manager, and her staff and the guests all loved her. She was happy with the way things were.

Harold came though town a few times a year after that, always trying to be a dad, always just managing to make our relationship even more uncomfortable. Every time he would leave again, I had to watch the hope in my mother's eyes die a little more.

By the time I was fifteen Harold had divorced

his wife. For a while I thought maybe this would finally be the time he came for us. The time he took the heart my mother had offered him over and over again and treated it with care.

But once again he disappointed me. He and his other kids, my younger half-sisters, stayed in Manhattan, living the high life, while my mother continued to work her way up within the Austin Spa.

When I graduated high school, she sat me down and asked what I wanted to do. Having grown up following her around at her job, I had long decided that hotel management was where I wanted to work. I had applied for several schools, and even received a few scholarships, though I would have to work hard to earn enough money to make up the difference.

That was when my mother told me that Harold had offered to cover my college expenses. I tried to refuse, saying that we hadn't needed him before, I damn sure wasn't going to start taking his money now. She let me storm around a bit, blowing my top as I always did, then reminded me that regardless of how I felt, Harold was my father, and had always tried to do right by me in the best way he could.

My mother was a friggin' saint. She put her own hurt aside every time.

So, in the end, I accepted, more for her sake than my own. Harold tried everything to get me to attend school at Cornell, but there was no way I was ever stepping foot in New York. That state had taken enough from my mother, I wasn't going to let it take her son, too.

So we compromised. I would let him pay if he let me choose a school in Texas. In the end, I got my degree in Hospitality Management at the University of Texas at San Antonio. I got the degree I wanted and I was less than two hours from home.

When I finished school, Harold offered me a job. I turned him down. I didn't want any more hand outs. But once again, my mother intervened. She encouraged me to take a position with Pennington Hotels, saying that it would be good for me to get to know my father more, to understand that side of myself and where I came from.

"You are more than just a cowboy, baby," she'd say to me every time I claimed that my New York blood didn't exist. So, when she pressed, I relented. And when I was twenty-three years old, I took a job at Pennington Hotels. Much to my fathers' displeasure, I insisted on using my mothers last name, Montgomery. I didn't want anyone thinking I hadn't earned my place.

I started at the Dallas location as the night manager. Then moved up to food and beverage manager, and finally on to general manager. At that point, Harold started to offer me promotions personally, but they were all at the head office in New York. I kept turning him down. Even stopped taking his calls for a while, until he reminded me that even if I didn't want to talk to my father, he was still my CEO.

I had spent the last few years as the regional manager for Pennington Hotels southwest division. I covered territory from Texas to California and all the states in between. It was a good place for me, and I had been happy. I thought we had settled this, until Harold came calling again.

"It's an incredible opportunity, son," he said, knowing I hated it when he called me that, but doing it anyway. "Pennington Hotels is branching out in to Casinos. I want to take the Las Vegas Strip by storm, and with you at the helm, we'll have a much better shot at doing just that."

I ground my teeth. The bastard knew this was an opportunity I would love to take. I just hated that he was the one to give it to me. I hated taking anything from him. I didn't need him, no matter what my mother thought.

"It will only be a four month stay in Nevada. You'll oversee the completion of the project. We have a top-secret theme that I personally picked. I think you'll love it. You will have final say in all the details. I'm sending someone from marketing out as well, so you will have someone completely devoted to this project exclusively. You will stage a few massive launch events, and then you can go back to Austin. Easy."

Truth be told, it sounded fantastic. Really getting to sink my project and put my own stamp on the finished product. Let everything I've learned in the last nine years come into play and really make a name for myself. I could maybe even use this project to pad my resume enough that I could leave Pennington altogether. Get a position with a company *not* run by the man who broke my mother's heart. All I had to do was give up four months. It couldn't be that hard.

Finishing with McNally's care, I popped a few

sugar cubes in my palm from the box I kept in the tack room to try and get back on his good side. I hate to leave him this way, on bad terms, as it were, but I had to catch that flight. McNally looked at my hand skeptically, ears back to show me his displeasure.

"I know, old man, and I'm sorry," I muttered, rubbing my other hand down his nose. "You know as well as I do that I'd rather stay here. But ma wants me to go. I've never been good at saying no to her." McNally gave a whinny and, if I didn't know any better, I'd think he was laughing at me. Dipping his head, he took the sugar cubes, letting me know we had reached a truce. "That's my boy. You hold a grudge like no one else, you know that?" He leaned forward and pressed his head into my chest. "I know. I'll miss you too. But you have to look out for Ma for me, alright? Keep an eye on things? Can you do that?" McNally gave another soft wicker and huffed out a breath in my face before retreating back into his stall and digging into his breakfast of hay and oats. "Thanks, my man. I'll be back before you know it."

Walking back across the gravel drive between the house and the barn, I paused and glanced around at the spread that belonged to my grandparents. What was a large and prosperous cattle ranch covering several thousand acres had been reduced to just a small parcel. My grandfather, Earl Montgomery, inherited the land from his father and worked it as a cattle ranch for a few decades. He and my grandmother, Sophie, had hoped for several sons to help work the land and pass the property on to, but after my mother was born, they were never lucky enough to conceive more children. That, combined with the rise of corporate farming and ranching, made it hard to continue on as things had been, so Earl was forced to sell off more and more of the property. By the time he passed, the land he did keep was all being rented out to neighboring ranchers for their stock. The only parts my mom still used were the house, the small garden behind it, and the barn, and only because I kept McNally. He was probably lonely, being the only resident, but he had plenty of space to roam, and mom visited him every day, even if she didn't ride anymore.

I tried to spend as much time out here as I could, but work was keeping me in the city more and more. Mom had retired from the Spa a while back, and I only kept a small place in Austin so that I could help out here with chores and maintenance and the like.

The sprawl of the Austin city limits was creeping closer and closer to our spot, but it still didn't sit well with me, leaving mom alone out here for four months.

In the distance, down the long gravel drive that ran to the highway, a pair of headlights turned my way, their mellow beams shining in the growing dawn light. Recognizing the truck immediately, I waited near the porch steps as it worked its way toward the house and parked beside my own vehicle.

"Didn't expect to see you here this morning," I said reaching for the outstretched hand of my best friend, Silas Harrison. Friends since middle school, Silas was the closest thing to a brother I had ever had.

"Don't even go there," he said, drawing me into an embrace, our hands clasped between us, and rapping on my back with enough force to knock the wind out of me.   Silas was a big dude; even his gentle hurt a bit.   "You know you're the one who can't roll his ass out of bed in the mornings.   I wanted to come and make sure you were even awake.   Didn't want you to miss your plane.   I know how eager you are to please dear old Dad."

He said it in jest, knowing exactly how I felt about Harold, but it still made my hackles rise.   "Cut that shit out," I said, stuffing my hands in the pocked of my jeans.   "You know the only reason I'm even doing this is for Ma.   Why that woman has to push him and I together, I'll never know.   She should hate him after all he's put her through."

"Your ma could never hate anyone, and you know it."   Silas had spent as much time at our place as he did his own.   He had two older brothers and their own spread was small compared to some of the other properties around the area, so he had more freedom to come and go than most of the other ranch kids we knew.   My grandfather was done working his place actively by then, so Silas and I were free to roam, finding all sorts of mischief to get up to.   "Seems to me like she's just trying to do right by you, let you get to know your old man before it's too late.   I think she just doesn't want you to have any regrets, is all."

I grumbled out a noncommittal noise because I refused to let the bastard know I thought he might be right.   I knew my ma always had my best interests at heart, but it didn't make it any easier to look past the way Harold had treated her. She deserved better from him.

Making our way up the porch and into the house, we both stopped just inside the doors, each taking a big inhale of the delicious aromas wafting out from the house. "Oh, man. I do love when your mama cooks," Silas said, a huge grin spreading across his face as he pushed past me and headed for the kitchen. I followed behind, watching as he gathered mom up in a huge hug, spinning her around.

"Silas Harrison, you put me down right this minute! The eggs will burn."

"Miss Ellie, your cooking is so good, I'd eat them even if they were burnt."

I scoffed. "Kiss ass."

"Stone! You mind your language in my house, now," my mom admonished, turning a scowl my way.

"Yes, ma'am," I said, leaning in to press a kiss to her cheek.

"You boys wash up, I have enough for you both."

Silas and I moved to the sink, then took our places at the table, already spread with toast and bacon, pancakes and an assortment of homemade jams and preserves. We began to load up our plates, filling them to the brim as we always had. Mom brought the skillet from the stove and placed a couple fried eggs on top of everything, then dished a small plate for herself before joining us at the table.

"Silas will be by to check on you in a few days,

ma, before he flies out to join me in Las Vegas."

Silas was not only my best friend, he was also a security specialist and I hired him for all the properties I was responsible for.

After high school, when I went off to San Antonio for university, Silas had enlisted in the Army, then went on to join the Army Rangers. He didn't talk a lot about his time as a Ranger, but I knew some shit went down that haunted him. He worked real hard at being the same guy I knew growing up, but I could see when he was in a dark place. His eyes weren't the same, growing shadowed and distant when the memories were nipping at his heels, but he never let it keep him down for long.

"You know I don't need to be babysat, boys," my mom interjected.

"I know that, Ma, but it's for my own peace of mind. Once Si comes out to Nevada, I'll have one of the Berkshire boys come by a few times a week to look after McNally and ensure everything is running smoothly."

"Stone, really, I will be okay."

"I know you will, Ma. But I'm paying the boys to keep up things around here, so let them do their jobs, alright? You can even feed them, if it makes you feel better about it."

She smiled at me, and knowing how much she loved to bake, I figured those Berkshire boys would be happy as pigs in mud to come here and load up their bellies.

Si and I finished our meals and helped with the

dishes, then he said his goodbyes and headed back to his place. He had some things to look after for the Austin hotel before he could come to Las Vegas and oversee the completion of the casino project with me. He'd be a week, maybe two, before he could fly out.

I packed the last of my things into my suitcase and loaded up my truck. Mom sat quietly beside me as I drove to the airport, her hands in her lap, and I just knew she was working up to a speech. Eleanor Montgomery always gave great speeches.

"Now, Stone," she started, and I tried to suppress my grin. "I want you to be patient with your father." My hands tightened on the steering wheel. If there was one topic my mother and I did not agree on it was Harold Pennington. "He's a good man, Stone, and you deserve to get to know him as such."

"Mom, I-"

"No," she said sternly, surprising me. My mother rarely raised her voice to me. She was always gentle and calm. "I want you to listen to me, just this once, Stone. You shut down conversation about your father every time I try to bring it up, but I'm gonna say my piece now, and you'll hear me." I could feel her eyes on my face as I drove, unable to make eye contact because my anger was boiling again. Rather than snap back at her, I simply nodded for her to continue. "What happened between Harold and me is just that; between Harold and me. I know you have always felt it was your job to defend me and my honor, and I appreciate that, but the choices your father and I made were our own. They have never affected how he felt about you as his son. He loves you, Stone. And if you'd let him, he'd like to show you that."

Taking a deep breath, I considered her words. True, Harold Pennington had never done anything but try to be a good dad. Even being away in New York, he always remembered my birthday, always called to ask about school and football and girls. He came to Texas as often as he could, as often as his marriage and family and work would allow. He asked every summer if I wanted to visit him and my half-sisters in Manhattan and my stubborn ass would decline every time out of pure spite.

But he was getting older now, and maybe Ma was right. If I wanted a chance to get to know him, I would have to decide quickly, before life and Father Time took the decision from me.

"I can't promise you anything more than that I'll try, Ma," I conceded, finally glancing her way and seeing the watery shine in her eyes.

"Thank you, baby. That's all I'm asking." I reached over and took her hand, bringing it to my lips for a quick kiss.

We reached the Austin airport and I hugged her goodbye, promising to call when I got to Nevada. I also made her promise to call me when she got back to the ranch so that I knew she'd made it alright. Then I watched as she climbed behind the wheel of the truck and drove away, my chest strangely tight. I loved that woman more than words could say. I'd have to threaten the Berkshire boys again, make sure they did right by her while I was gone.

Six hours later, after a brief stopover in Dallas, I found myself stomping my way through the concourse of McCarran International Airport. I was hot and sweaty and my legs were achy from being stuffed into a too small seat. All I wanted to do was get to the house and have a shower. Harold was offering up use of his own home while I was in town, and I liked the idea of a quiet space rather than being smack dab in the middle of the action on the Strip.

I was hauling my suitcase and making for the exit when the sound of raised voices caught my attention. Over near the baggage claim inquiry desk, a woman was getting more and more agitated with the staff. She was wearing jeans and a dress shirt, her blonde hair in a bun, and steam practically coming out of her ears. As I passed by, she stepped backward and turned, running directly into my chest, exploding her hot coffee all over the both of us.

Shit. What a way to start this job. Now I was pissed. Again.

CHAPTER FOUR
Penelope

"Can you please check again?" I begged, looking at the bored man behind the desk.   I had waited almost an hour at the baggage carousel, pacing and drinking too much coffee, but my suitcase never arrived.   "It was a direct flight.   How could it be missing?"

"Ma'am," he droned, the apathy in his nasally voice telling me he really didn't care about my predicament at all.   "If you'll just fill this out, when your bag does show up, we will have it delivered to your location."

"But everything I own is in that bag!"   I exclaimed, raising my voice.   I usually tried to be kind to service people, knowing just how hard they work, having worked minimum wage jobs for years myself. But the man, Trip, according to his name tag, was being so callous, I could hardly handle it.   Didn't he realize what a disaster this was?   How was I supposed work with only the clothes I had on?   There was no way I had the budget to go shopping and replace things. "Can you please check again?   Please?" I implored.

Trip let out an exasperated sigh, clicked on his

keyboard a few times, then rolled his eyes back up to me. "It's the same, ma'am."

"Stop calling me ma'am!" I practically shouted, surprising even myself. I had to get a grip here, or they would have airport security on me soon. Taking a sip of my too hot coffee, my third since I had arrived in Las Vegas, I took the form Trip had offered and wrote down the address Angelique had provided for Mr. Pennington's house in Summerlin South. Sliding the paper back to Trip, I watched as he took it and quickly set it beside his keyboard, already looking at the person in line behind me, and promptly forgetting about my desperate plight.

Gritting my teeth, I grabbed my coffee and my carry-on bag and spun from the desk in a huff, only to smack into someone. Hard.

The hand holding my coffee was trapped between us, crushing the cup and spraying both of us in a shower of scalding caffeine. Dropping my bag and stepped back, trying to hold the hot shirt away from my chest so it would stop burning my skin. I looked up at the person I had crashed in to, prepared to apologize profusely, but the words caught in my throat when I saw him.

He was tall, much taller than I was, and so broad it seemed like he was the only thing I could see. He wore jeans and a dark button-down shirt, tucked in, and a belt with a huge buckle. His dark hair peeked out beneath a black cowboy hat, a day's worth of stubble graced his cheeks, and I couldn't remember when I had ever seen a better looking man. Try as I might, I couldn't seem to voice my apology, my throat frozen like the air was trapped in my lungs as my whole body began to tingle. Even just looking at him had me feeling like someone had zapped me with a live wire. I had to get a grip.

The gorgeous cowboy didn't seem to be similarly affected. His scowl was dark as he glared down at me, his hazel eyes burning with anger as he shook his hands to rid them of the spilled beverage. When I continued to remain mute, he curled his lip in disgust and snapped, "What the hell is wrong with you?"

Shocked, I raised my eyebrows and asked, "Excuse me?"

"What, are you deaf as well as dumb?"

Seriously? What was this guys problem? "It was an accident," I tried, shaking my shirt to try to cool the coffee enough to let it touch my skin again.

"Listen, blondie," he sneered. My eyes widened. Was this guy for real? "Maybe if you were more worried about where you were going and less about your designer clothes, you wouldn't have crashed into me."

"Hang on, now," I started, but he was already walking away, dragging his massive suit case behind him. "Save it. I don't have time for your bullshit excuses. Just learn to pay attention." He tossed back over his shoulder, his work-dirty boots thumping on the floor as he passed through the doors and out of sight. I stared after him in shock for a moment, before the cooling mess on my shirt reminded me that not only did I no longer have my precious coffee, but now I had a massive stain on my only freaking shirt.

I flagged down an airport staff member to let them know about the mess on the floor, then I headed into the nearest bathroom to assess the damage.

And damaged I was. The entire right half of my white shirt was soaked in dark brown coffee. I quickly removed it, eying the redness of my chest and neck at the same time. Burnt, but not badly. More like a scald than a burn, with the skin a little sensitive to the touch, but nothing I was really worried about. Standing in the public bathroom in just my bra (which also had a nice coffee stain on the right boob, thank you very much, Mr. Grumpy Cowboy), I proceeded to run the blouse under cold water. I rinsed it several times, and while it was still stained, it was a bit better than it was before. After wringing it out, I held it under the hand dryer for what felt like hours until it was dry enough to wear again.

Putting it back on and looking in the mirror, I realized I was a disaster. Still make up free from my rush this morning, both my cheeks and my eyes were red. My hair was falling out of the bun and the stain on my shirt was still prominent. I wasn't fooling anyone.

Tucking my shirt back into my still slightly damp skinny jeans, I checked the time on my phone and was shocked to see that I was due at the hotel for the meeting with Mr. Montgomery, my boss here on this project, in less than half an hour.

I didn't know much about Mr. Montgomery,

other than he was regional manager for Pennington Hotels south west. He had a reputation of being difficult to work for, but I had a reputation for being pleasant and mostly agreeable, so I figured we would be just fine.

Dashing out of the bathroom, I ran outside and flagged down a taxi. Having never been to Las Vegas before, or anywhere, for that mater, I couldn't help but stare around in wonder as my taxi was driven along the busy streets. There were colors and sights and sounds and smells everywhere. I hoped this initial meeting would be over quickly, because I could not wait to take my first wander around.

Twenty-seven minutes after I left the airport, I was pulling up to the doors of the Pennington Hotel and Casino, Las Vegas.

To say it was huge was an understatement. I recalled the details from the fact sheet Angelique emailed me, a short list of items to know about the project before I arrived. The property itself consisted of thirty acres of prime real estate on Las Vegas Boulevard. The buildings were spread across the area, with a huge circular drive way leading up to the main doors. There was no landscaping yet, and the frontage of the building was mostly plain. I knew this was by design in a hope to keep the theme secret until the last possible moment. There were over three thousand guest rooms and suites, with a massive casino covering over one hundred thousand square feet. A multi-purpose business and conference center was built at the back portion of the property, with the pools and recreational areas in between. There were restaurants and theater spaces as well as several bars and two concert venues on site. It was a true testament to human innovation that places like this could be build in the middle of a predominately empty desert.

Paying the driver, I gathered my purse and my carry on, the sum total of my belongings here, and headed for the conference building at the back. According to Angelique's email, the hotel was not ready but the business center was. This was intentional, as that building housed all the administrative offices and would be where I was based for the duration of the project.

My heels clacked against the marble floor as I entered the building. I was immediately approached by a woman who was probably ten years older than me. She looked focused and a bit annoyed, but was dressed professionally and moved with purpose.

"Miss Lund?" she asked briskly. I nodded, and she motioned to the elevator at the back of the lobby. "This way please. Mr. Montgomery is waiting. The meeting was due to start thirty minutes ago."

"What? No," I gasped, my heart rate increasing. "The email from Angelique said two o'clock. It's just two now." We hurried into the elevator and she pressed the button for the third floor.

"There was an addendum sent out an hour ago, moving the meeting up. Mr. Montgomery wanted to leave early to attend other business."

"I have just come from the airport. I haven't checked my emails since I landed."

She glanced over her shoulder at me, one eyebrow raised, as if to ask how any of this was her problem. The elevator moved upwards, my anxiety climbing with it. This was not good. No way to make a good impression by being half an hour late on the first day. Taking a deep breath to calm myself, I listened to her give me details.

"My name is Moira, and I will be the liaison on this project between you and Mr. Pennington in New York. If you have any concerns that Mr. Montgomery can't help you with, any requests, or any ideas that we need to address, you are to bring them to me first. Is that clear?"

My brain wanted to say 'Yes, Ma'am," responding to her like the drill sergeant she seemed to be, but I managed to hold it in, instead giving her a solemn nod.

The elevator dinged, the doors opened, and Moira hurried out into another lobby then past a reception desk and across an open space, stopping before a set of wide double doors. She turned to look at me, running her eyes over my messy hair, my naked face, and my stained shirt. She pursed her lips in judgment, but kept her thoughts to herself. Meeting my eyes one last time, she said "Good luck. You're gonna need it." And with that ominous parting statement, she opened the doors and motioned me inside.

The rumble of voices halted as I stepped into the conference room. There was a large oblong table, surrounded by a dozen or so high-backed leather office chairs. Seated around the table were five men in suits and one woman, who was impeccably dressed, her long black hair in a sleek and stylish low ponytail, her eyes narrowed, gazing at me like I was something unpleasant she had stepped in. Did everyone in this town throw dirty looks around like confetti?

I ducked my head, preparing to move to an empty seat, when a low chuckle from the front of the room drew my attention.

"Well, well, well. We meet again, Blondie."

No. Impossible.

There is no way that this would be Mr. Montgomery.

Of all the rotten luck. Why would the universe curse me this way?

I froze mid step, and turned my head to look at the man standing at the front of the room next to the projector screen.

He had changed since the airport. Must be nice to have actually gotten your bags.

He now wore a tailored black suit with a smoke gray button down underneath, opened at the neck with no tie in sight. The cowboy hat and boots were gone, replaced with shiny shoes and a hair cut that looked like it cost more than my weekly grocery budget. He had shaved, as well, his strong square jaw now smooth and highlighting the natural tan of his skin. If I thought he was good looking before, this confirmed it. He was a god in either his suit or his jeans.

I kind of hated him for it.

I kept up hope that this was a mistake, that it

wasn't the jerk from the great coffee caper standing in this board room. There was no mistaking the hazel eyes, though, and they stared at me in malicious glee.

"Nice of you to join us. Miss Lund, is it? So pleased you could grace us with your presence. I hope we aren't keeping you from anything important." His comment drew quiet chuckles from around the table, the woman in particular smiling at me with a wicked gleam in her eyes. She reminded me of Constance, and I knew my dislike of her was growing thanks to that comparison. I glanced around the room, feeling my cheeks redden.

"No, Mr. Montgomery. Of course not." I continued on and found a seat. "Just a little trouble at the airport," I said, not wanting to go down without a fight. "Nothing I couldn't handle." I met his glare with one of my own. He stared me down for a second longer before someone at the table cleared their throat. It was the woman with the cold eyes.

"If we could please continue," she drawled, turning to face Mr. Montgomery, her face lighting like he was some sort of celebrity.

"Of course, Miss Carlisle, and my apologies for the rude interruption." Montgomery drawled, making me think the cowboy thing was real, as his gentle accent definitely sounded like he came from the south somewhere. Miss Carlisle beamed at him, then looked around the table.

"As I was saying, I will be leaving for Japan next week. My time will be spent between Tokyo and Osaka, and then from there I will head to Beijing, then

Hong Kong. Following that will be Moscow, Cairo, Dubai, and then on to London, and finally New York." She smirked at me, clearly proud of her busy passport, inflating her self-importance. "I will be back one month before opening with confirmations from our whales."

"Whales?" I asked, before I could think better of interrupting. Again.

Montgomery sighed. "Yes, Miss Lund. Whales. Did you not read your briefing package? A whale is a common term for a very wealthy hotel guest. They are our most lucrative and desirable visitors."

"I did not receive a briefing package, Mr. Montgomery. Angelique only emailed me the travel documents and a point form project summary."

He stared at me, dumbfounded. "So you have no idea what we are talking about? You literally do not know any information about this hotel or casino? What are you even doing here, Miss Lund, besides wasting our time?"

I opened my mouth to respond, but was saved when another man spoke up.

"I have extra packages right here, Mr. Montgomery. I would be happy to stay with Miss Lund and review all the pertinent information." He practically bounced in his chair, eager as a puppy, and smiled at me. At least someone was happy I was here.

"Thank you, Mr. Reynolds. It's nice to see at least some of my executive staff is both ambitious and prepared." He leveled me with a pointed glare, letting me and everyone else in the room know that I was the only one who had shown up with nothing today. "Now, moving on." And with that, Mr. Montgomery dismissed me completely, continuing with his discussion of the status of the food and beverage department.

Mr. Reynolds, who was seated directly across from me, discretely slid a shiny folder my way. Its thick pages were professionally coil bound and the glossy cover showed a digital rendering of the outside of the completed casino. My eyes widened and a laugh escaped my mouth before I could stop it.

Once again, all the attention was drawn to me.

With a dramatic sigh, Montgomery rolled his eyes, placed his hands on his hips, and growled, "What is it now, Miss Lund?"

I cleared my throat and schooled my features to what I hoped was a neutral expression.

"Nothing, sir. Please, continue."

"Oh, no. I think it is most definitely something." He looked at the package in my hands. "Is there a problem with the information you have been given? Something so important that you felt it necessary to interrupt Mr. Yates in his report on the status of the menus and kitchen services here? Please, tell us what is so very pressing."

He crossed his arms, leaned back against the wall behind him and stared, waiting for me to speak.

I couldn't. Once again, this man had me frozen. The pissed off look on his too handsome face had rendered me incapable of forming a sentence.

I blinked, looking around the table as the other

executive staff members all watched me with annoyed expressions of their own. Miss Carlisle was extraordinarily sour looking.

Only Mr. Reynolds regarded me with anything resembling kindness, though, if I were honest, it was probably more pity than anything.

Montgomery continued to stare my way. "Well, Miss Lund? Care to share with the class?"

Damn.

I took a deep breath and started.

"I was just looking at the rendering, sir. I was shocked, is all."

"Shocked about what, Miss Lund."

"It's just, a Western themed hotel? Really, sir? I was expecting something sleek and modern and, well, pretty. Not this."

A frown creased his face as he uncrossed his arms, stalking toward the table. "You have a problem with the theme of the hotel?" he questioned, leaning forward, pressing his closed fists against the polished mahogany of the table. "You have something against cowboys, maybe?" he challenged.

Sitting up straight, I met his glare and shot back, "Well, I have yet to meet a decent one, that's for sure."

He stood back up straight, his eyes assessing me, making me wonder if I just made a mistake.

"Well, Miss Lund, it could be that no cowboys have ever found you worth being decent to."

He spun from the table and headed for the door. "That's all for today. I want everyone to meet back here Wednesday at eight am with department updates.

Dismissed." And then he was gone.

I sat back in my seat, wondering what the hell I just got myself into. As the room cleared out around me, with glowers and glares thrown my way for good measure, I took a few deep breaths, closed my eyes, and rubbed my temples. After a moment, I felt movement beside me and looked up to see that Mr. Reynolds had moved and took the seat next to mine. He smiled companionably and extended his hand.

"I'm Toby. Toby Reynolds. Human resources, and you look like you've had quite a day."

I huffed out a laugh. "Mr. Reynolds, you have no idea."

"Call me Toby, please."

"Penelope," I replied, shaking his hand. "And you are the first friendly face I've seen all day."

"Yeah, it gets a bit intense around here. I've worked with Montgomery before, and a few of the others, but with this being the first Casino project, we have added tons of new staff and departments to the mix. Everyone is running on high anxiety right now. There is no room for failure here, you know?"

I did know. My entire career was hanging on this job. And I'd already pissed off the boss. Typical.

"Thank you for helping me with this," I said, indicating the package. "I don't know why Angelique neglected to send me the information." But I did have a hunch. Angelique had been quite pleased to see Constance that day in Mr. Pennington's office, and I had a feeling that she was actively working against me to try and increase Toddrick's chances of getting the VP position.

"It's not a problem," he said, leaning close to me. I stiffened slightly, but didn't move away, telling myself he was just trying to help. "So, should we start at the beginning?"

Working our way through the information package, I learned that the theme was most definitely western. In fact, they were calling the hotel *The Alamo*. It was going to be complete old west decor inside and out, with the grounds being landscaped to take the most advantage of the desert around us. The exterior of the building would be made to look like a classic street from the American frontier. Wooden stone and wooden facings, plank board walk ways, and hanging tin signs. The inside of the hotel varied depending on which area you were in, with varying degrees of old west cowboy or modern honky tonk, depending on what you were looking for.

The bars were made to look like Old West Saloons, with lots of wood, dim lighting designed like oil lanterns, and a long wooden bar. The serving staff was going to be dressed like the old time Saloon girls, with their brightly colored corsets, fishnet stockings, and garters.

The theaters were done in a Classic American design, with red velvet curtains and rounded balconies, opulently decorated with gilded plasterwork reminiscent of the theaters of the eighteenth century.

As I flipped through the pages of design, theme, food, and entertainment, I was totally taken aback. I had planned on marketing a sleek and modern themed hotel, with a cosmopolitan feel and lots of glass and chrome. This was something I was completely unprepared for. The walls were made of dirt, for crying out loud! I was going to have to completely rethink my strategy. My heart sank at the prospect.

As Toby and I finished going through the package, I was overwhelmed and completely disheartened. And I really wanted to call my mom.

Putting on a brave face, I turned to Toby with the biggest smile I could muster. "Thank you, Toby, for everything. I appreciate all you did for me today."

He stood and offered me his hand. Feeling obligated to take it even though I was perfectly capable of standing on my own, I released him as quickly as I could, turning from the table and gathering my things.

"I would be happy to continue this discussion, say over dinner, perhaps?"

My stomach clenched. Oh, boy. This was the last thing I needed to deal with right now. Holding on to my smile, I turned to him and said, "Thank you, Toby, but I am afraid I am going to decline. I have so much to do to get ready for Wednesday, and the airline lost my luggage so I have to deal with that as well." I hoped he would take the hint.

"Of course, maybe some other time, then?"

"Maybe," I said carefully.

He walked with me back to the bank of elevators, where he pushed the button and we waited in uncomfortable silence. Just as the doors opened, I heard my named being called and turned to see Moira walking toward me.

"You go ahead, Toby. I should see what she wants."

He frowned slightly. "If you're sure."

"Yes," I said quickly. "I am. Quite sure. Thanks again." And I turned to leave him standing in the elevator, his face confused as the doors closed on him.

I followed Moira to her desk across the foyer where she began to pile things on top, listing them as she went.

"Laptop, company phone with directory already loaded, marketing budget manual, and finally, the keys to the house in Summerlin South." She looked at me with a smile, her manner completely different from when I had first encountered her. "I figured since the rest of your package hadn't arrived, you would be missing these things as well. Turns out, after some digging, Angelique sent everything here instead of your home in New York. One might wonder if she did that on purpose, don't you think?"

My suspicions confirmed, I smiled back. "One just might, Moira."

I loaded what I could into my purse and carry on, eager to get to the house and have a shower. I had no idea what I was going to do about clothes, though. Turning to the elevator, Moira called me back again. "Miss Lund? If you'll just write down your sizes, I will have some things sent over to the house for you to hold you over until your luggage arrives. On Mr. Pennington, of course. It's the least he can do to make up for Angelique's...mistake."

My heart clenched at her thoughtfulness, and I had to blink to keep the tears at bay. I wrote the information down on the paper she provided, thanking her again, then asking, "Um, Moira? How did you know that my luggage had gone missing?"

"Mr. Montgomery mentioned it on his way out," she said easily, like the words weren't the most shocking thing I'd heard all day. "He said he had noticed you at the lost luggage counter while he was in the airport himself."

I thought about what she was saying, but decided I needed to file that away for processing later. For now, I just needed to get out of my dirty clothes and get my head back on straight.

"I am here for you, Miss Lund," Moira said with a gentle hand on my arm. "Don't let these sharks get to you. They can smell your fear, you know?"

So, with new resolve I made my way back down through the building and out to the front of the property, climbing into yet another cab, and headed to Summerlin South.

A hot bath and a quiet night would do me a lot of good.

CHAPTER FIVE

Stone

The hot water rolled down my back, hoping it would release the tension in my shoulders and doing a shit job of it.

Today could not have gone worse if I tried. I had told myself I was going to try to rein in my attitude, to not be a jerk to my new staff, and then she walked in and everything went to hell.

I didn't know what it was about her that riled me up. She really didn't do anything wrong. I knew the whole coffee thing was an accident. But when she stood there gaping at me like a freaking goldfish, I just snapped.

It had been that way for a while; my anger like a rabid dog, barely held back by the pitiful leash I try to keep it on. The only person safe from my wrath was my mother.

Turning off the shower and snagging the towel I brought in with me, I quickly dried off and slid on a fresh pair of jeans, leaving my suitcase to unpack later. Harold insisting I use his personal house was more than a bit awkward. I hadn't spent any time at a property he owned outside of the hotels. Staying in the same home he built for his other family made my hackles rise. I wanted to hate the place on principle.

As I headed down stairs, I thought again of the walking beautiful disaster that was Miss Penelope Lund. When Harold said he was sending someone from his New York marketing team, I pictured someone more like Ava Carlisle; slick, manipulative, willing to do anything to get ahead. I hadn't anticipated the gorgeous and delicate Penelope to be who walked through the door.

Yes, she was definitely gorgeous, with her golden hair and big blue eyes, even the coffee stain couldn't distract from the fact that under that dirty shirt was a body to die for. It was just a shame she had to be from New York.

My prejudice against New Yorkers wasn't unfounded. After all, people from New York had been ruining my family since before I was born. First Harold, then his awful socialite wife, Dierdre, and her ghastly daughter, Constance. Whenever I would make an attempt to connect with Harold as a child, whether on the phone or when he would bring my half-sisters to Texas to try to make us a 'family', Constance never failed to remind me that he was her father, and I was just a mistake.

The only person from NYC that I had ever forged any kind of relationship with was my youngest half-sister, Daphne. She was thirteen years younger than me, but she was caring and kind and always went out of her way to make me feel like I wasn't a blight on the family name, much to Constance's disgust.

Maybe, just maybe, I would find that Penelope was more like Daphne than the other two. And maybe I could find a way to not lose my cool every time I was around her. It would be difficult. She made me feel such conflicting things. First, the attraction, which was warranted, but unwanted. Second, the anger, due to her New York roots.

I moved through the ridiculously huge house and past the kitchen that no one with Pennington for a last name had likely ever actually cooked in. Snagging a glass of bourbon on my way, I stepped outside on to the back deck, the stone tiles warm beneath my bare feet.

The property was spectacular, even if I hated to admit it. With its impeccably landscaped drought resistant yard, sprawling pool, and an outdoor kitchen that would have been my grandfather's dream, it was exactly what you would expect of Las Vegas luxury. At the far west of the city in a gated golf course community, Harold's home looked out over miles and miles of gorgeous hills and scrub brush of the Red Rock Canyon National Conservation Area. The jagged low peaks in varying shades of reds and oranges and browns were almost enough to remind me of home, and the hills that McNally and I spent so much of our time in outside Austin. Leaning back against the house, my glass dangling from my finger tips, I took in the view as the sun began to set. This house, this location at least, was exactly the kind of place I would pick for myself if I had the opportunity.

That was another thing that pissed me off. Harold and all the ways he seemed to know me. I didn't want him to know me. He didn't deserve it.

Like with this project. *The Alamo Hotel and Casino* was a dream come true for me. Taking all the things I loved about the hotel business and blending it with all the things I loved about Texas, it was the project of a lifetime. And the bastard knew it, too. It was as if he custom designed it to torture me, reminding me that no matter how hard I fought it, he was still my father and he still understood me.

I hated it.

I watched as the sun made its way to the horizon, casting warm light over the surface of the pool, making the blue water sparkle gold and crimson. I was still lost in the view when I heard a sound from the front of the house. Turning back toward the massive glass door that connected the outdoor living space with the indoor, I moved into the shadows, wanting to see who was here before I announced my presence. I supposed Harold had a staff for this place. It wouldn't do to scare them off right away. I watched the front door as muffled sounds reached me, like someone fumbling with the key, when finally, the door swung open.

I stared in shock as Penelope Lund stumbled in the front door of Harold's house, her arms full of bags and boxes, each with a different designer label. Of course, the New York girl couldn't just head to Walmart and grab some shirts to tide her over until her luggage was located. She had to hit the expensive shops and load up on brand names to make her Instagram followers all really jealous.

What the hell was she doing here, anyway?

She set her packages down next to the door, looking around the place with wide eyes. Likely seeing the dollar signs in every piece of furniture and decorative wall hanging in sight. I sneered from my hiding place, my lip curling in disgust. Turns out she was just like every other New York bitch I'd met after all.

I watched as her gaze moved to the back yard, catching the sunset and turning to head in my direction. I stayed hidden, following her with my eyes as she passed me and moved toward the pool, her head looking side to side and appreciating the view, just as I had earlier. I went to move out of my hiding place just as she bent down to touch the pool water, trailing her fingers through the small rippling waves like she'd never seen a backyard swimming pool before. The soft sigh she released reached my ears, and she stood and turned, gasping as she finally noticed me, her hands coming up to protect her from what she undoubtedly thought was an intruder. That was a mistake, of course, because I was supposed to be here; she was the intruder.

Her second mistake was taking a step backward. In her haste to distance herself from what she thought was danger, she stepped backward and dropped directly into the pool, disappearing below the surface with a squeak and a huge splash.

Shit. This girl was a mess.

She almost immediately popped back up again, her blonde hair now plastered to her face and her white blouse now plastered to her breasts. I took a quick peek while she was wiping the pool water out of her eyes. I'd had a feeling was hiding a killer body under that dirty shirt, but having her shirt rendered almost transparent by her impromptu swim proved it.

She coughed and sputtered, looking at me as I stood above her, hands on my hips, and sent her my best glare.

We both spoke the same words at the same time.

"What are you doing here?"

I paused, letting her make her way to the shallow end. She climbed the steps, shoulders hunched and her head bowed, as the weight of her wet jeans made walking cumbersome. As she rounded the side of the pool and headed back my way, I could see panic in her eyes. I could also see that, while Las Vegas was likely a mite bit warmer than New York in the first week of February, the wind off the canyon was definitely cool, if her pebbled nipples were any indication.

She caught me looking and hastily crossed her arms over her chest. I raised my eyes to her blue ones with a smirk, letting her know I'd seen everything worth seeing and there was nothing she could do about it.

Clearing her throat, she met my glare and asked again, "What are you doing in Mr. Pennington's house?"

"I think the better question is what are you

doing here? I'm supposed to be staying here. You're breaking and entering," I threw in, even though I'd seen the key in her hand. But I was hoping to get a rise out of her. She didn't disappoint.

"Mr. Montgomery, I did no such thing!" She placed her hands on her hips in indignation and puffed up her chest, drawing my eyes back to her breasts. Realizing what she had done, she crossed her arms again before continuing. "Mr. Pennington had a key for me because I have been invited to stay here. I was expecting a roommate, but you are certainly not Daphne."

That had me frowning. "What do you know about Daphne?"

Penelope looked at me curiously. "Mr. Pennington said that she would be staying here at the house with me during the duration of the project. He said that the house was big enough we wouldn't even notice each other."

I growled deep in my chest. I had a feeling I knew what was going on. "Did Mr. Pennington," I said the name with a sneer in my voice. "Say that you would be staying with Daphne specifically? Or did he just mention a roommate?"

"I'm sure he mentioned her," she said slowly, but I could tell by the slowly dawning shock on her face, that she wasn't sure.

"Miss Lund, think hard. What did Mr. Pennington say, exactly?"

Penelope released a huge sigh, the color draining from her face as the implication of what was going on hit her too. "Kid," she said quietly. "He said that his kid would be staying here. But I had assumed…"

"Yeah, well, look what that got you. You know what they say about people who assume things."

Penelope took a step back, careful this time to avoid the edge of the swimming pool. The last of the sunset was shining over the mountains behind her, casting her in silhouette, so I couldn't see much, but I noticed when her eyes widened, taking me in again from head to toe. I also noticed how her gaze lingered on my shirtless chest. I guess I wasn't the only one affected.

She stopped her perusal at my face, squinting at me curiously, before she gasped again. "But, Mr. Montgomery, you're-"

"Stone Pennington, illegitimate bastard, at your service." I tipped and imaginary hat for effect, but saying it out loud made my stomach sour.

How I hated calling myself a Pennington.

Penelope stared at me for a moment more, her face moving through a series of rapid emotions before she finally settled on one. It just wasn't the one I was expecting.

Disgust.

She was looking at me with disgust. Well, fuck her, then. Like I was the only child born out of wedlock to a rich man. I didn't have a thing to prove to her or anyone.

"You got somethin' to say, Miss Lund?" I asked stepping into her space, my anger causing me to make stupid choices. I should walk away. I should get out of here and get a hotel somewhere away from her and the damn house.

But my pride wouldn't let me.

Penelope schooled her features into a polite professional mask before clasping her hands demurely in front of her. Everything about her posture said submissive and meek. Everything in her eyes said she hated my guts.

"Of course not, Mr. Pennington," she said, every word dripping with acid.

Studying her, I tried to read her face, but she was a closed book, cold and empty. Except for the fire in her eyes.

"You're determined to stay at this house, then?" I asked. She pursed her lips and nodded, never once looking away from me. "Fine, then the south wing is mine. Stay the hell out." And with that I turned around and left her standing there, cold and damp, on the deck in the newly gathered dark.

That was good. The darkness outside matched the growing darkness I felt inside me.

I stomped across the house to the central staircase, taking the steps two at a time as I headed for the master bedroom I had claimed when I got here earlier. Slamming the door behind me, I snatched my phone up from the dresser where it was charging and dialed a number I rarely ever used.

My father.

It rang and rang. I glanced at the clock. It would be late in New York, but I wasn't about to hang up. I waited for him to answer, his voice rough from sleep as he did so.

"H-hello? Stone?"

"Yeah," I said simply.

"It's good to hear from you, son."

I chose to ignore the term. Again. Instead I got right to the point.

"Why the fuck didn't you tell me that Penelope was going to be living in the house too?"

"Oh. Yes, that."

"Yeah. That. What the hell, Harold? I can't be living here with a member of my executive staff? Why would you send some snotty Manhattan bitch to get in my way?"

"Now, wait just a minute. You have no cause to speak about Penelope that way. She is a lovely girl and she is excellent at her job."

I scoffed. "You could have fooled me. The girl's a walking train wreck. A joke from head to toe."

"Stone, please. Just give her a chance. I know she will succeed at this. I *need* her to succeed at this." The desperation in his voice threw me. I didn't think Harold Pennington ever needed anything he couldn't get with a snap of his fingers and a flash of his gold card.

"What the hell is so important about her that we can't have someone else here to do the job? I've got three marketing guys in my region who could work circles around this girl." I really needed her gone. I wasn't even sure why at this point, but when it came to Penelope Lund, I saw nothing but danger signs.

And those perfect tits.

Shit. This was bad. I needed to hate her, but I couldn't get her blue eyes out of my head. The way she shot fire at me with every look.

This girl was nothing but trouble.

"I'm sure that Pennington Hotels has a whole array of talented staff in all our departments. However, Miss Lund is there for a reason, Stone. And while I can't tell you why that is, exactly, I can tell you that she is the only one I want on the Las Vegas start up campaign."

"That's a bullshit answer, and you know it."

"Yes," he sighed. "It is. And I do know it. But for once in your life, can you please trust me? And believe that I have your best interests at heart? Penelope Lund is perfect right where she is."

I didn't like it. At all. But he was the CEO. If this project was going to fail, it was ultimately his name on the building.

And mine, I guess, if we're getting technical.

Shit.

"Just for the record, I'm against this the entire way." I stated, wanting to get the last word for some insane and immature reason. Talking to my father always did this to me. Talking to him with Penelope Lund in the same house? I was going off the freakin' rails.

"Your grievance has been noted," Harold said with a laugh.

"Fine," I said, prepared to end the conversation, but as I moved my thumb to the disconnect button, he called my name.

"Stone?" he asked, the hope in his voice making me feel a small measure of guilt.

Very small.

"Yeah?" I replied, trying to soften my tone. Maybe I succeeded.

"Thank you," Harold said quietly. "I know you will do a great job out there in Las Vegas. I am so proud of the things you have already accomplished. I'm always proud of you, son."

Clenching my jaw against the strange and raw emotions now hurtling through me, it was a moment before I could speak. When I did, my voice was rough and choked. I hated that, too.

"Yeah," was all I managed. He was going to have to take it.

"Good night, son," Harold said, and then he was gone.

I stared at the blank screen of my phone, trying to process the day. There were too many things happening. To many strange events all crammed into twenty-four hours that I couldn't seem to get a handle on what I was feeling, so I went with what I knew. What I was comfortable with.

Anger.

I was angry that Harold insisted I keep Miss Lund on staff. I was angry that she would be sharing this house with me. I was angry she was apparently good enough at her job that Harold felt he needed her. And I was angry I found her so damn attractive when I was trying so friggin' hard to hate her.

The whole situation was shit.

Kicking off my jeans, I climbed into the huge bed, set my alarm, and leaned back against the small mountain of pillows that, for some reason, all smelled of the ocean. There wasn't an ocean around for almost three hundred miles.

Fuckin' rich people.

Sure, I made good money working for Pennington Hotels, but there was something about people who had grown up rich - like, never driving your own car rich - that just rubbed me the wrong way. They didn't understand struggle. The didn't know what it was like to sacrifice, to have to put your dreams on hold until you could obtain them the old-fashioned way, through dedication and hard work. Blood, sweat, and tears. That's what built character. Not trips to Europe and shopping on Madison Avenue.

Sighing, I stared up at the dark ceiling, wishing I was back in Texas. Wishing I was finished with this project and back where I belonged.

The good news was that Silas had messaged me earlier. He would be wrapping up in Austin sooner than anticipated and should be here tomorrow. If anyone could talk me down from this ledge, it was him. I hated to burden my mother with my emotional baggage. Especially after her speech this morning about giving this an honest try.

Rolling over and moving the pillows around - it really was a ridiculous number of pillows for one bed - I resolved to get through this as quickly and efficiently as possible so I could get my ass back to Texas as fast as I could.

I was starting to hate Las Vegas.

CHAPTER SIX
Penelope

"The girl's a walking train wreck.   A joke from head to toe."

My stomach sank as I heard the words Stone shouted into his phone, clearly not trying at all for discretion.   I could only guess that he was talking to Mr. Pennington.   *His father.*

How could it all have gone so wrong so quickly? Of course Stone was Harold's son.   Why would anyone besides his family have a shot at succeeding?   It's not like Stone had worked his ass off to earn a scholarship, then studied every waking minute of his university career because failure was not an option.   He was not the one with a mother back home who was counting on every penny he could make to save their home and keep them out of the poor house.

Why would all my effort even matter when all he needed was to have the right parents?

Nepotism.   How I hated it.

I couldn't fault his logic, though; I was a complete mess today.   Not even twenty-four hours and I had already pissed off the boss something fierce.

I came in from the back deck, dripping pool water all over the pristine house and headed for the north wing as instructed, gathering up the packages Moira had waiting for me when I arrived and made my way to one of the four bedrooms in the wing.

When the taxi had pulled up to the house in Summerlin, I thought I would be tired enough to just go straight inside to bed. But after a quick glance around I found the entire area so lovely that I had gone for a walk around the neighborhood instead.

The place was just so vastly different from anything I had ever known. The east coast was often gray and dreary, the sun finding it hard to reach the ground between the impossibly high towers of Manhattan. I was used to concrete and steel and glass, shades of gray and black that never really changed.

But Nevada was like an explosion of color. I couldn't believe all the different shades of red and brown and even green that I saw as I wandered the streets, admiring the low houses with their stucco walls and the terracotta roof tiles. Each house had a yard, which was something else I wasn't used to. Green space in Manhattan was pretty much non-existent outside Central Park. Even in Queens, where small front yards were more common, the houses were pretty much built right on top of each other. Space was always at a premium.

But as I made my way through the quiet streets of that gorgeous Las Vegas neighborhood, watching the families going about their evening routines and enjoying their time together, I could not get over the amount of open space there was around me. Each house sat separate from the next, with no shared walls between them to listen in on the arguments and too loud TV shows of your neighbors. The yards, while mostly landscaped in a drought resistant fashion, with rocks and shrubs and very little grass, were all done up in a way that was visually appealing, with decorative stones and pieces of art dotted throughout. They all fit the neighborhood aesthetic and everyone tried to maintain the area to the same standard.

The other thing I noticed was that there were barely any vehicles parked on the street. Every home had its own garage, keeping the cars and trucks out of the elements, and housing bikes and other family toys, from the light peeking I'd done into one or two opened bays as I passed.

But the truly amazing thing, the thing that I kept returning to again and again, was the sky. There was just so much of it. I was used to small glimpses of the sky, stealing moments between tall towers and subway stations. I hadn't realized how incredible the sky was until I came to Nevada. If I turned down the any street, I could find a place that was open, leaving nothing between me and that impossibly blue expanse but my own inability to fly.

The neighborhood was surrounded by a group of low hills, and while I didn't know their names, I couldn't wait to get a closer look at them. I figured hiking might be something I might like to try. After all, it's not like I had any friends to spend time with out here. I might as well start becoming one with nature.

My mother would be impressed by my adventurous spirit.

When I returned to the house where the cab left me earlier, I slowly wandered up the driveway, wondering again how I ended up here. The largest house in the neighborhood, and I had the key.

Stepping through the door was like entering another world entirely. The whole house was done in a warm tan, with light tiles on the floor, cream walls, and dark wood accents. The living room had a huge and comfy looking brown leather couch with enough room to hold fifteen people, while the kitchen was a glowing mix of white granite and stainless-steel appliances. But it was the glass wall at the back that caught my eye.

A pool. An entire swimming pool, and, for this moment at least, it was just for me.

I set the packages down, not caring one whit about what was inside them, and made my way to the back door, noticing it was unlocked, but not thinking about why that would be strange. I walked right up to the edge of the pool, taking in the breathtaking view of the canyons and hills, and felt my soul lighten. This was what I needed tonight. I moment to breathe.

From the second my mother burst in to my room this morning, it had been nothing but chaos. I hadn't had a second to catch up.

But here, with the sky an endless blue stretch above my head, I could feel like maybe things weren't so bad.

Maybe, just maybe, I could actually pull this off.

Bending down, I trailed my fingers through the sparkling waters of the pool, sighing at the cool water and looking forward to taking my first swim as soon as possible. Suddenly, a noise caught my attention. Realizing I wasn't alone, I stood up and spun around to see who was behind me, and my heart raced, adrenaline pumping double time as I saw a huge man, standing in the shadows.

Being a New York girl, I knew that when a man crept up behind you, it never meant anything good. I had only a heartbeat to register the massive shoulders and dark hair, instinct causing me to take an involuntary step back, away from my would-be attacker.

That was when I got my wish.

A swim.

So now here I stood, in a bedroom I wasn't familiar with, in a house I wasn't wanted in, on a job I had no chance of succeeding at, no matter how hard I worked or how well I performed, and I was wondering what I was even doing with my life.

Wandering into the massive bathroom, with its smoke gray granite and shower big enough for a family of five to live in, I caught sight of myself in the mirror.

Train wreck, indeed. My blonde hair was plastered to my head, my face was splotchy, and my eyes were red, both from anger and the chlorine. My shirt, still sporting the coffee stain, was now well and truly ruined, and it would probably take the jaws of life to pry the wet skinny jeans off my behind.

But underneath all that mess, I was still me. I

was still Penelope Lund, daughter of two blue-collar workers. Parents who, through their hard work and sacrifice, were the back bone of America. Without people like us, the Pennington family would never have made it to where they were today. I was still the girl who made it to the top of her class at NYU on her own merit, and who worked her way to the top of the marketing department in record time.

I had value. I had pride. And I had earned everything I had gained along the way.

So Stone and Toddrick and Constance and every other silver spoon, prep school, yacht club, trust fund jerk could take their nepotism and shove it!

That job was *mine*.

*   *   *   *

My alarm went off. I triple checked it this time.

Still, I woke up every hour or so all night long, just to be sure.

Today was a brand-new day, and I was going to make the most of it.

Hopping out of bed, I entered the bathroom and enjoyed every inch of that giant shower. I scrubbed from head to toe, then headed back to the bedroom to see what Moira had provided for me.

It was as bad as I had anticipated. The names on the clothes were ones I only ever saw in store windows and on Kardashian Instagram pages. But still, I had no other option.

Selecting what I thought was the simplest and

therefore least expensive option, I packaged the rest up again. I would have Moira return them later today. There was no need for all those things when my own clothes could be arriving any day now.

At least, I hoped they would be arriving.

But even if I never saw my suitcase again, I could go shopping and find some reasonable items to wear. I would lament the loss of the Jimmy Choo pumps, though. I frowned, wishing I had taken the time to at least try them on when mom presented them to me yesterday.

Putting on the plain black dress pants and simple pale blue button up blouse, I finished my hair and used the mascara and lip gloss that was included with the other items. I refused to use any of the other make up, however. I thought sixty-three dollars an ounce was a ridiculous amount of money to pay for foundation. I simply couldn't bring myself to even open it.

Sliding my feet back into the flats I had worn from Queens, I squared my shoulders, took a deep breath, and made my way out of the room and back down stairs to the kitchen.

Stone sat at the island, his suit jacket over the stool next to him, coffee in hand as he scrolled through his phone. He looked like a GQ cover model, and I hated that I thought he was handsome. Distressingly so. His dark hair and square jaw looked even more pronounced without the cowboy hat, although that was a look I appreciated as well. The sight of him sitting at the island, so casually, was doing weird things to my insides. It took more effort than I wanted to admit to keep my eyes off of his striking profile as I entered the kitchen and went about my morning, trying to ignore the low hum of attraction buzzing under my skin.

Making my way to the coffee machine, I selected a pod and inserted it. Placing a mug below and waiting for my drink, looking at him out of the corner of my eye as I did so. I didn't want to even acknowledge his presence, seeing as he seemed determine to ignore mine today. Just as well; we clearly had nothing to say to each other.

When the machine finished, I took my mug and moved again to the back door, taking in the spectacular view once again. In the early morning light, the hills appeared much darker, their low peaks soaked in crimson and the gnarled shrubs appearing almost black. I breathed deeply, letting the view and the smell of hot coffee fill me with energy for the day. I took a sip, never taking my eyes off the incredible vista, and heard the legs of the stool scrape back against the tiles as Stone stood up from the kitchen island. I watched his reflection in the glass door as he moved to the sink and I was surprised to see he was rinsing his own mug. He then shocked me further when he placed it in the dishwasher before heading upstairs, never once looking in my direction.

Not giving him another thought, I finished my own coffee, cleaned up my mess, and stopped at the fridge to grab an apple before gathering my purse and heading for the door behind the kitchen. Part of the package Moira gave me at the office yesterday included instructions to using the car that was kept in the garage. I grabbed the keys from the hook as I passed.

Stepping into the garage, my nerves picked up. Sure, I had a driver's license, but that was only a technicality. I had gotten it years ago in my high school drivers ed class. I renewed it every five years like I was supposed to, but I hadn't actually driven in almost nine years. Owning a car in New York was about as useful as owning snow shoes in Florida.

The car in question was beautiful. A sweet cherry red Mustang convertible, the top already down, the gorgeous tan leather seats on display. I moved around to the drivers' side and climbed in, careful not to smack the door into the large pickup truck parked beside me. After taking my time adjusting the seats and mirrors, I put the key into the ignition and turned.

Nothing happened.

I took the key out and reinserted it, turning again like I remembered to do, my foot on the brake pedal. Still nothing. This was bad. I didn't have enough time to call a cab if I wanted to make it to the office on time. Sighing in defeat, I dropped my forehead down on to the steering wheel, jumping when the car horn let out a quick blast.

"Having a problem?" drawled a voice from my right. I looked over to see Stone, now wearing his suit jacket, leaning against the door to the house, a smirk on his stupidly handsome face as he reveled in my failure once again.

"Not a problem," I said defensively, straightening up and turning the key a third time. Still nothing. "Not one I can't handle, anyway." I said, exiting the car and reaching for my phone. Maybe Uber was faster?

"Let me guess," Stone said, moving into the garage and stepping up to me, trapping me between the two vehicles. "You can't drive." He looked down his nose at me, like I should be ashamed.

I was not.

"I most certainly can drive," I countered, not backing down one bit. "It has just been a while, that's all. I'm fully qualified to operate a motor vehicle." I was rambling, but I couldn't seem to stop.

"Sure looks like it, Blondie." He stepped even closer to me, and I backed up before our chests touched. I was breathing hard, staring into his bright hazel eyes, trying not to let any emotions show on my face. Not my embarrassment at being once again found lacking, not my discomfort at being so close to him when he looked and smelled so good I could hardly think straight, and not my slight fear of being alone with him when he so clearly didn't like me in the least.

He continued walking toward me, and I continued backing up, when he suddenly grabbed the door handle of the pick up truck, opening it wide. "Get in."

I stared at him questioningly, a frown between my eyebrows, and he rolled his eyes in annoyance. "Look," he said, releasing a long-suffering sigh. "I'm going to the office. You're going to the office. You can either stay here all morning trying to figure out the difference between the brake and the clutch, or you can get in this truck and come with me. The choice is yours, but I ain't waiting all day for you to make up your mind."

With that he spun around, stalking to the other side of the truck, and climbed in. I stared at the open passenger door, wondering if I could risk the short drive with him and still keep my sanity, when he started the engine. The loud rumble of the motor startled me into moving, and a grabbed my laptop out of the Mustang and scrambled into the big truck. I had barely closed the door behind me and Stone had the vehicle in motion. After buckling my seat belt, I turned to look at him as he drove. One hand resting on top of the steering wheel, the other leaned casually on the console between us, he was the picture of cool confidence.

I mean, why wouldn't he be? He had a rich daddy who provided him with all the things he could ever want. He probably hadn't put in a single hard day's work in his life.

Letting out a soft snort of disgust, I turned to look out my window, watching as all the beautiful houses I had admired yesterday slipped past. It didn't take long for the residential area to turn back into the bustling hub that was Las Vegas Boulevard.

I was used to big, busy cities. After all, New York is known as the City That Never Sleeps. But seeing the amount of people out that early in the morning, going about their day in whatever capacity they chose, was really something to see. There were people wandering up and down the Strip taking in the sights, some of whom may have not even been to bed yet. There were municipal employees, already hard at work cleaning up after the last evening's revelry, and as we approached *The Alamo* building site, there were construction workers coming and going at a rapid pace. With the exterior of the building now nearing completion, it wouldn't be long before Mr. Pennington's secret theme wasn't a secret any longer.

It was time I got started on a roll out plan that made the most of the announcement. I had to control the narrative here, and reveal the information in a manner that was most beneficial to our plans. And to my hope of getting the VP position.

I was zoned out, busy going over ideas and strategies in my head, when Stone's voice cut in, causing me to jump again.

"You gettin' out, or what?" he barked. He had been so silent on the drive over I had almost forgotten he was beside me. Looking around, I realized we were parked in the employee lot at the back of the property, next to the administration building. Gathering my things once again, I lowered my self down from the truck - no easy feat; the thing was massive - and walked quickly to the doors. Stepping into the cool of the air-conditioned building, I was greeted by Moira's kind smile.

"Good morning, Miss Lund. I see the clothes were to your satisfaction."

"Yes, Moira. And thank you," I said. "But, please, there were way too many. If I could return the other things to you, I won't need them when my luggage arrives." Which I hoped would be soon.

"If you're sure, Miss Lund."

"I am, thank you. I don't know how you expected me to wear those clothes in the first place," I said. They were way out of my price range and therefore, out of my comfort zone. Moira smiled, understanding my plight.

Stone, however, seemed to completely misinterpret my meaning.

"What's the matter, Blondie? Those expensive brands aren't good enough for your Uptown ass?" he commented as he passed by me and headed for the elevator.

"Excuse me?" I sniped, but he ignored me, giving me his signature smirk as the doors closed, leaving me steaming in the lobby with Moira watching with a curious expression.

"Seems like things are going well at the house, then," she said sarcastically. I rolled my eyes, but didn't elaborate. As we stood there, sharing a smile that said more than I needed to, another young woman approached from across the lobby. She was younger than me by a few years, and her eyes were wide as she stared at the closed door of the elevator.

"Was that Mr. Montgomery? I was hoping to catch him. He's, like, ridiculously hot," she gushed, fanning herself dramatically. Moira and I shared another look, this time one of amusement.

"Yes," I said, then leaned in conspiratorially. "It was. And he is, like, ridiculously hot." I met Moira's eye with a wink, then threw in. "At least, his boyfriend sure thinks so."

Moira choked down a snort as she attempted to keep the smile off her face. The younger woman looked flabbergasted.

"He's gay?" she gasped, like this was the end of her world. "But, I thought I caught him checking me out yesterday."

"Oh, honey. He was probably just admiring your outfit. After all, you heard him commenting on my clothes a minute ago. It's like, his thing."

Understanding dawned in her eyes as she contemplated this new information. "Damn. I totally thought I had a shot. I mean, who wouldn't want a ride on that handsome cowboy?" she asked, pursing her lips as she looked again to where Stone had entered the elevator. "I'll have to tell the girls he's off limits," she added before walking back to the office she had entered from and immediately heading to the cluster of desks where three other young women sat at a bank of phones. They bent their heads together while she dished the gossip.

Moira finally let her laugh free, the sound of it bold in the quiet lobby. "Girl," she said with a small shake of her head. "I think you have some serious balls. I can't wait to see how this plays out."

Then she turned back to me, all business. "The reports you requested last night are all on your desk. Please, let me know if you need anything further."

"Thank you, Moira," I said with a smile. "I think today will be a good day. I can feel it."

CHAPTER SEVEN
Penelope

The morning flew by in a flurry of meetings and phone calls and emails.

I arranged to meet with each of the department heads, starting with Ava Carlisle, the head of VIP Services. We had a very brief discussion of her goals in bringing High Rollers in from around the world, all while she stared at me down her overly altered nose. Apparently, there was a certain group of men in the Far East who had a bit of a Wild West fetish. Ava was quite confident she could have all the suites filled for both the Soft Launch in three months, and the Grand Opening in four months, provided I could assemble the right materials in the teaser packages.

I made notes on hiring photographers, models, a video crew, and even a horse. I would have the packages to her before she left for Japan early next week. Ava left the meeting with a stiff nod, leaving my office door open as she went. I looked out into the reception space, noticing Stone standing by Moira's desk as they spoke to one of the call center girls from the first floor. The look on the young woman's face had softened and she resembled a dreamy teen girl, eyes full of desire. Her chest went out and so did her lower lip, pouting hard as she blinked rapidly at Stone as he and Moira spoke briskly about whatever it was they were discussing with her.

I held in a laugh as he looked at her blankly, staring without speaking until she gave up, deflating a little as she walked away. Poor girl. Someone should tell her that regardless of how appealing Stone was on the outside, his personality was enough to make you want to keep your distance.

After Ava, I met with Curtis Jones, Operations Manager. We discussed the retail shops that would be available, as well as staff uniforms and the pool area. The theme for the pool was "Desert Oasis" and according to the architect's renderings, it would be a lush tropical paradise nestled in the heart of *The Alamo* property, with the rooms on that side of the building all having nice pool views. I added all those points to my marketing notes as well.

Geoff Yates, who was already annoyed with me for interrupting his report at the meeting yesterday, basically dropped a list of restaurant menus on my desk and told me to email him if I had any questions.

Gideon Langford, a very attractive man who reminded me of Idris Elba without the accent, was the Casino Manager. He was in charge of all aspects of the gaming facilities, from the poker tables to the slot machines. We reviewed the tables offered and the themed dress of the dealers, who would look like old time gamblers, with their white shirts and black vests.

We agreed that as soon as the casino floor was ready we would arrange a photo shoot for some promotional shots.

Entertainment manager Carson Young sat with me while we discussed the exciting list of things to do while staying at *The Alamo*. He was tasked with finding and securing talent for the three different sized theaters on site, as well as all of the smaller events and the animal exhibits.

This perked me up quite a bit, having loved visiting the Central Park Zoo as a kid; animals had always held a place in my heart. We talked about the horses that would be kept on site, as well as a few donkeys, and, if he could arrange it, maybe even a couple goats. There were animals kept all over the Strip, of course, from the tigers at *The Mirage*, to the *MGM* lions and obviously, the flamingos at *The Flamingo*. But the experience here would be different. The availability of more domesticated animals would increase the accessibility of interactions with the guests, and the whole thing would have more of a petting zoo feel to it, allowing the guests to engage with the animals in a safe and monitored environment.

The theaters were another matter. For the mid sized theater, which was more of an arena than a true theater, Carson had signed a group of performers to do a variety show loosely based on Buffalo Bill's Wild West Show. It incorporated all the elements of the wild west with a *Cirque du Soleil* feel, including trick riders and acrobats, and it finished with a re-enactment of the final battle of *The Alamo* itself.

It sounded wonderful.

There was a huge concert venue which was booked for the next year with all the hottest country and country-rock acts available, all under contract to keep their appearances a secret until the hotel theme was revealed. There were quite a few names on that list I wouldn't mind seeing myself if given half a chance. Hotel packages including concert tickets would bring a ton of guests in. It was all shaping up for a great roll out.

There was also a night club, and Carson had several up and coming DJs lined up who were stars at mixing country and rock and Top 40 hits together to keep people dancing and drinking all night long.

The only problem remaining was the small venue. Modeled more like a dinner theater than a concert hall, Carson had been having a difficult time finding the right act for the space. We finished the meeting agreeing to both consider what we could do there.

My meetings concluded, I gathered up my things and prepared to head out. It was early afternoon, and I wanted to walk down Las Vegas Boulevard, enjoying the sunshine and taking in the sights on my way to meet with the photographer I had called earlier. As I headed for the elevator I waved to Moira, letting her know I had the cell phone she had given me and that I would be back in an hour or two. I pushed the button and stepped in when the doors opened, pressing the button for the lobby. The doors were almost closed again when an arm pressed between, causing them to open. Stone Pennington stepped into the elevator, his scowl firmly in place and barely looking in my direction as he stood beside me, his wide shoulders seeming to take up more space than he was entitled to.

But that was his way; taking more than he was entitled to. Him and all the other rich kids living off their daddies' hard work. I glanced at my phone, wondering how it could possibly take so long for the elevator to descend three short floors. I shifted my feet awkwardly in my flats, wondering how someone so good looking could possibly be such a jerk, just counting the seconds until I could escape the elevator and his angry presence.

Just when I thought I would make it, he spoke. "Leaving the office early, Miss Lund? We aren't paying you to sight see, you know?" Condescension dripped from every syllable, and my spine straightened.

"I know that, Mr. *Montgomery*," I fired back, letting him know exactly what I thought of his duplicitous nature using two names to hide the fact that he was only here because his father owned the company. "That is why I am currently on my way to a meeting. One I arranged earlier. While working. Like you pay me for." I refused to even glance his direction, not wanting the sight of his deep hazel eyes to distract me, instead staring at the numbers as they crawled to the bottom. Finally, the doors slid open and I made my escape, darting out of the elevator before he had a chance to move.

As I walked quickly but with as much dignity as I could muster so that I would not look like I was running - which I kind of was - I heard him growl behind me as he replied. "See that it stays that way."

I pushed through the doors of the administration building, stopping as I felt the sun on my face. Closing my eyes, I lifted my chin and let the light and heat wash over me, taking my crazy emotions with it.

Just being in the same space as Stone Pennington was enough to send me into crazy town. I couldn't control my snark when I spoke to him, which was a bad thing because, jerk or not, he was still my boss. It wouldn't matter how great my marketing campaign was if I was fired for insubordination.

Shaking my head to clear his ridiculously handsome and arrogant face from my mind, I set off toward the street, taking the long way to avoid the majority of the construction areas. The exterior was coming along nicely, with the store fronts starting to look like old west general stores with high end label names on the signs. I smiled politely as the workers waved and gave me nods, and at last found myself standing on the Las Vegas Strip.

It was busy, even for the middle of the week, but that was not unexpected. This was a twenty-four seven kind of town. Checking the address on my phone again, I set off in the direction of the photographer's studio, my head on a swivel as I took it all in. Towering hotels, each with their own unique architectural theme, were interspersed with open spaces filled with palm trees and fountains, the flowing water adding an element of calm to the chaos that was the busy thoroughfare. People of all walks of life moved around me as I made my way up the street; folks in costumes looking to earn a buck, parents hauling their reluctant children from place to place, couples holding hands, and groups of young people traveling in packs. They all made a colorful mosaic that was as fun as it was beautiful.

I was staring at a man-made volcano belching flames into the sky and wondering if anything could be more Las Vegas than a waterfall on fire, when a voice cut into my thoughts and drew my attention.

"Well, hey there, sugar pie," drawled the syrupy sweet voice steeped in country twang. I turned to see a very tall, very blonde, very buxom woman smiling at me, her hair as poofy as cotton candy and her lips a vibrant pink as she flashed me a huge smile. "Well, aren't you just as pretty as a picture? Where you from, darlin'?"

I couldn't help but smile back at her, taking in the gorgeous outfit of denim and rhinestones. "New York, actually," I replied. "How about you?"

"Oh, honey buns, every body 'round these parts knows that Dolly Parton is from Tennessee, deep in the Great Smokey Mountains. I'm just passing through on my way back to Nashville."

I was absolutely dazzled by this woman, who, while clearly not the real Dolly Parton, at probably six feet two inches tall, was an absolute joy to behold.

I wasn't the only one dazzled by her, either. As

I watched, tourists of all ages stopped in their tracks and asked Dolly for a picture. She smiled and posed and laughed her tinkling laugh as folks lined up for photos at five dollars a pop. It was amazing to see how just being in her presence could make people happy - and open their wallets.

And it gave me an idea.

"Nashville? Tell me, Miss Parton. Do you, by any chance, sing?"

Dolly smirked at me, her prominent Adam's apple bobbing as she laughed. "Darlin'," she sassed, cocking out a hip and flashing me a wink. "I may not be able to croon like the original, but I can lip sync with the best of them. And I promise you, no one shakes their bazooms like I do," she added with a shimmy, causing her rhinestone encrusted breasts to bounce and sparkle in the desert sunshine.

I laughed, loving every moment I was spending with this glorious woman. "Well, Dolly, I'll tell you what; if you are interested, and if you have any friends who might wanna tag along, I just might have an opportunity for you to shake and shimmy those bazooms for a crowd."

Dolly's eyes widened, then another smile spread across her painted face. "Alright then, sweet potato. You let me make some phone calls and I'll have you a whole troop of fabulous women who will knock your socks off."

"If they're even half as amazing as you are, I have no doubt!"

*   *   *   *

It was just before five when I headed back to the house. I had met with the photographer and made arrangements for her to come to the hotel in a few days to start preliminary teaser shots. I then located a local printer who would be perfect for printing the promotional materials I wanted to start handing out shortly. I used the internet to find someone who would meet me later in the week to start setting up digital edits to use for our social media campaign, and then I walked to a *Walgreens* and got some make up that didn't cost an entire paycheck.

I sent a message to Moira, telling her that I wouldn't be back in the office for the rest of the day. I hadn't heard a word from Stone, so I could only assume he was still working. I probably should have told him I wouldn't be riding back to the house with him, but I didn't want to be the one to attempt civility first. I had to hold my ground. He thought he could push me around and I needed to show him that I might not be uptown like him, but I was not a door mat either.

I arranged a meeting with Carson Young for Friday, as well, and I was hopeful he would like my idea for the smallest theater. I had been contacted by Dolly, and, from the sounds of it, she was going to have a multitude of ladies that I was confident Carson would love.

When my taxi dropped me off back in Summerlin South, I was ecstatic to see my suitcase sitting on the porch, tattered, but finally arrived. I hauled it inside with me, rolling it to the base of the stairs before heading to the kitchen. I'd skipped lunch, too focused on accomplishing things today, and my stomach had been growling at me for an hour. As I opened the fridge, I heard a voice call from up the stairs.

"Hey, Stone? You're home early. Can you grab me a bottle of water? I've had a killer headache all day."

I turned to look as a gorgeous brunette walked into the kitchen, typing away on her phone at a million miles an hour, short shorts and a tank top on, her tanned stomach showing in the inch or so in between. She was stunning, and I couldn't help but wonder how often Stone came to Las Vegas if he had a woman here who expected him home at a certain time.

She came looked up from her phone and stopped short when she saw me.

"Oh! You're not Stone," she said, tilting her head to the side and assessing me from head to toe.

Why did women keep doing this to me? "Neither are you," I replied, deadpan.

"So, what are you doing here, then?" she asked boldly. "You don't look like his typical booty call." I crossed my arms over my chest, arching an eyebrow. Who did this chick think she was?

"And I suppose you are?"

At that she snorted. "God, I freakin' hope not!" Moving forward, she extended her hand to me. "Hi. I'm Daphne Pennington."

Realization dawned, and I felt my cheeks turning crimson. Good grief, was I being possessive of Stone? Why? He was a jerk! A mean-spirited trust fund baby who talked to me like I was beneath his station.

So what if he was the best looking guy I'd ever laid eyes on? That didn't matter one bit.

Yeah, I'd always been a terrible liar.

More than that, I wanted to change the way he thought of me. I wanted to prove to him that it didn't matter that my parents weren't rich or that I went to school on a scholarship. I deserved to be here just as much as he did.

Likely more.

I blinked away that ridiculous train of thought and shook Daphne's hand, remembering that when I had thought it would be her that I was rooming with here, I'd hoped that we could be friends, or at least get a long. Stone and I certainly weren't managing that, maybe I would have better luck with Daphne. "Hi, I'm Penelope Lund."

"Oh, right!" she exclaimed, suddenly excited. "You're the one Constance was moaning about. I totally get it now." Daphne smiled like the cat that got the cream.

"Get what?" I queried hesitantly. Maybe I didn't want to know what she and Constance thought about me and my chances of earning the VP position.

"Why Constance is shaking in her boots," Daphne chortled, laughing uproariously. "She should be scared. Toddrick is as useless as an ejection seat on a helicopter!"

Picturing that, I laughed softly. "I highly doubt Constance is concerned about me. Toddrick may be useless, but she is still a Pennington. I wouldn't be surprised if this whole competition thing is just a big joke." I couldn't help but let my bitterness and self doubt show a bit.

"I don't think so," Daphne said, moving to the fridge and retrieving the bottle of water she was asking for earlier. I looked around idly for some food, not really hungry anymore. My stomach was in knots thinking about the slim chance I had of getting the promotion and making life easier on my mother. "My father may be a lot of things, but he is not a fool. Putting Toddrick in an important position just to please my uptight sister would not be a great move for his business."

"But everyone knows he wants to keep the company in the family. If not Toddrick and Constance, then..." but I trailed off. Of course. How could I have been so blind?

Stone. The secret Pennington. That was the goal all along; to have Stone take over Pennington Hotels. That meant that no matter how I did in the next four months, he was likely going to be my boss in the end regardless.

And he hated me.

Daphne looked at me, concern on her face. "Hey, what's that look for?"

Taking a deep breath, I shook my head. "Nothing. I just realized that your brother was going to be my boss some day." I glanced at her wryly. "He's not exactly my biggest fan."

"Ugh," she said as she rolled her eyes. "Stone is really no one's fan. He's such a grouch." She turned her back to the counter and hopped up, her bare legs dangling. "When we used to go to Texas to see him, he barely talked to us. It took forever for me to even get him to acknowledge I existed. The only reason he finally did is because we would make fun of Constance together." Daphne laughed, shaking her head. "I remember one time, when I was like six, we were in Austin for the summer. Constance hated going down there, but I loved it. She had to come, because she wasn't eighteen yet, and she was doing her best to make the whole trip as miserable as she was.

"Anyway, dad always tried to engage Stone in family activities, but he was so angry, he wanted nothing to do with it. If it wasn't for the fact that his mother asked him to, he would never have interacted with us at all. So we were out at the ranch where Stone and his mother lived, and Stone had me up on this horse. We're walking around the corral, and I'm happy as a clam, but Constance is fuming. She's sitting on the fence rail, reading some magazine, when this big old dog comes up behind her and starts barking like mad. Connie jerks and falls right off the fence rail face first in the mud." Daphne throws her head back and cackles. "She was covered. Even had it in her ears!"

I smiled as I pictured it, perfectly poised Constance Pennington face first in the dirt. "I bet that's not the type of mud bath she was used to getting." I laughed.

"It sure wasn't," the evil grin on Daphne's face told me everything I needed to know about her relationship with Constance. Perhaps we could be friends after all. "Anyway, as Connie was laying there, hollering her face off about how much she hated Texas and everyone in it, Stone and I were laughing our heads off. From that moment on, we've had an understanding. He may not be the most affectionate brother in the world, but I know he loves me. It's just hard for him, you know? Growing up without dad around. Being thought of as the mistake." Daphne looked away, her eyes growing distant as she got lost in her memories. "That's what Connie and my mother always called him, even to his face as a kid. A mistake." Daphne frowned, suddenly serious. I felt it too. The horrible way a little boy must have felt, being told those things by the women who were supposed to be his family. No wonder he was so defensive. He had probably spent his whole life deflecting emotional wounds.

I stared out over the pool, remembering our encounter there yesterday, how he was so quick to snap at me. Even at the airport, he assumed I was out to get him before I even had a chance to do otherwise.

As I watched the pool ripple in the desert wind, I thought that maybe I understood Stone Pennington just a little bit better now. And maybe I could forgive him for being such a jerk to me.

Then the front door swung inward, Stone

entered the house with another man by his side, and all my charitable thoughts went out the window when he opened his freaking mouth.

"What the hell are you doin' now, Blondie?"

CHAPTER EIGHT

Stone

Watching Penelope walk away in the lobby, I couldn't help but feel a little guilty. I knew she'd been working hard all morning. I had practically been camped outside her office all day, constantly finding excuses to be where I could see her. I didn't understand it.

On one hand, she annoyed me so badly, I wanted to throw things, with her fancy clothes and her New York attitude, she was everything I hated about that town.

But on the other hand, she was sassy and fiery and didn't take any shit. She stood up to me no matter how hard I pushed. I liked that. I was so sick of people always scrapin' and kissin' my ass. It was part of the reason why I didn't use the Pennington name. If it was this bad when they thought I was a Montgomery, imagine how ridiculous it would be if they knew it was my name on the front of all the buildings?

Then there was the fact that I couldn't stop thinking about how damn gorgeous she was. Those big blue eyes and all that golden hair she kept trapped in a bun like some school teacher. Even when I was fumin' mad because she was getting under my skin, I still couldn't stop picturing diggin' my fingers into that hair and holding tight while I kissed her.

And what the hell was that shit? There was no way I was gonna be kissing her. For one, she was a New Yorker, and I wouldn't kiss her on principle alone. And for another, she worked for the company. After seeing the aftermath of my parents doomed affair, there was no way in hell I was getting involved with someone who worked for me. Absolutely not.

Standing in the lobby, I watched and waited as the work trucks came and went from the parking lot. Silas had messaged me a few minutes ago, saying he was in a taxi and on his way to the hotel site. It would be damn good to have him here.

As I stood there, I couldn't help but notice that several women kept walking to and fro, flitting about like little birds. I would see them staring out the corner of my eye, and when I turned to look, they would avert their eyes and move along quickly. I turned to look into the room where they gathered. It was the main business office and call center. All the incoming calls and packages came through there, then were forwarded to the appropriate department. There were about half a dozen women employed there, and they were all staring at me like I was a zoo exhibit. What the hell was going on?

I forgot all about them when the door opened and my best friend walked in. Silas was dressed as he usually was, in jeans and a long-sleeved Henley. He had his hair freshly cut, still according to army regulations, and he wore aviator sunglasses, his black duffel bag slung over his shoulder.

He entered the lobby, looking around until he spotted me, then pulled off his sunglasses and gave me a mocking smile. "Well, look at you, all suited and booted. I hardly recognized you, looking all big city like you are." He exaggerated his Texas accent for effect, and I scowled at him.

"Yeah, you keep talking like that, you'll have to find yourself another place to stay. I don't have room in my house for mouthy bastards like you." I attempted to keep my scowl, but I couldn't hide the jest underneath.

Silas boomed out a laugh and dropped his bag, grasping my outstretched hand and pulling me in for a hard slap on the back. "Good to see you, man. Looks like Vegas is treating you well."

As we released each other, I heard a round of giggles coming from the call center. Looking over my shoulder, I saw all of the women were staring openly, dreamy looks on their faces. Silas and I shared a confused look, then headed for the truck. The girls all strained to watch us go.

Bizarre.

"I know you probably want to jump right in and get to work," I said, knowing my friend well enough by now to know he prided himself on his work ethic. "But I thought we could grab a late lunch. I have a few things I'd like to talk about."

"Uh oh," Si said, climbing in the passenger seat

with much more ease that Penelope had this morning. "Sounds like you have a Harold problem."

I frowned at him. "What's that supposed to mean?"

"Stone, in all the years I've known you, the only time you ever want to have a serious conversation is if it's about your father."

"That's not true," I insisted, even though it probably was. Even work conversations weren't as dire as the discussions Silas and I had had about Harold Pennington. I guided the truck down the side streets, getting us to the restaurant I wanted with as little traffic as I could manage. It wasn't far, but I didn't think we would be going back to the office today, so I brought the truck.

I had another moment of guilt over giving Penelope shit about ducking out early when that was exactly what I was doing now. Christ, I really was an ass.

"It is and you know it," Silas said, laughing. "Dude, if you had any more daddy issues, you'd be a stripper!"

"Fuck off," I said, but laughed anyway. "Besides, this isn't about Harold. Well, not directly."

"It's not?" Silas looked skeptical. He stared at me for a moment, then his eyes went wide. "Holy shit," he breathed.

"What," I said cautiously.

"It's a woman."

"No." I was immediately defensive. "It's a work thing." It happened to be about a woman I worked with, but I wasn't going to give him the satisfaction of being right.

"Bullshit. This is a woman problem." Silas had a smug grin on his face.

"It's a problem with a woman at work, yes," I tried, but he wasn't buying it.

"Stone Pennington. I'll be damned. You caught some feelings here in Sin City?"

"Absolutely not," I insisted, probably too quickly. "I haven't even been here two days." He just laughed.

"Oh, just wait until your mama hears. She's gonna be over the moon. She's been waitin' on you to settle down for ages, boy."

"Don't you dare tell my ma nothin'! She'll start planning a wedding, for Christ's sake." This conversation was going all wrong. I parked the truck and turned off the engine, turning to my friend and just coming out with it. "There is a woman working on this project. She's a walking disaster. Harold has her staying at the house with me."

"You two are already livin' together!" Silas snorted, clapping his hands. "Oh, this just gets better and better."

"Not like that, you moron. Harold set her up at the house but she thought she'd be staying with my sister. She's, I don't know, she's a mess and she's beautiful and she hates me already, and she's... she's from New York."

"Ah," my friend said and nodded sagely. "There it is."

I frowned again. "There what is?"

"The thing holding you back about this girl. She's from New York, so in your mind, she's automatically the devil incarnate."

"That's not true," I protested again. But it was. I knew it was.

"Stone, man, when are you gonna wake up and realize that Harold did the best he could by you. The best that you would allow him to do." Silas shook his head. I knew he saw my situation differently. His own family had been a mess, with a mother that left when he was little and a father who liked to get drunk and knock him and his brothers around. As far as he was concerned, Harold had offered me a golden ticket time and time again, and I had foolishly refused it.

And maybe he was right, but that didn't mean my concerns about Penelope weren't valid. Although, I was having a harder and harder time believing them myself.

We headed into the restaurant and got a seat. It was a middle of the road place, but their Yelp reviews said they served good steak, so I figured it was the place for us. After ordering our meals and a couple of beers, Silas started in again.

"So, aside from being an evil New Yorker, what is it about this girl that's got your tail in a twist?"

I took a deep breath. "She is just constantly getting under my skin, ya know? Like, she's always in the way, interrupting me at meetings and questioning my decisions. It's inappropriate." God, I even sounded like an asshole to myself.

"Is she wrong?" Silas asked easily.

"What?" I said, thrown by his question.

"When she questions your decisions, is she wrong?"

I swallowed, feeling like a complete heel. "Well, not my decisions, exactly. But she questioned the theme of the hotel. I think the old west theme is perfect, but she wanted something slick and more *big city*."

"So she didn't so much question you, as where you come from," Silas stated, that smug grin back on his face. "You felt slighted by her opinion of your roots. Let me guess; you immediately took it out on her?"

I sighed, remembering how I had cut her down in front of her colleagues. "Yeah. Shit." I took another swig of my beer, rolling the bottle between my hands as I stared at the table.

"And how did she respond to this verbal admonishment?" The ass was enjoying this.

"She fired right back at me." She had too, calling me out for being an asshole to her at the airport. She was right, but that was beside the point.

"So, let me see if I have this right? This girl – she's beautiful, smart, sharp, and she puts you in your place when you're being a belligerent ass?"

"Yes," I ground out thought clenched teeth.

Silas slapped his hand down on the table. "Well, shit, Stone. If you don't want her, I sure as hell do. Any woman who can take what you dish out and give it back just as good has got to be one hell of a catch."

I narrowed my eyes at my friend, the thought of him and Penelope together making my jaw clench. He didn't miss it, and it only made him laugh harder. "Oh, hell. You got it bad, boy." He was saved from the beating I wanted to give him by the arrival of our food.

Throughout the rest of our meal, I steered conversation away from Penelope and back toward the project. Silas was as excited about the theme as I was, and we reviewed some of the aspects of security he wanted to handle while construction was still happening, things like camera placement and emergency exits and the like. I told him he had complete control and that I would arrange a meeting with the head contractor as well as his staff tomorrow. Then we settled into regular bullshit conversation, the type we'd been having since high school.

It was early evening when we headed for the house. Walking in, I heard Penelope's laughter coming from the kitchen and immediately saw a suitcase sitting at the bottom of the stairs.

What the hell? Was she inviting guests to the house? Without asking me?

Then another thought hit me. Did this bag belong to her boyfriend? Some yuppie schmuck from SoHo or something? Some pale man-boy with a sweater vest and horn-rimmed glasses who insisted on eating vegan and drinking artisan beers.

I hated him already. She could do better than that loser.

Well, I'd show them. There was no way that asshat was gonna be staying in this house. She was here to work, not traipse around with her beatnik boy toy. He was taking his piece of shit suitcase and he was outta here. Tonight.

"What the hell are you doin' now, Blondie?"

Silas hissed quietly behind me. "What the fuck, Stone?" I ignored him. My anger was up and there was no stopping me.

Penelope came into the foyer, a confused look on her face. "Is there something I can do for you, Mr. Montgomery?" she said, her tone docile, her eyes full of contempt.

I pointed at her boyfriend's busted up suitcase. "Get that piece of shit out of here." He needed to leave. Now.

Penelope looked at the bag, confused. "Excuse me?"

"You heard me. He needs to leave." Silas stood beside me, shaking his head.

"Who needs to leave?" Penelope asked, looking at Silas. "He's *your* guest."

"What?" I said, and Silas looked at me, eye brow raised. Yeah, we were all confused. "Not him." I hooked my thumb at Silas. "Him," I said, again pointing at the bag.

Penelope frowned. "My bag? Why? And why do you keep referring to it as 'him'?"

Now I was the one who was frowning. "Your bag?" There was no way. A New York girl would never have such a busted-up suitcase. Constance had always insisted on Louis Vuitton or some other smarmy brand. This thing looked like it was from the seventies, all worn brown leather and large buckles. There was no way this was Penelope's.

But as she walked over to it, I realized I was wrong. The tag hanging from the top was purple and had flowers all over it. "Yes," she said, grasping the handle and pulling it away from me. "My bag. I realize that it may not live up to your standards, but I would appreciate it if you would not give me any grief about it. It's not any concern of yours."

We stared at each other for a moment, her face defiant, mine baffled. What the hell was going on?

The tension was broken when Silas slapped me on the back, then moved past me toward Penelope, his hand extended. "Hello. I'm Silas Harrison, Security Manager for *The Alamo*."

Penelope faced Silas, a brilliant smile on her face. "Hello Mr. Harrison. Penelope Lund, marketing. A pleasure to meet you. Now," she said and turned to me, a look of barely restrained violence thrown my way, "if you'll both excuse me, I have to take my 'piece of shit' bag and go to my room. Good night, Silas," she said politely, granting him another smile. It dropped from her face as she glared at me again. "Mr. Montgomery." And with that, she heaved the bag up the stairs, stomping the whole way.

Silas and I watched her go. When she was out of sight, he turned and punched me full force in the arm, my bicep going numb with the hit. "Ow! Shit, man. What the hell?"

"What the hell, is right, you sorry fuck. What the hell was that?"

Rubbing my arm, I put on my signature scowl. "Nothing."

"That girl didn't deserve one ounce of the shit you just flung her way. You wanna tell me what that was all about?"

He was right, the ass. But how could I tell him what went through my head? How could I possibly explain that at the sight of the ratty suitcase, my stupid brain had conjured up an entire scenario, spiraling me into a vortex of rage over a man who didn't even exist? That just the thought of Penelope having a boyfriend had made me so angry, I blew up at her again.

I was so screwed over this girl. I knew it, but I still denied it.

After all, the best lies were the ones we told ourselves.

"That was me, wondering why she was having some sort of party in a house she doesn't own." I tried for believable, but Silas wasn't buying it. He just shook his head at me in disappointment. To be fair, I was disappointed in myself, too. But I just got so mad when I heard Penelope laughing in the kitchen.

Come to think of it, who the hell was in the kitchen anyway?

Moving past Silas, I turned that way, stomping through the hall and entering the room prepared to take on any intruder in there.

But a smile spread on my face at the sight of my half-sister, Daphne, perched on the counter top, staring at me like I was the worlds biggest moron.

Yeah, there was a lot of that going around.

"Well, hey there, big brother," she said, shaking her head. "You about done beating your chest like a big old gorilla?" I laughed, moving to give her a hug. She opened her arms for me, but stopped when something over my shoulder caught her eye. She froze, eyebrows shooting up, her cheeks going pink, as she gazed at my friend as he entered the kitchen. Looking at Silas, I saw the same expression of amazement on his face as he took in my sister.

Oh, hell no.

Daphne and Silas hadn't seen each other in over ten years. Apparently, a lot had changed since then.

"Silas," I barked, snapping him out of it. He cleared his throat, looking at me sheepishly. "You wanna close your mouth and come over here. I'm sure you remember, Daphne. My *baby sister.*" I said the words with enough emphasis that he immediately caught on. His face went blank, and he looked at Daphne as if she were any other person he had just met on the street. Good. That was another issue I didn't have time for. Daphne and I might not have been very close growing up, but there was still a code among best friends. Little sisters were off limits.

Period.

It hadn't been an issue when we were kids. Silas was only a year younger than me, which still made him twelve years older than Daphne. But, apparently, that age gap was starting to matter less and less.

Silas simply nodded his head and muttered,

"Daphne."

Daphne frowned, looking from Silas to me and then back again. When she realized what had passed between him and I, she sighed, her shoulders falling, as she shook her head.

"I guess I'll just go up to bed myself," she said as she jumped down from the counter, pushing past me.

"What? Why?" I asked. "It's still early, and we just got in." I hadn't seen her in months. I was looking forward to talking about her classes and UNLV.

"Well, Stone, it may be early, but your *baby sister* needs her sleep," she spat, making it clear I had pissed her off now too. "I'll just go up and see how Penelope is doing. I think between the two of us, you've done enough damage for one night." And with that she stormed off for the stairs.

Silas and I watched her go. When she was out of sight, we both blew out a breath.

This might just be the longest four months of my life.

CHAPTER NINE
Penelope

Glancing at the clock on the wall once more, I tried to swallow down my rising panic. Carson Young and Stone Pennington were staring at me, Stone with his usual stern scowl on his face, and Carson with a mixture of apprehension and discomfort on his.

I couldn't blame him. The tension in the room was practically choking me; I couldn't imagine how Carson felt, not knowing the true cause.

When I arranged to meet with Carson to discuss my idea for the final open theater space, I had assumed it would be just him and me. But when Stone found out I had organized something without telling him, he insisted on being a part of the meeting. And, because he's my boss, I couldn't very well tell him no.

Stone and I had barely spoken since Tuesday evening, when he went nuclear on me for having an ugly suitcase. I was still not sure what it was about my bag that set him off, and since neither of us had wanted to initiate any actual conversation, it was unlikely I would ever actually find out.

The one bright spot in my life had been Daphne.

She was spending her evenings at the house, rather than her dorm room, and we had gotten to know each other pretty well considering it had been less than a week. She was bubbly and vivacious and I couldn't help but smile when she was around.

And, good grief, did I need some smiles.

Living and working with Stone Pennington was absolutely exhausting. Avoiding him was even more so. I constantly felt like I was walking on egg shells, always trying to evade a confrontation. In the mornings we passed like strangers, moving from the coffee pot to the door without actually acknowledging the others existence. I started using Uber to the office because the thought of being in the vehicle alone with him for the twenty minutes it would take us to get from the house to the office was excruciating.

If he cared about my change in my transportation, he hadn't said anything.

For his part, Stone has been avoiding spending time at the house as much as possible. He and Silas seemed to constantly have things to keep them occupied, leaving Daphne and I to spend some quality girl time together.

I had found her really easy to talk to. She loved that we were both from New York, though very different versions of it, and we spent hours discussing our favorite places to hang out, shop, and eat. That was how I wound up telling her about my dad; we had been discussing Central Park, reminiscing over wine about what we missed the most. She said she missed weekend brunch at the Tavern on the Green. I'd never been there, but from the way she described the Eggs Benedict Florentine, it was more than outside my prince range. It was then that I mentioned the Central Park Zoo, my birthday tradition, and the loss of my father.

I didn't realize until that moment, but I never really talked about my dad to anyone but my mom. People have a strange reaction when you say you lost someone you love; they get uncomfortable. It changes the dynamic of your relationship irrevocably. They suddenly view you as vulnerable, a breakable thing that requires careful handling.

I hated the pity in people's faces when they learned about my father. The distant look in their eyes that told me they wanted to leave the conversation, but weren't sure how to do it without looking like a complete jerk.

Daphne didn't have that look. She smiled sweetly when I told her my fondest memories and stated that it was high time I got back to the zoo. She insisted that the moment we were both back in New York we would arrange a date and treat each other to our favorite Central Park experiences, brunch at the Tavern and a day at the zoo.

It sounded lovely.

I almost let myself believe it would happen.

But I knew better. Daphne was lovely, but I knew our different lifestyles would separate us once I was done squatting in her father's guest bedroom. Once I was back east, she would be in her borough and I would stay in mine.

It was probably for the best.

"Any chance you'll actually start the meeting you called, Miss Lund?" Stone's dry sarcasm drew me out of my musings. I frowned at him.

"The meeting was between Mr. Young and myself, Mr. Montgomery," I said, wiping my sweaty palms on my skirt. "If you have something more pressing to attend to, please don't let me keep you."

He opened his mouth to say something, eyes flashing with indignation, and I braced myself for a cold reply, but a commotion in the hall brought him up short.

"Wait," I heard Moira's voice, her tone strained. "You can't just go in and-" The door burst open in a cloud of glitter and denim. I saw Stone and Carson's jaws drop wide open, and a smile spread across my face.

"Well, listen here, puddin' pop," drawled Dolly in her exaggerated country twang. "I can go any which way I please. Don't you know who I am?"

"It's alright, Moira," I interjected. "She's with me." Dolly smiled my way, her bright pink lips stretching wide.

"Hey there, pumpkin pie!" she gushed, her signature giggle filling the conference room. "Don't you look a treat! Those shoes! They are to die for." I flushed as Dolly fawned over my magenta pumps. It was the first day I was wearing them. I figured if they were going to work their magic, as my mother and her friends insisted, then today would be the day.

Stone scoffed, his eye roll telling me everything I needed to know about his opinion of my shoes. I shot him a frown, then turned to Carson. "Mr. Young, may I introduce you to Dolly Parton. Dolly, this is Carson Young, entertainment and events manager for Pennington Hotels Las Vegas." Dolly turned her brilliant smile on Carson, eying him up and down.

"Hi there and hello, sugar. Aren't you just as cute as a possum on prom night!"

Carson stared open mouthed at Dolly, a bright pink flush creeping up his cheeks, not entirely sure what was going on. Stone's face was a mixture of confusion and annoyance.

What else was new?

"Dolly," I said, drawing her attention from Carson and intentionally failing to introduce Stone. "Thank you so much for joining us. If you please," I gestured to the chair nearest me. Dolly sat, exaggerating every movement like a pin up girl, her extraordinarily long legs looking even longer in the short denim skirt and exceptionally high heeled shoes. She crossed her legs and settled back in the chair, looking every inch a Queen on her throne. I smiled again, then turned back to the two men sitting before me.

"Gentlemen, I have been working with Dolly this week to develop a strategy for the final theater venue here at the hotel."

Stone immediately cut me off. "That's not your job, Miss Lund. I believe Mr. Young is in charge of acquiring talent."

I bit the inside of my cheek to keep myself from replying in the way I truly wanted, and instead drew in a slow breath before responding to Stone's unnecessarily sharp remark.

"Yes, Mr. Montgomery, he is. However, after my discussion with him earlier this week, I was made aware that he had not secured an act for the small theater venue as of yet. When a chance encounter brought Dolly and I together, I saw an opportunity and I took it. Mr. Young may be in charge of acquiring talent, but my job is attracting visitors and their dollars. I believe Dolly will do that."

Carson was now smiling slightly, assessing Dolly from a business perspective and not just as the beautiful spectacle she was.

Stone, on the other hand, continued to scowl. "And how do you expect one drag queen to fill and entire theater? Talented though she may be," he added, with a nod in Dolly's direction. She raised one painted eyebrow at him but didn't respond.

"I don't expect one talented drag queen to fill an entire theater," I said, smiling at Dolly. At my nod, she brought her fingers up to her lips and gave a shrill whistle.

"Ladies!" she said, standing again, one hand on her cocked out hip. "Saddle up now, and show these boys what we're made of."

Stone and Carson turned to the door of the conference room as a parade of exceptionally beautiful queens entered the room, strutting their gorgeous stuff around the table. There were at least a dozen ladies, some celebrity impersonators, some simply incredible characters, and they were all dressed to the nines.

I crossed my arms as the line of women stood arrayed out behind me. There were women of all shapes and sizes and colors and ethnicities. They wore pants, and dresses, and gowns, and boots and platform shoes. Their hair was sky high and their make up was outrageous.

And I loved everything about them.

Smiling again, I turned back to Stone. His face was blank as he studied the women in front of him. Carson was now grinning broadly.

"Allow me to introduce you to *The Queens of the Alamo*," I said proudly. Reaching into my briefcase, I withdrew some of the promotional materials I had drawn up earlier in the week. The photographer I hired had met Dolly and her ladies for some great shots in the desert, and then I'd done some mock ups and had them printed. I handed the items to Carson and Stone, watching as Carson's face lit up and Stone's eyes narrowed. "I'm thinking a dinner theater and variety show. A mix of lip sync, cabaret, burlesque, and stand-up comedy. There would be some audience participation, and even a little slap stick. It turns out that these are some seriously talented ladies." I gesture to the women behind me, who all preened and posed like a bunch of brightly colored birds.

"Penelope," Carson exclaimed brightly, getting up and wrapping me in a hug, squeezing me so tightly my ribs ached and my feet left the floor. "This is brilliant!" He let me go just as quickly and turned to Dolly. "I would love to work with you guys, uh, gals on some musical numbers. I have some ideas for original songs you might be interested in."

"Listen, darlin," came a voice from behind me. I turned and gazed up - way up - in to the beautiful face of Cher. Her long black hair hung straight on either side of her face, falling almost to her waist. She was wearing purple corduroy bell bottoms and a flowered cropped peasant top. Her huge eyes, painted in shades of bright purple to match her pants, blinked down at us. She must have been close to six and a half feet tall, skinny as a rail, and absolutely gorgeous. Cher batted her eyelashes and dramatically licked her lips. "If anyone here is gonna be talking about original songs, it's me." She swept her hair back off her shoulders, doing a perfect impression of Cher's signature move.

"Oh," stammered Carson. "Uh, yeah." He grinned at her, one side of his mouth ticking up. "I'd love to discuss options. Penelope, these fliers are great. I'd like to talk about a schedule and get Geoff in on the menu side. I'm thinking four nights a week and a matinee on Saturdays. Also, I want to-"

"Miss Lund," Stone's booming voice broke into the conversation, halting everyone as we swung our heads in his direction. I looked at him, tapping my flier on his knee as he sat, leaned back in the chair, one ankle crossed over his other leg. Standing tall, my lips pursed as I awaited his judgment, I tried to anticipate what he'd hate about my idea. Would it be too cliché? Too over the top? Or perhaps he'd hate it for no other reason than it was my idea. I crossed my arms and regarded him coolly, but I could feel my pulse racing in my throat.

Finally, after staring at me silently for a few long moments, he spoke. "This idea, did you come up with it all on your own?"

I was taken aback. His tone seemed purely professional, with no sign of his typical snideness or mockery. His face held nothing but honest businesslike curiosity.

I cleared my throat. "Yes, Mr. Montgomery. Although, once I started to develop it, Dolly and her crew provided a lot of inspiration."

"And these numbers," he said, pulling the sales estimates I drew up out of the package I provided. "You think these are going to be accurate."

"According to the statistics chart that was provided with *The Alamo* business dossier I was given, they are, yes."

I waited again as he assessed the assembled ladies, each one more outrageous than the last. There was Dolly and Cher, but also a Madonna impersonator and some famous TV personalities as well. The program the women had put together with their assembled skill set was quite entertaining. I imagined with some polish and a few tweaks from Carson it would be a knockout production.

At last, Stone stood, gathering the package I have given him back together. "If you can reach numbers anywhere near what you've projected–" he said, his face serious but not scowling like I was used to. I didn't really know what to do with him at that moment. How did I handle him if he wasn't spitting out snide remarks with every other breath? "I think you just might have a hit on your hands."   And with that, and a shocking twist of his lips I might even have called a real smile, Stone turned and left the conference room without looking back.

Carson and I stared after him for a beat, before we both look at each other in confusion.   Carson spoke first.

"What the hell just happened?"

"I, um, I think Stone Montgomery just complimented me," I said, still not quite sure if I believed it myself.

"Honey cake," Dolly chimed in, her sweet voice breaking through my shock.   "If that man is half as surly as he looked, you better get yourself to a casino and place a whopper of a bet.   Because, considering the smile he sent your way, I think this might just be your lucky day!" she finished, and all the ladies cheered.

The only problem was, I didn't know if I'd consider what happened lucky at all.

But it was damn confusing.

*   *   *   *

That night, after watching the sun set in another spectacular display of brilliant crimson and gold across the hills of Red Rock Canyon, I sat by the pool, a blanket across my lap as I curled up on one of the lounge chairs and called my mother.   We had been communicating mostly via text messages during this first hectic week, and I found I just really needed to hear her voice.

"Hey, there," she said excitedly. I could hear how tired she was by the way her voice was a bit strained. Part of the reason we hadn't talked much was that she was working nights lately. It was hard on her physically, but there was a wage premium paid to nurses who took the overnight shifts, and we needed all the help we could get. "How are things out in Sin City?"

"Oh," I said slowly, not wanting to really burden my mom with my problems. She had enough to worry about. "Things are as good as can be expected."

"Penelope," she said sternly. "Tell me everything."

I took a deep breath and started from the beginning. I told her about losing my luggage, and the coffee incident, and stumbling late into the meeting to find that Stone was my boss. I told her about falling in the pool, and the uncomfortable living situation, and how Stone seemed determined to cut me down at every turn. She made all the right noises of outrage, her mama bear instincts kicking in.

"But something pretty great happened today, Mom."

"Well, I should hope so," she stated. "It's been a heck of a week. I wish you were home, I'd get you some ice cream and put on an episode of The Bachelor." I chuckled, thinking how right she was; sweet treats and trash TV often solved all our problems. "Tell me about your great thing, honey."

"Well," I said, drawing the word out to create suspense. "I wore the shoes!"

"Yes!" my mother exclaimed. "I knew it. I knew they would help. Tell me, what amazing thing did that fabulous footwear accomplish?"

So, in an excited rush, I shared with her my idea for *The Queens of the Alamo*. My mother laughed with me as I gushed about all of Dolly's terms of endearment, and asked for pictures when I told her how spectacular Cher looked in her purple bell bottoms. We laughed at Carson's reaction, and I told her all about the show I had dreamed up in my head, how I planned to market it, and how successful I wanted it to be.

"These women are just incredible, Mom. They are the most confident people I have ever come across." I paused, remembering the way the ladies had each strutted into the room today, not caring for one moment what anyone else thought of them, the type of clothing they wore, or how they were 'supposed' to look. "Watching them, seeing how they command the attention of everyone in the room, it's inspiring."

"Confidence is supposed to be inspiring, honey," my mom said sagely. "That's what makes someone a good leader. But there is a difference between confident and cocky. No one likes an ass."

I burst out laughing. My mother rarely swore, and hearing her drop a simple word like that without missing a beat shocked me something fierce.

It also sent a pang of homesickness through my

chest. I clutched at my phone, blinking back the tears that threatened to fall. I lay back in the lounge chair, staring up at the sky over the darkened hills, and I thought of home. Of sitting beside mom on the couch, sharing a laugh and a bottle of wine after a long week of work. I thought of walking to the train station in the mornings, waving to the neighbors who had lived near us for as long as I could remember. I thought of the sounds and the smells and the sights of our street in Queens. The kids playing in the school yard on a Saturday afternoon, watching them race their bikes up and down the same roads that I used to ride on when I was their age. I thought of visiting my dad at St. Michael's, wandering the familiar silent paths through the cemetery and spending my quiet moments with him.

I missed it all. So much it hurt.

But under that hurt was my determination. I was not going to be pushed aside for something I worked so hard for. I was not going to give up the hope that mom and I could finally get out from under our financial burden and maybe, just maybe, get some breathing room.

And I was definitely not going to let a snooty cow like Constance use her name and her husband to take something that neither of them deserved.

My mother sensed my emotional struggle. She sighed into the phone. "Oh, Penelope. I am so proud of you."

I smiled, my tears coming again, but for an entirely different reason now. "Thanks, Mom."

"I mean it," she confirmed. "You have worked so hard, and I am so proud of the things you have accomplished. But, Penelope, I want you to know something; you don't have to do this for anyone but yourself."

"Mom, I-"

"No," she interrupted me. "Please hear me out. I love you. We have always been a team, you and me, and I appreciate everything you do. But, honey, I want you to start taking care of you first. I want you to make choices that make you happy, not the choices you think are going to be best for us, or for our bank accounts. All the money in the world wouldn't mean anything if you were unhappy while you made it." She took a deep breath and I held mine, waiting for whatever she would say next. "Just be sure that you are happy, Penelope. That's all that I want for you out of this life. It's what your daddy would have wanted, too."

I smiled sadly, another tear escaping and tracing its way down my cheek. I swiped it away before continuing. "I love you, too, Mom. And I am happy. I promise. Just a little...stressed right now. But, it'll be okay. All of it. I'll finish here soon and be back in New York before you know it."

"Good, honey. That's really good. Now," mom said, and I could just picture her squaring her shoulders and dusting her hands in the way she did. "I am on my way to work. I'll tell the ladies the shoes are doing their job. You keep wearing them. I know you'll keep doing great things, honey. I love you."

"I love you, too."

Ending the call, I leaned back again, staring up into the clear night sky, looking at the stars as they stretched across the heavens for as far as I could see.

I will get through this. I will complete this launch and create the best damn marketing campaign anyone has ever seen. I will get the VP position and no one, not Toddrick, not Constance, not Stone - not even myself - will stand in my way.

CHAPTER TEN

Stone

The following weeks went by in much the same manner as the first; me, working and stomping around in a shitty mood. Silas, giving me shit for said shitty mood. Daphne, giving me stink eye at every opportunity. And Penelope, avoiding me at all costs.

She had been getting to and from the office on her own. She was gone before I got up in the morning and I would find her at her desk every day, head down, drawing up plans and making phone calls. She'd been working with the art department back in Manhattan and some of the specs coming across my desk were fantastic. Her social media teasers were also working wonders. I had to admit, her hashtags had been popular and, according to the report she delivered at our most recent weekly meeting, our Instagram followers were up by several thousand.

By all accounts, she was doing a wonderful job. The fact that she was doing it with cold and focused determination should have made me happy, but in reality, it didn't. I missed her fire. I missed the snark and sass that she would deliver, even when she was giving me shit. Now she only spoke to me when I asked her a direct question. Even then, it was "yes, Mr. Montgomery" or "no, Mr. Montgomery". When I saw her at the house, she refused to make eye contact and didn't even acknowledge my existence. I would hear her having conversations with Daphne or I would see them sitting in the living room, or at the kitchen island, laughing together. While Daphne had gone back to talking to me like her brother, Penelope would make a quick exit from every room I entered.

I couldn't decide if it hurt or just pissed me off.

A knock at my office door brought me back to the present. I looked up to see Silas standing there, a grin on his face as he took in my messy desk.

"Whoa." He sounded astonished, and I didn't blame him. "What the hell happened in here?" There were reports and media briefings spread all over my desk, as well as several stacks of fabric samples from the decorator and a pile of shipping boxes in the corner, their contents spilling out all over the floor. Silas walked over to the nearest box and opened it. "Horseshoes?"

"Yeah," I sighed, shaking my head. "Horseshoes. Real ones. Used and everything."

He moved to the next box and reached inside. "And this?"

"That," I replied, gesturing to the coil of rope in his hands, "is apparently the bull rope used by six-time National Finals Rodeo Bull Riding Champion Sage Kimzey."

"Where did you get all this stuff?" Silas gestured

to the other boxes, each one filled with more and more surprising items.

"Harold," I said dryly. "Apparently, he has been going around the country for the last year, collecting western memorabilia. He has been sending me things for weeks. Said he wanted to use them to 'decorate the new hotel'. He's like a kid on Christmas with this shit."

I had heard more from Harold in the last month than I had in the entire time I'd been employed by Pennington Hotels. He had jumped into this theme with both feet. It actually surprised me, seeing as he spent little to no time in Texas with us. Yet, he was acting like he had been a cowboy all his life. The other day, he called in the middle of the day to ask me which Spaghetti Western film was my favorite. I was totally shocked by the question, but managed to spit out *A Fist Full of Dollars*, not only because it was the seminal classic of the entire genre, but because it had Clint Eastwood in a poncho, and you just don't get shit like that anymore. John Wayne movies were great, but there was something about Clint Eastwood and that short cigar that just made the whole Spaghetti Western classic.

My father and I talked about it for almost half an hour, and I couldn't remember a time when we had just...talked. It was strangely comfortable, and as such, made me strangely *un*comfortable. I was not used to talking to him like a dad. And as I hung up the phone, feeling a mix of things I wasn't sure what to do with, I realized that a big part of the reason Harold had never been a dad to me was my own stubborn pride.

"Anyway," I went on, shaking off the thoughts of my father. "What are you doing here? It's late."

"Exactly. Everyone left hours ago. I came to drag you away." Silas walked over and seated himself in one of the chairs facing my desk, leaning back. Even relaxed as he was, you could see the coiled strength in him. His eyes were alert and constantly moving. He never turned it off. It was what made him such an excellent security chief.

It was also the reason he didn't sleep at night, but he didn't know that I knew that.

"I still have a shit-ton of work to do," I stated, gesturing broadly to the piles of things scattered around my office. The final decisions on things like curtains had to be finished by Monday. We had an interior design department, but I wanted to have Daphne take a look at their final choices. She had been going to school for this stuff and I wanted her opinion. I asked her to come by the office today when her classes finished, but she said she had plans. I was going to bring the samples to the house for her to look over.

"And that shit-ton of work will still be there when you roll up here on Monday," Silas countered. "Come on, man. You have been busting your ass for the last month. You have spent hardly any time at the house, and that's not just because you are trying to avoid your hot roommate." He threw a sly grin my way and I scowled.

"I've been working." I tried to defend myself, but he wasn't buying it. "I have less than three months to get this roll out completed.   There are still so many things to do and I am just, well, trying to... you know. Work," I finished lamely.

He raised an eyebrow at me.   Yeah.   Neither of us were buying that one, but he let it go.

"Come on.   You and I are going out on the town.   I have been here all this time and you haven't shown me the bright lights of Sin City yet."

"It's really not my thing," I protested.   "I much prefer the quiet of the house."

"Sure.   The house you spend no time in."

"The quiet of the office, then." I tried again. "We could order in.   Any restaurant in town will send food over here.   I have an almost fully stocked bar over at the main building.   And it's completely empty right now."   I tried to entice him into staying, but I could see by the look on his face he was determined.   I sighed. "Alright, Si.   Where do you want to go?"

Silas clapped his hands together.   *"Hooah!"* he shouted, giving the standard US Army cheer.   "That's what I'm talking about."   As he stood, I noticed for the first time that he was dressed differently than he had been when we left the house together in the morning.

"Si," I questioned.   "Did you go shopping?"

He smoothed his hands down the front of his perfectly pressed black button-down shirt.   "As a matter of fact, I did.   You're not the only country boy who can rock some fine city threads.   Now, get your ass down to the truck.   We are hitting a club."

Thirty minutes later we were seated at a booth in one of the hottest bars on the Strip.   It was Friday night and it was packed. Not that there was really any such thing as a quiet night in Las Vegas, but the weekends seemed to bring out the party animals.

This place was a bit classier, the cover charge alone being enough to dissuade some of the rowdier party goers. I sat at the comfortable booth, my own dress shirt not as nice as the one Silas was wearing simply because I worked in it all day, but the glass of bourbon in my hand was quickly making it so that I didn't care. I stared idly around the bar, taking in the crowd of beautiful people dressed in their best, rolling the glass of bourbon around on the table top. There was a woman standing at a high-top table near ours, her skin tight silver dress and her long dark hair making her look like she belonged on a red carpet and not by herself in a bar. She glanced our way once or twice, but the perpetual scowl on my face must have convinced her I wasn't worth the trouble because she eventually moved on to another group of guys a few tables down from us. Silas watched her go, then shook his head at me.

"What?" I said, already knowing what he was going to say.

"You are never gonna find yourself a lady if you keep looking like you're mad at the world."

"I am mad at the world," I said petulantly.

"I know you are," he replied thoughtfully. "And I love you, man. I really do. But you have got to get a grip on all that anger and shit."

We were distracted from our conversation by a pair of young ladies who stopped at our table. The were obviously past tipsy and they clung to each other for support as they giggled at me.

"Oh, my god. Did he just say he loves you?" the first one asked me.

"Um, yeah, but-"

"Oh!" squealed the second, her face scrunching up as she looked at Silas. "That is so sweet." She looked back to me. "Mr. Montgomery, you are the luckiest guy, like, ever."

"Excuse me?" my eyebrows shot up. "Do I know you?"

"Yes," the first girl said. "I mean, maybe. We work for you. In the call center and mail room."

Recognition hit me as I realized these two were a part of the group that was giggling and staring in the lobby on the day Silas arrived.

"Right." I said, trying to end this conversation and move these two on with their night. The last thing I needed was to be seen with inebriated employees. That was a law suit waiting to happen. "Of course. But, you see, we were just leaving, so..."

"Oh," gushed the second. "We're sorry. We didn't mean to interrupt. We just wanted to say we thought you were so cute together. We'll let you get back to your date. See you Monday." And with that, they wobbled off on their high heels, I assumed to find more drinks.

I stared after them, unable to completely comprehend what just happened. "Date?"

Silas started to laugh, his head thrown back. "Oh, shit."

"What?" I questioned, raising my glass to finish off my bourbon.   Coming out tonight was a bad idea.

"That day," he said, running his hand over his short hair.   "The day I arrived in town.   All the girls in the office were staring.   That's why!"   He exclaimed, like it was a revelation.   "They think we're a couple."

I choked on my bourbon.   Slamming my fist into my sternum, I coughed until the fire cleared out of my lungs.   "Why would they think that?"

"Well," Silas said thoughtfully.   "Let's think about what they've seen.   The first time they saw us together we were hugging."

"That was a bro hug," I qualified.

"True," Si conceded, nodding.   "But it was an enthusiastic bro hug.   I can see where they might have misinterpreted it."   I grinned as he continued listing all the reasons people would think we were romantically involved.   "You and I arrive to the office together every morning, we eat lunch together almost every day, and we leave together in the evenings." He finished ticking off the list on his fingers.   "All in all, I'd say from the outside it looks like we are in a very happy and committed homosexual relationship, Stone.   And those gals are right about one thing," he finished with a smug grin on his face.

"Yeah? And what's that?"

"That you, Mr. Montgomery, are the luckiest guy, like, ever."

With that we both burst out laughing.   I really was lucky to have a friend like him on my side.

My laughter cut off as I caught a glimpse of two

women standing at the bar, my eyes drawn to the one with long golden blonde hair. I could only see her from behind, and as she leaned over to tell the bartender her order, I couldn't help but stare at her perfect ass, covered by a tight black skirt, the lace trim at the bottom only accenting her long sexy legs. Her hair fell almost to her waist, and I was struck by a sudden vision of running my fingers through it, fisting it tight as I pressed into her from behind.

The image was so strong, so realistic in my mind, that I felt my blood pumping hard and my body responding to the thoughts in my head without my permission. As I sat there, staring at the gorgeous blonde and letting my imagination run wild, my eyes tracked down her long legs to see the bright pink shoes she had on.

Shoes I recognized.

I dragged my eyes up her body again, this time really looking hard.

It couldn't be.

But it was.

It was Penelope. And she was a fucking Blonde Bombshell.

As the bartender handed her the drink she ordered, she paid him and turned around. And there stood Penelope, her hair down for the first time that I had seen, wearing a sexy skirt and those freaking heels. The smile on her face wide as she laughed at something the person beside her said. Looking at her companion, I realized with a shock that it was Daphne. My sister was standing there in a dress that was practically scandalous as every man in the room stared at the two of them like they were lunch.

My fist tightened around my empty glass. Penelope hadn't spoken to me in weeks, but here she was, looking hot as hell for any guy in town to drool over.

And Daphne! She'd barely turned twenty-one. Neither of them should be here.

Silas looked at me, and seeing the change in my face he followed my gaze. I could see his eyes widen as he took in what I just saw. His jaw tensed, and I wondered if it was because of Penelope or Daphne. However, that was a conversation best saved for later.

We watched them from our booth, laughing and enjoying their drinks. Penelope looked incredible. Her hair, out of its bun for the first time since I'd known her, fell like a waterfall of sunshine, and her bright blue eyes were shining even in the dim light of this ridiculous club.

She was stunning. Absolutely glowing, and it took me a moment to realize that it was because she was happy.

It was the first time I'd seen her without her defenses being on high alert, and the difference was striking. Seeing her now, carefree and light, I could tell just how much strain our bickering had been putting on her. Watching her laugh with my sister, I was struck by just how much I wanted to bask in the light she gave off. I was drawn to her like a moth to a flame.

And I just knew I was gonna get burnt.

Shutting down any further thoughts of

Penelope, I moved to stand. I wanted to leave the bar and head back to the house where it was quiet and I could sit in my room and think of all the reasons why I hated Las Vegas and this project and how badly I wanted to get back to Texas. But as I was pulling a few bills out of my wallet, I saw a trio of guys approaching Penelope and Daphne. I stilled as I watched the douchebags, probably a group of dude-bros here on vacation from whatever Ivy League school their daddies got them into.

"Stone," Silas warned. "Whatever you're thinking of doing, man, don't. Just walk away."

But I barely heard him. I stood and watched as the tallest of the guys leaned down and whispered into Penelope's ear. Daphne had another guy on her side. He was yammering away but she seemed to be ignoring him. Penelope was listening to what ever that douche was saying, then she threw her head back and laughed. She nodded, and suddenly he wrapped his arm around her shoulder and held up his phone with the other hand. Just as he was about to snap the selfie, he leaned over and pressed a kiss to Penelope's cheek.

And I snapped.

I headed off across the bar, Silas hot on my heels. As I pushed my way through the crowd, I could see the guys stepping away from Penelope and Daphne, but I didn't let them get far.

"Hey, asshole," I shouted, drawing the attention of just about everyone, including Penelope. Her mouth dropped open as she stared at me storming through the crowd. The guy with the phone turned back, looking around like a dope as he considered who I could possibly be talking to. "Yeah, you, dipshit." He raised his eyebrows as I stopped in front of him. Silas was behind me, his hand on my arm to call me back, but I shook him off. "You always go around putting your mouth on women who don't belong to you?"

"I, um, dude, we were just-" he stammered, looking to his buddies for help, but neither of them wanted to step in. I couldn't blame them; I was raging.

"You were just looking to get a punch in the mouth, that's what you were doin'."

"Stone," Penelope hissed from my side. "What the hell are you doing?"

"Hey, I didn't know she had a boyfriend, man," the goofball said, like that made what he did any better.

"Stone!" Penelope tried again, tugging on my arm. I continued to glare daggers at the kid, his friends backing away slowly. I rolled my eyes. *Nice crew.*

I took a step toward them and they all backed up three steps. Penelope moved in front of me, positioning herself between me and the losers I was trying to accost. "Seriously! What do you think you are doing?"

"That moron touched you when he had no right to do so. I am about to teach him how to treat a lady."

She snorted, crossing her arms over her chest, her eyes throwing fire at me. "Right, because that's your specialty, is it?" she asked sarcastically. "You wouldn't know what to do with a lady if you had an instruction manual."

The trio behind her all gave a round of low "Ohhhhhhs" which just served to piss me off more.

I sent them another glare, which shut them up. Looking back at Penelope, I tried a different approach. "I just think it's poor manners to touch someone with out askin' their permission."

"He did ask," she said, shocking me. "I said yes."

"What the hell would you do that for?" I demanded before I could think better of it.

"I don't see why it's any of your business," she replied coolly.

Seeing I wasn't going to get any answers from her, I turned my attention back to the offending moron. "What do you have to say for yourself?" I barked. He held his hands up, trying to placate me.

"Honestly, dude, it was totally innocent."

"Really?" I snarled.

"Yes!" He reached in his back pocket and withdrew a folded piece of paper. "Here, look."

Taking the sheet, I scanned it with a frown. Shit.

"A scavenger hunt?"

His shoulders drooped in relief. "Yes. A scavenger hunt. See, Benny here–" The guy reached for one of his friends, dragging him back in front of me. "Benny is getting married next month. This is his bachelor party. And to commemorate the occasion, I was tasked with item number fourteen: a kiss with a beautiful lady. And I mean, dude. Like, look at her."

He gestured to Penelope, his eyes roaming up and down her body salaciously.

This was ridiculous. I pinched the bridge of my nose. "Just get the hell out of here, alright?"

All three of them bolted like their asses were on fire. I turned around and caught the glare from Daphne.

"Stone, I love you," she said, shaking her head slowly. "But you really are an asshole."

"Daphne, I-"

"Just save it, Stone." The disappointment in her eyes killed me. Both her and Penelope were looking at me like I was the worst person they knew.

I might have to agree with them.

"Come on, Penelope. Let's get out of here. I have a friend who can get us VIP at a place I know." With that my sister turned and headed for the door. Penelope gave me one last agitated look, then turned and followed my sister.

I watched her walk away - *again* - and wondered how I could have possibly handled that any worse.

Turning, I looked at Silas. "Thanks for the help, *friend.*"

"Oh, I think you did quite fine on your own." He shook his head at me. "For a man who dug his own grave."

"Shit."

"Yeah, Stone," Silas said, slapping me on the back. "My sentiments exactly."

CHAPTER ELEVEN
Penelope

The night air was cool as it blew in from across Red Rock Canyon. Standing at the edge of Harold's property, I allowed my gaze to pass over the shadowed hills as I tried to shake off the emotions from my disaster of an evening.

When Daphne called me just before I finished work for the day, she sounded so excited. She wanted us to go out, spend some time on the town. I hadn't been out the entire time I had been here in Las Vegas, instead focusing on the work and creating the promotional materials needed for the launch. But my mother's words played in my mind, how she wanted me to live a little while I was here, so I had agreed. Daphne met me at the house and I dressed in my best clothes. I had sent all the things Moira purchased back to her once my suitcase arrived. There was no way I was going to need all those items. I even insisted on paying her for the pants and top I had worn, the cost of which was an entire week's worth of my mother's nursing salary, but I didn't want to be indebted to anyone, especially Harold Pennington. It was bad enough I was living in his home.

When Daphne and I arrived at the club in my Jimmy Choo heels and the skirt my mother had altered for me by hand, I was feeling pretty good about myself. We headed to the bar and I ordered a drink, and I was just starting to relax when out of no where came Stone Pennington, barreling in and throwing his weight around like he always did.

Once the drama was over, I begged off going to the next club with Daphne and we both decided to call it a night. I was just tired of all of it. Tired of ignoring Stone, tired of dealing with his snide remarks and his constant asshole comments. Tired of feeling attraction to him when all I should feel was annoyance. Tired of fighting for a job that would likely never be mine regardless of how hard I worked.

I was just tired.

Standing there looking over the barren desert landscape, the normally beautiful reds and oranges now painted in shades of muted gray and black in the darkness, I was contemplating my next move when I heard the foot steps approaching behind me. Letting out a huge sigh, I turned and met Stone's eyes in the dim light from the pool. Crossing my arms over my chest, I watched him approach.

"Penelope," he said, looking supremely uncomfortable. I felt a little bad for enjoying his discomfort. But only a little. "I, um, I wanted to apologize."

I waited for him to continue, and when he didn't, I pressed him. "Apologize for what, exactly,

Mr. Montgomery?"

He cringed at my use of his last name, a sure sign that we were not on good terms right now.

"For tonight. For getting involved where I wasn't wanted. I just assumed..."

"Yeah, well, you know what they say about people who assume things," I quipped, throwing his own words from the first time we stood by this pool back at him. He didn't miss my dig, pressing his lips together in discomfiture. Turning back to the silent desert, I stepped away from him, moving farther from the property and into the sand, feeling the small rocks and stones shifting beneath my shoes.

"Penelope, you should maybe-" Stone started, but I cut him off.

"Don't tell me what to do, Stone," I threw over my shoulder, not taking my eyes off the darkened silhouette of the mountains in front of me, taking another step away.

"Yeah, no," he said, and I could practically hear the eye roll in his voice. "I won't, of course. I would never dream of suggesting you do something you don't want. But, if I may, Blondie, I think I should bring to your attention that the further you go into the desert, the more likely you are to encounter something unsavory."

I scoffed. "There is no one out there for miles, Stone. I walk the streets of Manhattan every day. I think I can handle unsavory."

Stone chuckled lightly. "Unsavory people, sure. But I was referring to the snakes."

I froze, a chill creeping up my spine. He had to be joking. "Snakes?"

"Sure. Rattlesnakes, likely. We have a bunch in Texas. But that's not the only thing out there."

I gulped, moving backward slowly, my eyes scanning the ground at my feet. "What else is out there?" I whispered.

"Scorpions," he stated flatly, and that was it.

I turned, intending to race back to the safety of the patio, but Stone was right there behind me. I slammed into his chest with a thud, instantly surrounded by the warm scent of his cologne. Stone's arms came up around me, grasping me tight to steady me on my heels. I looked up, meeting his eyes, seeing the question in them. My pulse pounded in my throat, and I thought for sure he could hear it. I didn't move, my eyes dropping from his heavy lidded ones down to his full lips. Seeing them slightly parted, I could feel his breath as it skated across my face. Stone moved one hand from where it rested against my back, bringing it up and running his knuckles down my cheek, and I felt my skin grow warmer at the contact.

"Penelope," he said quietly, his eyes searching mine again.

"What?" I breathed, not daring to speak louder and break the spell we seemed to be under. Every moment we spent like this, my muscles tightened, anticipation of what he would do next sending my adrenaline through the roof.

I wanted him to kiss me.

I wanted him to let me go.

Those conflicting desires battled inside me, leaving me frozen in this strange emotional limbo, the feel of his arms around me the only solid thing in my life at that moment.

Stone looked at my lips again, then said, "I have no idea." With that, he crushed his lips against mine and all my questions vanished.

He was warm. That was the first thing I noticed. His lips seemed to sear mine as they pressed against me. The hand he had been touching my cheek with moved, his fingers sliding into my hair and fisting it tightly at the back of my neck. The sudden pain, mild but shocking, caused me to gasp, and Stone took full advantage of my surprise, sweeping his tongue into my mouth. He tasted of alcohol, warm and smoky, and I melted as the flavor of him seeped into me. Curling my fingers into his shirt, I pulled him tighter against me, not thinking of anything besides getting closer to him. Wanting to feel him pressed against my body, the firm length of his chest as he used his other hand to draw me toward him. I moaned softly when his hand slid down my back and his large, warm palm landed on my ass, giving it a gentle squeeze.

I couldn't believe that this was happening. Stone was kissing me. And I was kissing him back. Stone Pennington.

Shit.

Stone freaking Pennington!

The realization of what I was doing slammed into me like a bucket of ice water and I pulled my head back. Stone opened his eyes, his gaze clouded as he looked at me. He reached for me again, but I stepped back and again crossed my arms over my chest.

Seeming to come to the same awareness I just had, Stone blinked the lust fog out of his eyes, replacing the soft look on his face with his usual scowl.

And I couldn't take it anymore. His anger and confusing mood swings were just too much.

"I have to go," I said quickly, and started for the door.

"Penelope, wait," Stone said, reaching for my arm as I went. "I just - shit!" He sighed, looking conflicted and defeated, an expression I was unused to seeing on his face. "Can we just talk?" He gestured helplessly to the seating area near the house.

Sighing, I moved past him and sat on one of the loungers, drawing my knees up to my chest as I sat. He watched me for a moment, then sat on the lounger next to mine, his feet on the tiled pool deck, his elbows on his knees as he looked at me intently.

Neither of us spoke for a while, me staring into the sparkling waters of the lit pool, him staring at me. I was the one who broke the quiet first.

"I just don't understand, Stone," I said quietly. "From the beginning, you have been nothing but a jerk." He hung his head and blew out a breath.

"I know," he allowed. "It's kind of my default setting."

"Yeah, well, it gets a bit tiresome," I replied, raising my eyebrow at him. He had the decency to look ashamed. I drew off my shoes one by one, setting them on the lounger next to me. I curled my toes in and stretched them out, over and over, working my sore feet. "For the last month, I have been walking on eggshells, trying to avoid your ire, and I don't even know what I did to earn it."

"Shit, Penelope," he said, looking at me. "I don't even know. I just...I always do this. I take my bullshit out on everyone. Even Silas. I don't know why. I just get so fuckin' mad. About everything."

He stood, pacing beside the pool, his agitation clear in the tension in his shoulders and the way he was fisting his hands. "I just, I see you," he huffed, the words coming quickly now. "All shiny in your designer New York clothes, walking around all perfect, knowing you represent everything I hate about that city."

I was completely taken aback. "Excuse me? Everything you hate?" He couldn't be serious. "What, exactly, do you hate about me, Stone?" I said coldly, narrowing my eyes as I watched him pace, looking for all the world like a cornered animal.

"Everything!" he shouted, turning to me and throwing his hands in the air. "Your perfect hair, your ridiculous shoes, your expensive wardrobe, and every other thing your rich daddy likely bought you to make you think he loved you, when he's really just an asshole who loves his money the most."

He was panting when he finished, and as I stared at him in the darkness, I realized there was a lot to Stone Pennington he didn't want people to see. But here, under the cover of night, he was showing me everything. The scars he wore that had never healed.

The wounds that bled every time he breathed.

It was no wonder he went by a different last name. Stone Pennington was hurting, and he had been for a long time. Daphne had hinted at this the night we met, but now I could see for myself how Stone had suffered.

And though his assessment of me was way off base, I understood what he was trying to say. He wanted to hurt me because Harold Pennington had hurt him.

He stood there, glaring at me, daring me to say something, to fight back and lash out in return, as I had in all of our previous confrontations. My reactions had fed his inner beast.

But that was not what he was going to get tonight. Instead, I tried a different tactic. Taking a deep breath, I pushed aside the walls I usually kept in place to protect me, and I showed him my own pain.

"The day the planes struck the towers in New York, I was seven years old," I started quietly. I could see the confusion in his eyes. He was expecting my rage. I was giving him something else. "My father had been a member of the NYPD my entire life, and when the call went out, the whole department responded. His precinct was the 108th, in Queens, where we lived, and there was never a question. Every member of the NYPD, the NYFD, even the Port Authority, they all ran to Ground Zero."

Stone slowly resumed his seat, his own anger forgotten as he stared at me open-mouthed. I couldn't look at him, so I watched my toes clenching and un-clenching as I recited the story I hated to tell.

"The first days were terrible. The following months were worse. The recovery effort was beyond comprehension. Those men and women, they worked in the rubble and debris, day and night, looking for survivors at first, then bodies at the end." I squeezed my eyes closed, picturing my fathers face, the lines of sorrow that got deeper every time he returned to the house. "At first, everyone was so focused on the folks who didn't survive, the ones who were lost in an instant, that no one stopped to consider the toll things were taking on those who were left behind."

I swallowed thickly. "They called it Toxic Dust, but that's a really bland name for something that contained over two thousand contaminants. Jet fuel, concrete, glass, rubber. You name it, they breathed it. For days, months on end. Every volunteer, every first responder, every office worker that made their way back downtown as the world tried to carry on. They all spent their days in a poisonous cesspool."

I chanced a glance at Stone, finding him watching me, his eyes wide and his face blank. I couldn't read anything in his expression, so I turned my gaze back to my toes, finding it easier to talk now that I had started.

"When I was nine, my father started showing symptoms. My mom is a nurse, so she was pretty on the ball about those things. She had him in a doctor's office quickly, but even then, it was close." I could feel the tears threatening, but I made no move to hide them. My father deserved my tears. He deserved my pain.

It was how I knew I had loved him.

"There are over fifty-five thousand people listed on the Word Trade Center Health Registry. They try to help; they do. But there is just not enough money to go around. And cancer treatment?" I scoffed humorlessly. "That shit's expensive. Like, twelve thousand dollars a month, expensive. Add to that the wages my mom lost because she was taking care of dad, and it makes for a pretty bleak picture."

I paused when I felt Stone's hand on my shoulder. Turning my head to look at him, I rested my temple on my knees. I hated to see pity in people's eyes when I told them about my father, but I didn't see pity from Stone. I saw sadness and pain. He felt what I was feeling, and he shared my sorrow. I took strength from his touch and told him the rest.

"I was eleven the day we buried my dad. The cemetery was packed with his brothers and sisters from the department, all standing side by side in their uniforms. I remember thinking how nice they all looked, their white gloves so bright against their dark blue clothes." I could still see it, the rows of uniformed officers, all there to say goodbye to my dad. I could feel my mom, squeezing my hand for all she was worth. "It really was a beautiful ceremony."

"Penelope, I-"

"There is a lot more to me than just being from New York, Stone. I got my first job at thirteen, because between the bills and the medical debt, mom's paycheck was tapped out, and it was up to me to make the grocery money. By fifteen, I was working two jobs to try and cover the utilities as well." I could see the blood draining from his face, but I pressed on. "I can't drive a car, Stone, because we never owned one. I got my license in driver's ed when I was in high school and that's the last time I was behind the wheel. I earned a scholarship to NYU and started at the bottom at Pennington Hotels because the company holds a special place in my heart. I have struggled, sweat, and cried my way through life. I have worked for every thing that I have, and I am still fighting for everything I want.

"So, when you see me, Stone, try not to just see the things you want to see, simply because of your own experiences." I stood, looking down at him as he stared at me blankly. Gathering my shoes in my arms, I was moving toward the door when he called me again.

"Penelope." I paused, then slowly looked over my shoulder to see him, standing, his arms hanging limply by his side. "I'm sorry, Penelope. Truly."

I looked at him, his handsome face seeming so sad in the dark, and I sighed. "So am I, Stone. So am I."

Carrying my shoes, I entered the house, hoping that a hot shower would help put this entire night behind me. Padding barefoot up the stairs, I paused when I reached the upstairs landing. My room was to the left, in the north wing, and I started in that direction when a noise to the right drew my attention. I knew Stone and Silas were occupying the south wing, so it was no surprise when the door to Silas' room opened.

What was a surprise was seeing Daphne

slinking out of his room. Still wearing the club dress from earlier, Daphne turned and froze when she saw me, her eyes going wide and her mouth falling open.

"Uh, hey," she said awkwardly.

"Hey, yourself," I replied, raising my eyebrows, hoping she'd divulge a bit of information.

"So, if you could just, um, not mention this to Stone…"

"Got it," I smirked. Daphne let out a relieved breath, then gave a crooked little smile and a shrug and darted past me, headed to the room that was actually hers.

Looked like I wasn't the only one with complications in my life.

CHAPTER TWELVE

Stone

Shit.

How could I have been so wrong?

I felt like a complete asshole, which was saying something, because people generally thought that about me.

But this was bigger. I had taken one look at that woman and decided I knew everything about her, just because of where she lived. And I hadn't even gotten that part right. I judged her unfairly and treated her poorly because of it.

Which was ironic, because I hated when people judged me by my father's last name. I hated when people heard that I was a Pennington and felt that they knew everything about my life because of it.

What an asshole.

I ran my hands down my face and blew out a big breath.

I couldn't believe the story she had just told me. I mean, everyone knew about the attacks on September 11th, but down in Texas, we knew them in an abstract way. The way you knew about the First World War, or the Mount Saint Helens eruption. Those were things that had happened and, yes, they were tragic, but they hadn't directly impacted my life in a real way. Sure, we had stricter security measures at the airport, but by now, it just felt like that was how it had always been.

But Penelope had lived through that horror. She had watched her father, his friends and coworkers, people she had known and interacted with her whole life, suffer the physical and emotional after effects of the disaster. I tried to put myself in her place, a seven-year-old child, waiting at home every day hoping that her father would return. Listening to the news and seeing the images and knowing that he was down there, digging through the damage, and wondering if he was going to make it back to them.

And then to have him survive all of that only to succumb to a related illness a short while later? That was a different kind of tragic.

But even after all that, she had overcome.

She worked hard, she persevered and came out the other side stronger.

And I gave her shit for it.

Pushing myself off the lounge chair, I made to follow Penelope into the house. I had to talk to her, to see if the kiss was as good for her as it had been for me, and if we could try to start over.

I had wanted her before she told me her story. True, that had been in a mostly physical way, because she was beautiful, there was no doubt about that. But knowing how much strength went with the fire in her eyes? I was addicted to her now.

Just as I reached the open door into the kitchen, my phone rang. I slipped it out of my pocket, prepared to send whoever it was to voice mail, but I hesitated when I saw it was Harold, who, as he liked to remind me, was both my father and my boss. I would have sent him, regardless, but having listened to Penelope's story, I was feeling like an extra big heel at the moment. Perhaps I could give my father the benefit of the doubt, just this once.

Cursing, I drug my thumb over the screen and accepted the call.

"Yeah," I growled. Hey, baby steps.

"Stone," my father greeted me jovially. I looked at my watch, wondering why he was so chipper considering the time in New York. "How are you, son?"

"Fine," I said cautiously, wondering what the deal was. I wandered into the house, staring at the stairs and wanting nothing more than to end this conversation and go after Penelope. I was tired of watching her walk away.

"Good, good," Harold replied. "Listen, I'm hoping we can catch up. I'd like to see the progress on the hotel, you know, walk around and really get a feel for the place." I froze, not quite sure what to do with that information. "I feel like I should show my face around a bit, you know, for morale."

"Sure thing," I said vaguely, hoping to wrap the conversation up. "Let me know when you plan to be around and I'll make arrangements."

"Actually," Harold hedged, dragging the word

out awkwardly. "I'm in town now, as it happens."

I froze. "You are? Where are you?"

I was given my answer when the doorbell rang. Moving robotically, I walked from the stairs to the front door, opening it slowly.

There on the front step, was Harold Pennington.

"Stone!" Harold threw his arms wide, his brittle smile telling me he wasn't sure if this was going to be a good surprise or not. "Good to see you, son."

"Harold." It was all I could think to say, and I could tell it was the wrong thing when his face fell a bit. But he recovered quickly,

"Sorry for the late arrival, but we thought it would be good to surprise you."

"We?" I questioned as he bustled past me into the foyer. My brain was struggling to keep up. "Who is we?"

But I had barely finished the question when my half-sister Constance strode through the door after him, her nose in the air as she looked at me with disdain.

"Yes," Harold said, oblivious to the tension in the room. "Connie and I thought we would take the weekend, come out and see you, and check out the progress. A little family reunion, if you will. I know Daphne is here right now. It will be lovely. You'll see."

"Yes," Constance blurted, crossing her arms over her narrow chest. Everything about her was narrow, including her mind. "Toddrick would have come as well, but he's so very busy. The Atlantic City project is going so well, but they couldn't possibly have spared him for the weekend. He's vital to the project's success." She looked at Harold, waiting for him to validate all her claims, but Harold merely blinked at her, smiling blandly. I'm sure Toddrick was vital, alright. Vital to keeping his dealer's pockets flushed with cash.

The awkward silence dragged on until another person appeared at the front door; a man in a suit, carrying the luggage.

"Oh, Frederick," Harold said, rushing over to the man, who I now knew was Frederick. "Thank you, my man. Just inside here will do nicely." He gestured to the side of the foyer, and Frederick placed the bags there.

"If there is nothing further, sir."

"No, thank you, Frederick. I'm sure Stone won't mind driving me around tomorrow," Harold gushed, slapping me on the back. "You enjoy your weekend. I'll see you here Sunday afternoon."

"Very good, sir."

When the door closed behind him, the three of us were left once again standing staring at each other, not sure what to say. I was about to suggest that we all just go to bed when a noise from the top of the stairs caused us all to turn.

There was Penelope, her hair wet from what I assumed was a shower, wearing some sort of silky shorts and tank top set that was probably her pajamas. I should have warned her that we had company, but the sight of her long, toned legs sticking out of those lavender shorts caused all the blood in my body to head south and I couldn't make my mouth work.

"Stone," she started cautiously, moving down the stairs toward me. "I think we should talk about what just - Oh!" Stopping short, Penelope froze on the bottom step, her eyes darting to the two newcomers in the foyer. "M-Mr. Pennington. I'm so sorry, sir. I didn't realize you…"

"No," Constance drawled, an evil smile on her face as she took in Penelope's state of undress. "I bet you didn't."

"Mrs. Pennington-Grover," Penelope said flatly, her face shuttering at the sight of my half-sister's calculating look. "What a pleasant surprise."

Constance snorted, indicating exactly what she thought of Penelope's false words of greeting.

"Miss Lund," Harold chimed in. "So lovely to see you. The work you've been doing out here is very impressive. I've been watching those online numbers closely. The board and I are very impressed, indeed."

Penelope blushed hotly, pulling her hair around and draping it over her shoulder. The damp strands caused a droplet of water to run down her neck and over her collar bone. I couldn't take my eyes off of it as it trailed across the curve of her breast and disappeared into her cleavage. That was not helping the situation in my pants one bit. Snapping my eyes back to Harold, I attempted to think of anything but Penelope and her sexy attire.

"Thank you, Mr. Pennington," she said graciously. "We have a wonderful team here in Las Vegas. They have all contributed to any success the board has seen."

Something in my chest tightened at her words. She was so selfless. Any other person in her position would have jumped at the opportunity to make themselves look better in front of the company CEO. But not Penelope. She was modest in her thanks and gave credit to those who helped achieve the success.

I couldn't wait to talk to her. We needed to clear this up between us, because I had so much to learn about her. I wanted to know everything. I wanted to climb into her head and scour every nook and cranny and find out what made her tick. How someone who had experienced the things she had could possibly still see the world as bright and shiny.

And how I could maybe start to see it the same way.

As Harold continued to wax poetic about Penelope's great work, I watched Constance. The way she narrowed her eyes at Penelope told me everything I needed to know about Constance's presence here in Las Vegas.

She was working reconnaissance. I bet Toddrick was up to his neck in a disastrous marketing plan. His hotel theme was different, a 1920s gangster themed place. If I had to guess, I'd say he had already blown his entire budget on what would be the opening night party. The expensive champagne, the music, the girls; a real Prohibition style blow out. He'd plan it like he was planning the bachelor party of the century. It wouldn't surprise me if he even had strippers.

But it would be flash in the pan. There was no

long-term success with a focus like that.

That was where Penelope was ahead of the game. She was slowly drawing interest. Making it a tantalizing mystery that people couldn't wait to solve. Little hints and teasers to keep them on the hook.

It was genius.

And Constance hated her for it.

By the time we all headed to bed, I could practically see the smoke coming out of my half-sister's ears.

It was going to be a hell of a weekend.

*   *   *   *

Saturday found me walking around the hotel property with Harold, showing him the progress on the exterior, the rooms we had completed, the restaurants and bars, as well as the theater areas. Wandering around the site, he stopped and shook hands with everyone, from construction workers to kitchen attendants, the landscape crew and the ladies working on the cleaning staff. He treated every one of them like they were important, and I had to admit my respect for him jumped another notch.

He also adored Penelope's *Queens of The Alamo* idea and couldn't wait to meet Dolly and her girls. Harold held a meeting with the executive staff, who were less than happy about being called in on a Saturday, but they all showed up on time and presented their status reports. Harold was more than satisfied with all the progress being made, and his praise brought morale up around the entire hotel, just as he knew it would.

When the meeting ended, Harold announced that he wanted to take the entire executive staff for lunch at one of the restaurants run by a celebrity chef he was friends with. We would meet downstairs where he had arranged cars to take us all down the Strip. I was the first one out of the board room, heading to my office to respond to an email from Ava Carlisle before I headed out. Her whale hunt was progressing nicely, and she had secured some serious high rollers for our Soft Launch event as well as the Grand Opening that would follow a month later.

I was stomping my way toward my office when I noticed movement out of the corner of my eye. Turning my head, I saw that the door to Penelope's office was cracked open and there was a shadow moving on the wall. Knowing that she was still in the board room, likely getting hit on by Toby again (that guy couldn't take a hint, but so far hadn't crossed any lines), I stepped toward the door to see who was in there. It could have been Moira, but my gut told me it wasn't.

Moving slowly, I approached the open door, pressing close to the jam and trying to stay hidden. Just as I moved to push the door open, it swung back, revealing a startled Constance, staring at me open mouthed.

"Oh, Stone," she said, her face paling for a moment before she regained her cold composure. "Why are you sneaking around?"

"I could ask you the same question, Constance," I said, narrowing my eyes at her. "What are you doing in Penelope's office?"

"Is this her office?" she replied, feigning innocence. "I suppose I should have recognized the smell of discount store clothing when I stepped inside." My scowl increased. Constance had no idea what Penelope had been through; I wouldn't let her talk shit about my woman.

Whoa. Where the hell had that come from?

My woman?

There was a lot to unpack there, but now wasn't the time. I had to figure out what Constance was doing.

"Cut the crap, Constance. What are you up to?"

"Why, dear brother," she snarked back, her sarcasm letting me know exactly what she thought of us being related. "Why would you immediately assume I was up to anything? Perhaps I just got lost on my way to the bathroom." Her smile was filled with spite as she shouldered past me, stalking for the elevators. As she went, I watched her drop something into her ridiculously expensive, yet inexplicably ugly designer bag. Turning around while she waited for the doors to open, she stared at me, no longer trying to disguise the hatred in her eyes. "And you can tell that little gold digger that it will be a cold day in hell before she gets anything that belongs to me. Including my last name."

As the elevator doors closed on her angry glare, I knew that Constance was going to be an even bigger problem than usual. I'd have to keep an eye on Penelope this weekend. Constance would use any opportunity to try and make her look bad in front of Harold and our team.

And I'd done enough of that in the last month to last a life time. From now on, I was on Penelope's side the whole way.

Moving back into Penelope's open office, I glanced around to see if Constance had taken anything. Whatever she dropped in her purse, it couldn't have been very big, but I didn't notice anything out of place. Not that there was much in the room to begin with. It looked like Penelope hadn't added any personal touches at all. The company laptop was open on the desk, as well as a stack of files and flier mock ups she was preparing for the printers. Everything appeared just as it should be.

"What are you doing?" Penelope's voice startled me out of my inspection. Looking up, I found her standing in the doorway, her arms crossed, the look on her face part suspicious and part nervous. It was past time to change both of those.

"Hi," I started lamely. I was standing behind her desk, looking suspicious as fuck, so I guess she was right to be wary. "I was waiting for you, actually. I'd like to talk, if you have a moment."

Penelope looked over her shoulder into the hallway. "I'm not sure this is the time or place for this conversation, Mr. Montgomery," she replied quietly, her use of my last name stressing her need to keep things professional. I would respect that.

For now.

"Fair enough, but I'd like us to have some time to talk. Alone. Can I take you to dinner tomorrow night?" When she hesitated, I added, "Please."

Penelope's lips flattened into a line, her indecision clear on her face.

"Just dinner, Penelope. That's all I'm asking."

She assessed me, her blue eyes staring hard into mine, as if she was trying to read my mind. Whatever she saw must have been enough, because she nodded. "Fine. Dinner. Tomorrow."

Then she turned and walked away, her blonde bun bobbing as she strode to the elevator. I followed her, closing the office door behind me, and watched as Toby moved up beside her. Whatever it was he said, she gave him a polite smile before stepping into the elevator. As the doors closed on them both, she met my eyes again. And while there was still caution, there was also heat as she looked me up and down.

Yeah, I could work with that.

I was still staring at the closed elevator doors when I felt a hand clap on my back. I turned to see Harold smiling up at me. My father had been a big man in his younger years, and our broad shoulders and barrel chests were an indication of our shared genes. But time had shrunk him. He was in no way small now, but the strength that came with youth had faded, leaving behind a mildness that I guessed he hadn't possessed when he was my age. But his eyes were bright, their hazel still matching my own, and his mind was as keen as ever. And I didn't like the way he was smirking at me now.   It was too reminiscent of my own cocky expression.

"Well, son, I can't say I'm surprised."

"Surprised at what?" I asked gruffly.   I told myself I was going to try with my father, Penelope's story having resonated with me where years of my mother's pleading had failed.

"That girl is a spitfire, that's for sure.   She's honest and hard working and dedicated and loyal. You won't find a better woman anywhere.   I hoped sending her out here would be the catalyst she needed to push her into the next stage of her career.   If it wasn't for this silly Toddrick business I would have promoted her already. I never suspected…" he trailed off, making me glance at him.   He was staring at the elevator doors, a far away look on his face.

"Never suspected what?" I asked again, trying to mellow my tone.

"Just promise me something, Stone," Harold said quietly, his face suddenly serious.   "Don't waste time.   Don't allow my mistakes to scare you into making your own."   The sadness in his eyes rendered me speechless, and I couldn't think of a thing to say as he moved away from me to catch the next elevator to the lobby.

I don't know how long I stood there considering his words, but I was jolted back to reality when Silas moved up beside me.

"You ready to head out, boss-man?"

I regarded him, my best friend for more years than I could remember.   He'd been with me through all my family drama, just as I was by his side through his.

"Silas, I gotta say, my family just gets more and more bizarre every time I'm around them." I shook my head in exasperation. "Harold may be losing his marbles, Constance is the devil incarnate, and Daphne is-"

"Daphne is perfect," Silas cut me off, glaring at me and daring me to say something negative about my youngest half-sister. When I didn't speak, he nodded and stalked off to call the elevator for us.

Shit. I was gonna have to do something about that. But with all the other shit piling up on my plate, I didn't have it in me to take on my best friend right now.

Hopefully, he would wise up all on his own.

Daphne may be my half-sister, but she was still my sister in all the ways that mattered. Silas was gonna have to remember that.

CHAPTER THIRTEEN

Penelope

I was nervous.

There was no denying it.

I had no idea what to expect. I mean, Stone was my boss. This dinner could very well be a prelude to my termination. I couldn't imagine that the human resources hand book looked too kindly on coworkers sharing illicit, somewhat angry, kisses.

Although, if Toby's gentle flirtation was any indication, maybe human resources wasn't as fussy as one might think.

Giving myself one last glance in the mirror, I tried to gauge if my outfit was appropriate. Not that I'd ever been on a date in Las Vegas, but I didn't imagine we would be going to a burger joint.

Not that this was a date. It wasn't. It was just dinner. A casual dinner.

With a really, really good-looking guy who got my blood pumping and caused fluttering in my heart…and other places.

Okay, focus.

I left my hair down, and Daphne added some

soft curls with a curling iron she had with her. I'd never been good at doing my hair – I only kept it long so it was easier to put up and get it out of my way – but I had to admit, the girl was a master. It looked soft and shiny and I wanted to take her home with me so that she could do it like this every day.

My simple black dress fell to just above my knees, flowing gently when I walked. Grabbing my small black purse, I slid into my favorite pink shoes and headed out.

Reaching the top of the stairs, my breath caught in my chest when I spotted Stone standing in the foyer. He was in a pair of lightly worn jeans, their deep indigo color contrasting nicely with the smoke colored button down he paired it with, the sleeves rolled up revealing the tanned and corded muscles of his forearms.

When did forearms become sexy?

His hair was combed, the dark brown locks looking slick, and he had shaved, his face stubble free for the first time in a long time. For the moment, he hadn't seen me, replying to someone on his phone, and I took a few seconds just to look at him, drinking in the rugged masculinity that was Stone. He was so different from the men I interacted with in New York, with their fancy suits and their stock portfolios doing the talking for them. Stone's strength came from a different place. He was big, yes, with his muscular arms and broad shoulders, but there was an inner strength that I hadn't experienced before. I didn't know if it was the Texas in him, with the southern ideals and the farm-worked muscles, or if it was the fact that he had always felt like he had to prove himself in order to be a Pennington.

Whatever it was, I got the feeling that Stone's gruff exterior hid a lot of things that I wouldn't mind exploring.

Taking a deep breath, I started down the stairs.

Finally catching his attention, I saw Stone turn, his eyes widening as he saw me. I felt the heat of his gaze as he took me in, starting at the top of my head and finishing with my pink shoes, which he smirked at. As I neared the bottom, he held out his hand, helping me down the last few steps.

"Nice shoes, Blondie," he said quietly, and the word didn't hold the same connotation it once did, giving me a small thrill at having a nickname from him.

"Nice boots, Cowboy," I replied, eying the well-loved boots he paired with his jeans.

"I thought at least one of us should be comfortable tonight," Stone said with a smile. "You look incredible, Penelope."

I felt the blush creeping over my cheeks as he drew my hand to his elbow. "Thank you," I replied softly.

"Shall we go?" At my nod, he led me to the garage. I went to climb into the big truck, the vehicle he drove every day, but he surprised me by opening the door to the convertible.

"Oh," I gasped, staring dumbly at the passenger seat. Stone waited for me, one eyebrow raising as I hesitated, not even sure why I was. Something about him choosing to take the Mustang instead of the pick up truck seemed significant, but I couldn't stop to analyze it right now. I only knew that this move felt like taking our casual dinner and moving it a step closer to actual date territory.

Putting those thoughts aside, I slid into the seat, tucking my dress beneath me. Stone closed my door then made his way around to the driver's side and started the car. The engine gave a throaty purr that echoed loudly in the enclosed garage. Turning my head, I glanced at Stone as he drove us forward and out into the late afternoon sunshine. It was March, so the sun still went down relatively early, and here in the desert that made for some spectacular sunsets, many of which I'd had the pleasure of watching from the pool deck at the Summerlin house over the last month.

As Stone drove us out of Summerlin and toward the Strip, I thought about how things had changed in the last few days. Stone and I had spent the better part of a month at each other's throats for the simple fact that we had both made assumptions about who the other person was. I hoped that after we talked at dinner tonight, we could clear the air about everything, including that kiss.

That kiss that I could not stop thinking about.

It had been more than awkward to have to spend all day Saturday and most of today with Mr. Pennington and Constance, knowing that they had to at least suspect what had happened before I came downstairs Friday night. If he did suspect, Mr. Pennington was gracious enough to at least pretend he had no idea. Constance, on the other hand, shot daggers at me every chance she got. Of course, she shot daggers at me the last time we were in the same room together, as well, so there might be no correlation to the situation with Stone at all.

The whole thing was confusing and overwhelming and I just wanted to clear the air. Hopefully tonight we would do just that.

I watched the city pass by, the warm desert air tossing my curls around as Stone made his way up Las Vegas Boulevard, until he pulled in at the Paris Hotel, winding the Mustang past the replica *Arc de Triomphe,* with its beautiful carved panels and imposing arch catching the last of the sun. I had passed by the Eiffel Tower a few times when I walked up and down the road, but I had never ventured inside the hotel. Now, as we pulled up to the valet and Stone handed over the keys, I found myself getting excited. Las Vegas was the first place I had ever really traveled to, but this was likely going to be the closest I ever got to visiting Paris, so I couldn't help but feel giddy.

Stone came around to my door and gave me his hand. I took it, letting him guide me inside the main entrance to the casino.

It was like entering another world; all the casinos were. Walking in the doors was like being transported to another place, another time, and you couldn't help but suspend belief while you were there. As I looked around at the incredible decor, the ceiling painted to mimic a beautiful blue sky, the shops and restaurants made to replicate the two hundred year old architecture of the streets of France – with the narrow arched windows, exteriors painted bright colors, and the trees and flower boxes looking almost real – I couldn't help the smile that stretched across my face. The entire casino floor was lit with soft bulbs, the iron lamp posts serving to highlight the contrast between the Parisian decor and the neon lights of the slot machines scattered throughout the space. The check in desk was a beautiful scene with its marble floors, large Persian rugs, and at least a dozen beautiful chandeliers hanging above the guests waiting in line. As I walked with Stone though the casino, I could see the legs of the Eiffel Tower where they passed through the roof of the building before connecting to the tower itself outside.

Entering the designated elevator, I took in the view as we ascended, the glass walls showcasing a three-hundred-and-sixty-degree view of the surrounding area, each of the hotels standing out against the desert sand with their individual designs and motifs. I could very much appreciate how the western theme of *The Alamo* would do well here.

Las Vegas was a place where fantasies came to life.

Stone and I followed the hostess as she directed us to our place, a half-moon shaped table for two that overlooked the Strip and the Bellagio hotel with its incredible main street fountains. Once we were seated, she took our drink orders and left just as quickly as she had appeared.

The silence was awkward as I stared at the scene before me, the setting sun casting the hotels across from us in silhouette and painting the sky in a brilliant combination of colors like fire.   It was breathtaking.

Stone finally broke the silence.

"Thank you for coming out with me tonight, Penelope," he started, toying with the fork at his place setting.   "I know we didn't really get off to the best start, and I take responsibility for that."   He looked up at me, a self-recriminating look on his handsome face.   "I know I'm not the easiest guy to get along with. Daphne and Silas will tell you it's been like that my whole life."   I felt my heart climbing into my throat as he stopped playing with the cutlery and reached for my hand.   "But I'd like the opportunity to start over, if you'll allow it."

Blinking my surprise, I was saved from having to answer right away as the waiter delivered our drinks. Stone had ordered a bottle of wine, something I had never heard of, and I had ordered a club soda with lemon.   The server poured our drinks then made himself scarce again, leaving me with no other distractions and Stone looking like his whole existence was hanging on my response to his statement.

"Stone," I started lamely, not entirely sure what I was going to say, even though I had been thinking about this dinner for almost three days.   I knew Stone was gruff and antagonistic, but I had also seen glimpses of the man I was sure he hid underneath all the anger and pain.   The way he was with Daphne, for one.   He adored his little sister, and you could see it when he teased her.   Having been an only child, I had never had a sibling to have a relationship with, but watching Stone and Daphne interact for the last few weeks had shown me that, although they didn't spend a lot of their childhoods together, he cared for her in the way that an older brother should.

He had also shown compassion for me on the first day me met, though he may not remember it. After the first staff meeting, the one where I had slunk in late and stained with coffee, he had mentioned to Moira about my missing suitcase, ensuring that she helped me get a clean outfit until my own things had arrived.

These were just two of the many examples I had seen over the last month. I hoped that, given the direction this conversation seemed to be going, I'd be able to see many more.

"I appreciate you saying that. I think starting over would do us both some good." He smiled, a full and brilliant smile like I'd never seen on him before, and my chest constricted at how gorgeous he actually was. I'd thought him handsome since the first moment in the airport, but when he flashed me a real smile, I couldn't help but melt.

"I judged you unfairly, Penelope, and for that I'm sorry," he said as he absentmindedly rubbed his thumb back and forth over the back of my hand, sending sparks from the contact zinging throughout my body. How could such a simple touch create such chaos in my body?

Trying to control my breathing, I focused on him as he continued to talk. "I'd like to get to know Penelope Lund, from Queens. Tell me everything."

And so we talked. Over four courses of the

most incredible food I'd ever eaten, we shared stories of our childhood, our parents, and our friends. I talked about my time at NYU and he told me about his days partying at UT San Antonio, when he had actually visited the site of the real Alamo. His life in Austin was full of crazy stories, mostly because in his younger days, Stone spent a lot of time in an area he referred to as Dirty Sixth, which, he informed me, was basically nine blocks of bars and music and entertainment in the heart of downtown Austin. Apparently, Stone had quite a love for music, and hung with many bands and artists there before they went on to make it big.

Over dessert, I finally talked more about my dad, and why Pennington Hotels meant so much to me. I told Stone about my birthday tradition and the Central Park Zoo. He listened with rapt attention as I talked more about my dad's cancer diagnosis.

"Once dad started treatment, it was really hard on mom, trying to split her time between her work at the hospital, taking care of dad, and still being my mom. I was only nine when he was diagnosed, and we were really lucky because the ladies mom worked with at the hospital rallied around us. They would take turns babysitting me when mom had to work nights, would bring food by, and even took me back to school shopping." I smiled, thinking of the love I felt every time I walked it that hospital.

"They were even more helpful after dad passed. Mom was a mess, trying to be strong for me, you know, but barely holding in together. Between the nurses and dads' colleagues at the department, we had a veritable army of people pulling together for us. It was-" I blew out a breath, blinking away the tears the threatened whenever I thought of those days right after the funeral when everything was raw and painful. "It was the hardest and yet, some of the most wonderful times of my life. I have never felt more loved than I did in those days."

Stone stared at me, my hand clutched in his again, as I took a moment to let the emotions settle. He squeezed my hand, sliding his chair closer and draping his other arm across the back of my chair. I looked out the window ahead of us, watching as the incredible Fountains of Bellagio put on another astonishing performance for us.

When I had gathered myself again, I continued. "That's why these shoes, ridiculous though they may be, mean so much to me." I looked at Stone and I could see the apology in his eyes. "No," I cut him off before he could voice it. "You're not wrong. They are crazy expensive. I would never, ever have purchased them for myself. But that's just the thing; I didn't purchase them. When my mom learned that I would be working out here, she told the ladies at her work, and they all took up a collection. They pooled their money to get me these shoes, telling me that they would bring me luck, and let me look the part. Dress for the job you want, you know?" I huffed out a laugh. "Anyway, these shoes are the physical embodiment of the love I feel back in Queens. My extended family, cheering me on from all the way back east." I shrugged, feeling Stone's arm against my shoulder, his hand under my hair, fingers tracing gentle lines along the back of my neck. My entire body lit up with electricity, goosebumps running up and down my arms.

"I get it," Stone said softly, his breath dancing along my naked shoulder. "Family is important, regardless of blood ties. That's how I feel about Silas." Stone tilted his head closer toward me, his forehead almost touching my temple. "He's been like a brother to me since we were just kids. He spent more time at my place than he did his own. I'd do anything for him." I could hear the commitment in his voice. He meant it, but I still thought I'd push him a bit.

"Even let him date your sister?"

Stone's fingers froze where they touched me, his whole demeanor locking up. "That is a conversation for Silas and I to have." With that, he removed his hand from my neck and signaled for the bill. I missed his warmth immediately.

The sun had long since set, the streets of Las Vegas lit up like the carnival that they were. As Stone led me back down the elevator and along the street, I let my eyes wander to the spectacle that was Las Vegas Boulevard. Holding my hand casually, Stone drew me down the street, both of us content to let the city around us talk for the time being. We reached the corner and took the escalator up to the crossing bridge. I stopped half-way across to take in the view, cars passing below me at a steady rate.

"I know New York is busy, but this is like a whole other level," I stated, taking in the throngs of people on all sides. "Manhattan is always moving, but something about it always feels, I don't know, aggressive maybe? Like, the people there are so driven to do more, work harder, earn the most, that they rarely stop to have fun." I leaned on the railing, taking in the crowds on either side of the street. "Whereas this is a non-stop party." Stone came up behind me, his warm palm on my lower back. "Everyone here seems like they're living their best life all the time. Maybe it's because everything here is temporary. It's a world of hotels, and New York is a world of apartments. People come to Las Vegas for an escape, and people go to New York to become something."

I sighed, feeling foolish in my ramblings. "I know that doesn't make sense." I shook my head at myself.

"No," Stone said thoughtfully, his chin resting on my shoulder as he stood looking with me. "I think it makes perfect sense, actually. And you're right–" his arm came around my front, his hand now on my hip, that thumb drawing maddening circles through the fabric of my dress. "Las Vegas does seem very temporary." I took in his words, thinking that there was a deeper meaning to them than what I had meant when I said them. "So maybe we should try to blend in and just have fun. After all," he said, one side of his mouth hitching up in a smile as he turned us to look at Caesars Palace. "When in Rome."

I burst out laughing at his goofy joke, but stopped short when Stone leaned toward me.

"Penelope," he breathed, his eyes dropping to

my lips.   "I'd really, really like to kiss you again."

My tongue darted out to lick my lips, remembering the feel of Stone's kiss against them and tingling with anticipation at the prospect of a second try.

"Yeah," I replied, feeling exceptionally lame as I did.   "I think I'd like that too."

He only paused a moment, searching my eyes for something.   I guess he found it, because he dropped his head and pressed his lips to mine.   I sighed at the warmth, his full lips feeling lush and firm at the same time, and when he ran his tongue across the seam of my mouth, I opened for him gladly, welcoming him in as I wrapped my arms around his neck.   Stone took control of the kiss, his hand finding its way back into my hair and holding my head at the angle he liked best.   His other hand snaked down my spine, his hand once again landing on my ass.   His squeeze was not quite as gentle this time, practically lifting me off the ground as he pressed my body against his, and I couldn't help but notice the tell-tale bulge prodding me in the stomach.   Just the thought of it sent shivers across my whole body, and I moaned at the thought of where this kiss could take us.

Stone seemed just as happy as I was to continue exactly as we were, but a shrill whistle from a passing group snapped us from the fog of lust we both seemed to have fallen into.   I pulled back, dropping my hands down his shoulders and resting them on those sexy forearms I had admired earlier, the light dusting of hair tickling my palms.   Stone drew back as well, but refused to let go of my ass.

"Come on, Blondie," he said, pressing a kiss to my temple as he used the hand on my behind to guide me further along the walkway. We made our way across the street and found ourselves standing in front of the Bellagio Fountains. We had watched several performances during our dinner, but they were set to music, and we hadn't been able to hear it from our table. I was excited for the next show to start.

I walked along beside Stone, my arm wrapped around his waist, his hand still firmly on my butt, as he guided us down the street. The crowd was thick, with tons of people pressed against the granite railings, vying for position to view the show. Stone finally found a spot he was happy with, a little alcove where the railing bowed in toward the water and had a large tree standing near the sidewalk. Positioning himself against the metal ring protecting the tree, he pulled me against him, nestling me against his still hard erection.

"Won't be long now," he whispered, his quiet words sending goosebumps down my arms. "The good part will start soon." Again, I couldn't help but read deeper into his words. He surprised me once more as he dropped one hand to the hem of my dress, trailing his fingers up my thigh lightly. I leaned back against his chest, weaving my fingers with his where his other hand caged me in at my belly. The people crowded in around us, all looking out over the dark water. We were lost at the back of the crowd and hidden in the shadow under the tree.

The hum of chatter around us grew to an excited

buzz as the bell tower on the hotel began to chime the hour, and a sound like thunder came from the lake in front of us. Without warning, columns of water shot into the air, reaching into the night sky like cannon fire, as the opening strands of *"Fly me to the Moon"* by Frank Sinatra began to play from speakers all around. People everywhere gasped as the water jets began to dance in time with the song, lights below the surface accompanying each note of music.

I gasped as Stone slid his hand farther under my dress, his fingertips dancing along my inner thigh, feeling like lightning at every point he touched and creating static in my brain. His lips dropped to my shoulder, pressing kisses along the sensitive column of my neck and up behind my ear, their warmth working counterpoint to the chills his touch was causing. I squeezed his hand, looking around wildly for fear that someone would see, but every single person was focused on the water show. Every one, that was, except Stone, who was solely focused on me.

"Fuck, Penelope, you just smell so good," he whispered in my ear, taking the lobe between his teeth and biting lightly. I rolled my head to the side, giving him more access, and he growled in response, the sound sending shivers down my spine. He continued to press kisses on my sensitive flesh, the warm heat of his lips feeling exquisite against my neck, and all the while his fingers were creeping toward their goal. Stone hummed his approval as he brushed his knuckles across the already damp fabric of my panties. I moaned, shamelessly widening my stance to give him space, and he didn't hesitate. Slipping his fingers under the delicate lace of my underwear, he began to work me in time to the music, his fingers spreading my own moisture around and bringing me closer and closer to the edge.

As Frank crooned and the fountains danced, Stone worked his magic on my clit, his mouth on my neck playing back up to the main event that was his incredible fingers. I lost track of the moment, forgetting the crowd around us, and just let Stone take me higher, grinding my ass into his ever-growing erection as he did so.

The song approached its crescendo and Stone took his cue, thrusting two fingers inside me as the trumpets filled the air. My cry was lost as the water again boomed in time with the song, Stone holding me tight when my legs turned to jelly. When the show came to an end, Stone brought me down gently, working me through the orgasm and then he discreetly slid my panties back in place before removing his hand from beneath my dress. As the crowd cheered the end of the performance, my face was red in the dark as I realized just how exposed we actually had been.

But that only made the whole thing hotter.

I took a few deep breaths as Stone turned me toward him and wrapped me tightly in his arms, pressing a chaste kiss to the top of my head.

After a moment, he took my hand and simply said, "Come on, Blondie. Let's go home."

CHAPTER FOURTEEN

Penelope

I stared at my laptop screen, trying to focus on the email I was composing, but it was difficult. My mind kept wandering back to my date - yes, I guess it was officially a date now - with Stone.

And how things had completely changed in the span of half a day.

After our little bout of exhibitionism, Stone had walked me back to the *Paris Hotel*, holding my hand the whole way, and retrieved the car from the valet. Driving back to Summerlin, his hand casually resting on my thigh, Stone and I talked about music as he used the steering wheel controls to flip stations on the satellite radio. It was a short drive, but we finally settled on some 90s alternative when we stumbled on an *Everclear* song we both liked.

Stone had parked the car in the garage, escorted me inside, walked me to my room, placed a sweet kiss on my lips, and wished me good night.

At which point I began to completely freak out.

What the hell was I doing?

There was no world where this situation was a

good one, for so many reasons, not the least of which was that Stone Pennington was my boss, in every sense of the word. Not only was it inappropriate from a professional standpoint, but I was here to work, to achieve something specific for myself and my mother. I couldn't afford to muck it all up, no matter how handsome Stone was, or how incredible his kisses were.

I barely slept, running through every worst-case scenario my over-active brain could possibly concoct. By the time the sun started creeping in the window, I was certain that this whole experience was a one-time thing, and that ignoring it was the best choice. I would simply pretend that the entire thing had never happened and Stone and I would go on as we had for the last month; with thinly veiled contempt.

Except, I didn't feel contempt toward him anymore. At all.

And that was the scariest part.

I hadn't dated a ton of guys, and any that I had spent time with had always been of the causal sort. And that was by design. I was not the type of girl who wanted emotions and commitment and *feelings*.

Feelings were dangerous. Feelings were how you got hurt. Feelings were what happened when you made room for someone in your heart, in your very soul, and when they were ripped from your life you had nothing left to fill the gaping hole that remained.

Feelings were to be avoided at all costs.

So, after I had showered and dressed, I prepared to make my way to work as I had for the last several weeks - in an Uber. Alone.

I was completely unprepared to walk downstairs and find Stone standing in the kitchen, to-go mugs of coffee in his hands, while Daphne, sitting at the granite island, looked on with a sly smile. Silas stood at the far end of the kitchen, eyes on Daphne and a scowl on his face.

That was unlike him. Scowls were usually Stone's department. But, before I could think on that any farther, Stone stepped forward and handed me one of the coffee mugs.

"One cream, one sugar," he said, looking decidedly uncomfortable.

"Oh," I replied, shocked that he knew my coffee preference. "Um, thank you."

"We should get going," Stone barked, moving toward the garage.

"Going where?" I asked, thoroughly confused.

He turned seeming just as confused as I was. "To work."

"Oh," I repeated dumbly. "I, um, called an Uber."

Stone froze, his hand on the doorknob, and stared at me, his brows furrowing. "Well," he said slowly. "Okay, then." And he turned, opening the door.

Christ, we were bad at this.

"Or," I shouted, making him pause and turn back. "I can, you know," I managed to finish at more reasonable volume. "Cancel it."

"Sure," he said, eyes darting from me to Daphne at the island, who was failing to hide her laughter.

"So...we should get going."

"Right."

Following him into the garage where he unlocked the truck, I glanced at the Mustang, remembering how comfortable our drive home was last night. Worlds apart from this fumbling, awkward morning after scene.

Just another reason why pursuing this was a terrible idea.

As Stone guided the truck through the morning traffic I stared straight ahead, trying to find the words to tell him that last night had been a one-time thing. That there was no reason to be awkward because I was prepared to forget the whole thing.

And, yes, a part of me wanted to end things with Stone now so that he wouldn't be the one to end things with me. It was cowardly, but I couldn't help it. The last thing I wanted was to be stuck for the next three months working with the stern, grouchy, and oh, so hot guy who had patted me on the head and said "thanks, but no thanks".

That was a level of humiliation I wasn't prepared to deal with.

I had almost compiled my speech as we pulled into the parking area. I licked my lips, ready to say something as we exited the truck. I opened my mouth, standing near the hot grille, needing to end this before we entered the building, me as the employee, him as my boss.

But as Stone met me at the front of the truck, looking like he just walked out of *Western GQ magazine*, with his boots, jeans, and suit jacket over a crisp white button up, he did the very last thing I could have expected.

He took my hand.

Like, he reached down, grasped my hand, threaded his fingers through mine, and started walking into the office.

I had absolutely no response to that.

As I trotted along behind him on legs that were practically numb, I wracked my brain for clarity and found none.

We entered the building, moving swiftly to the elevator. I heard a quiet gasp and turned my head, finding us the center of attention as the entire call center team stared at us. Feeling heat rise in my cheeks, I dropped my eyes to our joined hands, once again questioning if this was real life.

The elevator deposited us on the third floor, and Stone moved swiftly toward my office. When we reached it, he turned to me, searching my eyes for something, then leaned in and gave me a swift peck on the lips.

"I have a lunch meeting," he said, like there was nothing unusual about what had just happened. "But I'll meet you here at five; we can pick up dinner on the way home if you want."

"Right," I said, blinking owlishly. "Dinner. Five. Right."

One side of his mouth quirked up slightly and he released my hand, drawing the back of his knuckles down my cheek. "Have a good day, Penelope."

Then he turned and was gone. I stood, my mouth open, staring after him for probably a full minute, before someone quietly cleared their throat. Jumping at the sound, I spun quickly to see Moira, a knowing look on her face.

"Good weekend, then?" she asked cheekily.

Remembering myself, I smoothed my skirt and pressed a hand to my bun, making sure all was in place.

"Fine, thank you," I said, sounding like I'd just run a marathon. "And yours?"

To that she just smiled. I pressed my lips together and strode to my desk, firing up my lap top and getting to work.

The day passed quickly as I exchanged emails with several vendors regarding the Soft Launch event that was planned. We were going to host an opening week bash, but prior to that, we would be hosting a smaller, more intimate gathering, to get the word out and get people talking. It was going to be by invitation only and consist of some of Ava's high rollers, as well as industry big shots, other casino owners, and all the right media. Celebrities would be contacted, Instagram feeds would be filled, and hopefully - *hopefully* - it would drum up even more interest for the Grand Opening Event.

The Soft Launch party was going to be one month earlier than the actual hotel debut, and that put it only eight weeks away. Carson and I had been organizing entertainment, which included Dolly and her girls, as well as some of the Cowboy acrobat troupe, a live show that was made to look like a shoot out at high noon, and even a staged robbery, with masked bandits and such. The 'robbers' were going to 'hold up' the guests, but any money collected was going to a local charity.

All in all, I felt like we were on the right track for both events. I was starting to feel really good about my role here and I could practically taste the promotion. I could see my office in Manhattan just waiting for me to come and take a seat.

But while I pictured that office, I couldn't help but think of the way Stone's hand felt in mine as we walked together this morning, or the possessive way he fisted my hair when he kissed me.

Shaking off those thoughts, because there was no possible way that Stone and Manhattan would ever go together, I looked at the clock, realizing it was nearly five. I made one last run through my list of projects, ensuring that I had accomplished everything I hoped to do today, when a soft knock at my door distracted me. Glancing up, I saw that it was Toby.

"Hi, Penelope," he said, a gentle smile on his face as he moved to stand in front of my desk. He was always so happy, smiling and interacting with everyone he came across in the most positive ways. I wondered if that was a prerequisite for being a Human Resources manager.

"Hey, Toby. Long time, no see." With all the hiring that had been going on recently, Toby had been working full speed with interviews, hiring packages, training courses, and benefits packages. We would pass occasionally, but hadn't really had time to chat in a week or two.

"I know," he said with a chuckle. "It's been kind of crazy. But I have all the department managers and their assistant managers hired now, and training for the second wave of workers started today, so it will slow down a little from here on."

I laughed. "I bet. It's been crazy here, too." I leaned back in my chair, rolling my neck from side to side. I hadn't realized I was so stiff, but sitting at my desk, on the phone and computer all day had taken its toll. Not to mention the constant thoughts of Stone and what was or was not happening between us. It was no wonder I was tense.

"I bet. What is it?" he questioned, stepping farther into my office. "Only a few weeks to the big show?"

"Yeah, crazy, isn't it?"

"You'll be out of here in no time," Toby said, unaware of how his casual statement caused a bolt of unease to shoot through my chest. "I bet you can't wait to get back to the city."

"Yeah," I said, though I wasn't sure I believed it anymore. But that didn't make sense. I had dreaded leaving Queens, and I was counting the minutes until I could be home, in my apartment, with my mother. Where I belonged. Wasn't I?

So why was I so uncomfortable thinking about that now?

"So, listen," Toby went on, completely unaware of my inner turmoil. "I was wondering if we could get dinner sometime? I know this great Indian place down just a few blocks from here. Really authentic." He stared at me with hope glittering is his eyes.

Oh, jeez. This was bad. I had a feeling that Toby had been flirting with me, testing the waters so to speak, but I hadn't expected him to just outright ask me to dinner.

"Toby," I started. "I appreciate the offer, but I think we should keep things strictly professional." I tried to be as diplomatic as possible.

"Sure," he said, playing unaffected. "Of course. That's probably best."

"Thank you, Toby. I appreciate-" but I didn't get to finish.

Without knocking, Stone entered the room, his head bowed over his phone as he typed frantically.

"Penelope, if you're ready, I ordered take out from that Italian place. I know you prefer the lasagna from there. We can pick it up on the way home and- Oh. Hi, Toby," Stone ground out, his usual formal boss-man tone in his voice. "How's things in the HR department?"

There was an awkward silence as Toby looked from me to Stone and back again, his gaze full of accusation.

"Things are fine, Mr. Montgomery," he said, no trace of the casual and friendly Toby who had entered my office only minutes before. "I'll see you both tomorrow then." And with one last cold look thrown in my direction, he turned and left.

"What was that about?" Stone asked, taking a seat in the chair facing my desk and sounding like he knew exactly what Toby had been talking about. He looked good, because of course he did. He had shaved again this morning, and his chin was just now starting to show the shadow of his beard. I tried not to think about how great that stubble would feel on my skin.

I was unsuccessful.

"Nothing," I replied, attempting not to look at his warm hazel eyes because they tended to distract me to speechlessness. "Toby was just-" I cut off when my lap top pinged a message at me. Our inter office messaging system had a distinctive chime, and right now mine was chiming all over the place. I glanced at my screen and felt the blood drain from my face.

"No," I breathed, forgetting for the moment that I was completely distracted by my ridiculously good-looking boss, who was also an amazing kisser. "That's not possible."

"Penelope?" Stone questioned, and I could hear the concern in his voice. "What's happened? Who messaged you?"

"Ava Carlisle," I said, my eyes scanning her messages again.

"The Whale Hunter?" Her nickname suited her, but right now, I couldn't appreciate it.

"Yes," I said, clicking out of the messaging program and into my office email. "She said that some of her whales have been given different dates for the Soft Launch and the Grand Opening. She's getting a flurry of calls saying that the dates are changing. Her people are pissed because they've made travel arrangements."

"Have you changed the dates?"

"No, I haven't." I scanned the inbox, seeing several messages responding to an email that went out earlier in the day.

An email I hadn't sent.

"What the hell?" I muttered under my breath. Opening one of the new messages, I saw that it was from the personal assistant of a well-known World Series of Poker champion. He was both a high roller and a celebrity, and therefor, a valued attendee of our Soft Launch. And he was pissed.

"Penelope," Stone said, having come to stand behind my chair. He rested one hand on the back, one on the desk, and leaned over, scanning the screen. "What's going on?"

"I don't know," I answered honestly. "There are several messages regarding an email I apparently sent that changed the date of the Soft Launch. Moved it up two whole weeks, in fact."

"Are we moving it up two weeks?" Stone asked, though he knew the answer. There was no way we could achieve being ready two weeks early. I would never have sent this message.

"Not a chance." Opening the sent folder, I scanned for the original message. Buried in the multitude of messages I had sent out all day was one that I had definitely not sent. "Here it is. But, Stone," I said, reading the email and then turning to look up at him, likely giving off waves of the panic that was currently coursing through me. I was terrified that this would be the thing that would cost me my job, never mind the promotion. "I didn't send this email. I have never seen it before."

Stone stared at me, his eyes darting back and forth between mine, then his stern face softened slightly, his lips curling up on one side. "I believe you, Blondie." The relief that washed through me was a physical thing. I huffed out a breath, turning to look at the screen again.

"This says it was sent at 12:47pm. I know for a fact I was in the staff room at that time. I took a fifteen-minute lunch break with Moira. She brought iced coffees. Whoever sent this email did it when I wasn't in the room."

Stone looked thoughtful for a moment. He pulled out his phone and fired off a text.

"I'll have Silas look into it. He can check the cameras, show us exactly who went in your office at that time." He was still leaning over my desk, and I could smell his musky cologne, spicy and woodsy, and totally Stone. I took what I hoped was a discreet sniff, enjoying having him so close. "Contact the people who received the bogus email. Offer each of them one thousand dollars in casino credit for the mix up and confirm the correct dates."

He was so decisive in his decision making, so sure that the mix up wasn't my fault. I was afraid I would get fired for this, and he never doubted me for a second. That information sent a warm feeling through me and I turned to look up into his face, my eyes widened in surprise.

Stone smiled down at me, his face so handsome

my heart clenched. "It's alright, Penelope." He raised one hand and gripped my chin gently with his thumb and forefinger. "I have faith that you'll sort this out." With that, he leaned forward and pressed a gentle kiss to my lips, lingering for a long moment and scrambling my senses once again.

When he pulled away, his half-lidded gaze filled with something I could only call hunger, he left his fingers on my skin until the last possible moment. As our connection finally broke, he shook his head slightly, then straightened, reaching again for his phone.

"I'll call the restaurant, have our order delivered here. You do what you have to do, I'll make sure you're fed." He moved to the office door, turning back once more, his lustful look gone, replaced with one of contemplation. "It's gonna be alright," he uttered quietly, but I wondered if he was telling that to me, or himself.

CHAPTER FIFTEEN
Stone

I wanted her.

I couldn't even pretend it was just a physical thing anymore. Everything about her intrigued me and turned me on. She was amazing at her job, she was kind, caring, selfless, and yes, fucking beautiful. I couldn't wait to make her mine. It wasn't even a question of if, but when at this point.

But right now, she was focused on her job. Whatever had happened, we couldn't afford to lose the high roller clients that Ava was securing, either for the Soft Launch or the Grand Opening events. So I would let her work, and while she did, I would take care of her, make sure she was fed, and then I would take her home.

As my imagination began to draw up all sorts of possibilities for the rest of the evening, Silas knocked on my door. He had been distant since our conversation about Daphne. At the time he said he understood where I was coming from, that he would break off whatever it was they had going on between them, and that we were still cool. But I couldn't help but feel that

I'd broken something in our friendship when I asked him to stay away from my sister.

The worst part was, I didn't know how to approach him to fix it. Avoidance seemed to be our best bet right now.

"You wanted to see me, Stone." Cold. Almost rude, but not quite. I would let it lie for now, but I wasn't sure for how long.

"Yes, if you have time. Someone sent an email from Penelope's computer. She insists it wasn't her, that someone must have been in her office when she was away from her desk. Can you pull up the video feeds from today and see who was in her office at 12:45 or so? That's when the email went out."

"Of course," he said, and with nothing further, he turned and left. Fine. He could be mad at me; I could take it.

Picking up my phone, I arranged for the meals to be delivered, then popped up my computer to see what work I could accomplish while Penelope did what she needed to do. I had several messages from Ava as well and assured her that things were being handled. I also checked in with the other properties and managers I dealt with in my regular duties as regional manager. Everything was running smoothly, as I expected. Things tended to go well when you had a reliable team in place, and I was proud of my people.

It didn't take long for Silas to return with his tablet. He set it down on my desk, the video all queued up.

"Are you sure about the date and time?" he

asked, and the lack of irritation in his voice told me that he found something else to focus on, and it likely wasn't good.

"According to Penelope's out box, the email in question was sent at 12:47 p.m. today."

"Well, I went through the entire day. The only person other than you and her to enter that office, was Toby Reynolds, and he was never alone. That was also almost four hours after the time the email was sent." Pressing play on the computer, he showed me a sped-up video of the hallway outside Penelope's door. I watched her go in and out several times, as well as other staff members moving up and down the hall, but at no time did anyone but Penelope go inside her office. I watched as Toby walked up, and then watched myself move into the office shortly after him. Everything matched up with Penelope's story, but none of it explained how or why that email got sent.

"Is it possible she sent an email and accidentally mistyped the information?" Silas asked when the footage had finished.

"I suppose," I said, although it would be very unlike her. Sure, she tended to be physically clumsy, but even that was only when she was nervous. Her work was her element, and she took great pride in doing it well. I couldn't see her making that kid of error. "Anything is possible."

Silas picked up his tablet and headed for the door. "Let me know if you need anything else."

"Si," I called, making him stop, but he didn't turn and look at me. "Are we...alright?" I asked awkwardly. I thought I could let this go, but apparently, I was wrong.

Silas took a deep breath, his chest expanding beneath his shirt, and I realized that if he wanted to, my very good friend could kick my ass. Badly.

After another breath, he turned and looked at me. "We will be, Stone." His eyes met mine, and I could see a whole host of emotions there: hurt and anger, sure. But there was also love. The love that said that we were best friends for life, and he would do anything to protect that. Even if it hurt him.

Shit. Maybe I was too harsh on him. He was my best friend, I trusted him with my life and all my secrets. Perhaps I could trust him with my little sister, as well.

I wanted to open my mouth and tell him that, but he closed his expression and turned, storming out of my office. I'd find a way to talk to him again; I couldn't let my stubborn pride hurt my best friend.

I got back to work and it wasn't long before security informed me that our meals had arrived. I met the delivery guy at the elevator, giving him a hefty tip, then took the food back to Penelope's office.

I paused at the door to watch her. She had her head down, typing furiously at the key board, her frown creating an adorable wrinkle between her eyebrows. Penelope gnawed on her lower lip, something I'd seen her do numerous times when she was concentrating, and she looked adorable as hell. Moving further inside, I caught her attention and she looked up, smiling slightly at the sight of me.

"Dinner is served," I said with a smile and a mock bow. "How are you making out?"

Penelope leaned back in her chair with a groan, rolling her neck from side to side. "It's fine. Most people are pissed until they learn about the thousand dollars. Then they're happy as clams. None of them have canceled, which is good, because Ava would probably murder me if they did."

"You know," I replied thoughtfully, popping the lids of the take out containers open and passing out the disposable forks. "I think she actually would murder you. She seems like the type who would know how to hide a body."

Penelope laughed out loud at that, sliding her lap top to the side to make room for her lasagna. I pulled the chair in front of her desk closer and open my own dinner, a simple spaghetti Bolognese.

"Thank you for dinner, Mr. Montgomery," Penelope teased playfully, and I shot her a smirk. "Actually," she started cautiously, loading pasta on her fork. "I've been meaning to ask you why you go by Montgomery and not Pennington."

I grimaced, not liking the direction the conversation had taken. But Penelope had shared so much of herself with me, I thought that maybe it was time I returned the favor.

"There are a couple of reasons, actually," I started, deciding to go with the easiest first. "When I started working for the company, I didn't want anyone to think that I was there for any reason other than my ability to do the job. If people know who my father was, they would think less of me and my own merits."

"Huh," Penelope said softly. "I'm ashamed to admit that's exactly what I thought when I learned who you were. After seeing how Constance and Toddrick worm their way around the office, I figured you were just another product of the Pennington nepotism game." She smiled warmly at me. "I'm glad I was wrong." Our eyes locked for a few seconds, hinting at things neither of us was ready to speak out loud. Penelope broke first, her gaze darting back to her meal, a blush rising in her cheeks. I let it go, continuing to answer her question.

"The second reason is much less noble and unfortunately way more petty," I muttered. I didn't want to tell her this part, knowing she missed her father as much as she did. It seemed ridiculous now, looking back on all the years I wasted by turning down all of Harold's attempts to be a parent to me, when Penelope would probably give anything just to speak to her father again. "Harold didn't know about me until I was almost four years old. My mother never tried to keep me from him, but all her attempts to contact him were side tracked by his staff, who were well paid to keep scandals like an illegitimate son out of the headlines." I didn't look at Penelope as I spoke, not wanting to see the pity in her eyes as I told her about my sad childhood without a dad. "He left my mom without a backwards glance, and over the years, I watched her heart continue to get broken by him. She gave me his name when I was born, but using it felt like an insult to her. To the fact that she raised me on her own, and I wanted to honor her for it. So whenever possible, I went by Montgomery instead of Pennington."

Finishing my story, I exhaled a heavy breath, then raised my eyes to gauge Penelope's reaction. I was pleasantly surprised when I didn't see pity but something like admiration on her face.

"Stone," she murmured, her hand reaching across the desk to clasp mine. "Your mom must be very proud of you." I didn't say anything, just watched as she moved her thumb across the back of my hand, her skin so pale compared to mine. "You care about her a lot. She sounds like she is a great mom."

"The best," I said quietly, a tightness forming in my chest. We ate in not-quite awkward silence, each lost in our own thoughts.

Penelope said that she had made assumptions about me, and I know that I certainly had made several about her. The thing was, I couldn't have been more wrong. She was nothing like Constance and her mother, Deirdre, the women who constantly made me feel like garbage for being Harold's illegitimate son. Penelope was warm, and caring, and kind. She worked hard for everything she had, and held no bitterness over the things she didn't have.

The more I thought about it, the more I realized I had never met someone like her. Someone who had endured so much pain in life, and yet, offered nothing but happiness back. I certainly hadn't dealt with my own losses as well as Penelope had, and the thought shamed me now.

Harold didn't intend for things to go the way they did for my mother. Hell, the minute he learned what had happened, he tried to be in my life, and my stubborn ass rejected him at every turn. My mother never held a grudge against him, knowing that some things in life are just out of our control.

It was probably time I put my petty bullshit aside and follow Penelope's example. I needed to finally own up to my own behavior and get to know my father.

Before it was too late.

While I was coming to these life altering conclusions, Penelope and I finished our meals. I gathered the empty containers while she shut down her computer.

"Ready to head out?" I asked, watching as she turned off the office light and closed the door.

"All set."

We headed down and climbed in the truck, the silence only broken by the alternative rock station we had settled on as acceptable to both of us. I glanced out the corner of my eye, watching as Penelope rolled her head on her shoulders again.

"You should try the hot tub," I said, trying not to picture her wet and warm in a bathing suit…or out of it.

"Hmmm," she moaned, and the sound shot straight to my dick. "That sounds lovely, actually."

"Tell you what," I said, trying not to shift as my pants got tighter. "When we get to the house, I'll grab the wine, you meet me out back."

She looked my way, her eyes wide. "Together?" she murmured quietly.

"You bet your ass, together."

She stared at me open mouthed for a minute longer, then nodded slightly. "Okay."

Half an hour later I stood on the pool deck, two glasses of wine in hand, waiting for Penelope to come down and join me. The house was quiet, which was strange given that Daphne and Silas had been around almost constantly since I'd arrived in Las Vegas. But Daphne had moved back into her dorm room, and Silas was spending less and less time at the house, a fact that reminded me I needed to make things right with them both sooner rather than later.

My thoughts were cut off abruptly when the door to the house opened quietly and Penelope stepped on to the darkened patio, her bare feet silent on the tiles. She was wearing a robe, one of the plain white ones Harold kept in each bedroom, like the hotel kingpin he was, and her hair had gone from its tidy low bun to a messy knot on the top of her head. Her skin shone in the moonlight, looking like flawless porcelain, and I was struck again by just how beautiful she truly was.

She padded over to me, her hands gripping the knotted belt of the robe tightly, and smiled shyly when I passed her the glass of wine.

"I figured a nice cold white would be our best bet," I told her, gesturing to the in-ground hot tub at the end of the deck. Setting my glass on the stone, I removed my shirt, standing in just the swim trunks I had put on when we got back to the house. The jets were already going, but I still heard the small gasp Penelope made when I was undressing. Smirking to myself, I kept my face away from her as I entered the tub, sitting on the bench on the side by my drink and stretching my arms across the edge. I managed to get my face back to neutral by the time Penelope reached the stairs, still in the robe, hesitating at the entrance.

I watched her, one hand gripping the bulb of the wine glass, the other still clenching the knot of the bathrobe, as her eyes darted from me to the bubbling water and back again. After a few moments, I figured she needed a bit of a push. "You comin' in or not, Blondie?" I said, watching as she jolted out of wherever her thoughts had taken her. Making a decision, she tipped the glass up, gulping down a hefty mouthful before setting it beside mine on the slate tiles. Standing straight again, she quickly undid the robe, placed it on a nearby lounge chair, and moved as fast as she could to the stairs into the hot tub.

As she gingerly entered the water, blowing out a few breaths at the temperature, I couldn't help but take a few breaths of my own. Penelope had the body of a goddess.

I had always had some idea, and after having her in my arms last night at the fountains, I was fairly certain she was gonna be a knock out. But actually seeing her standing in front of me in that tiny pink bikini, so delicately tied at the hips in small bows that just made me want to tug at them, I could hardly hear anything but the pounding of my heart in my ears. I shifted on the bench as my cock responded to the sight as well. Letting my eyes trail over her, from her slender calves disappearing into the illuminated water, up over her curvy hips with their pretty pink bows, and then along the dip of her waist, the narrow curve only accentuating the lusciousness of the rest of her. She finally settled on the bench seat across from me, her cheeks red, whether from the hot water, the wine, or the situation, I didn't know, and met my eyes through her lashes. The look she delivered carried so much inside it; heat, desire, and a touch of fear. Not of me, I was almost positive, but of the place we found ourselves. Of the fact that we were here, after a month of conflict, me as her boss, her my employee, on the cusp of whatever this was. There were so many things that could go wrong; so many ways that this could blow up in both our faces.

And I didn't care about a single one of them.

"You look incredible, Penelope." I moved to the next bench over, sitting perpendicular to her so that our knees touched under the water.

"Thank you, Stone."

I watched her, the light from the under-water bulb casting inverted shadows on her face as the steam rose around us. Penelope leaned back against the tub wall with a soft sigh, and cast her eyes up to the sky.

"I can't get over how many stars there are here," she said softly. "You hardly ever see stars in New York, obviously. This is…" she trailed off, raising one hand to gesture at the night sky.

"Beautiful," I finished for her, not taking my eyes off of her face.

Penelope turned to me, catching me looking, and her blush deepened. "We should probably talk, Stone."

"I disagree," I murmured, reaching out so my fingertips trailed along the back of her neck. I watched, fascinated, as goosebumps rose in the wake of my fingers. "I think we communicate much better when we don't talk at all." My fingers increased their pressure, feeling the tense muscles she was stretching earlier. I worked my thumb and fingers in firm circles up and down the column of her neck, and Penelope's head dropped forward, a soft moan escaping when I reached the junction of her neck and shoulder.

"That may be true," she whispered, eyes closed as I stared at her, watching as her breaths started coming faster. "But it's still the responsible thing to do. Talk, I mean."

I could barely hear her words over the sound of the jets, so I moved closer, shifting myself on to her bench. Penelope twisted her body away from me, but only to grant me better access to her shoulders. I raised both hands, massaging her warm skin gently, even though every possessive instinct in me wanted to press her to me, wrap my arms around her, protect her and claim her. But I forced myself to go slow, knowing that she had so much more riding on this situation than I did.

"I think," I whispered, my mouth against the shell of her ear. She shivered when my breath caressed her hot, damp flesh. "That you have spent way, way too much time being responsible. I think," I repeated, trailing my lips from her ear, down her neck, over her shoulder and back again. "That you should let me worry about things for a while."

I closed my mouth on her skin, just behind her ear, and she melted against me, resting against my chest. I moved my hands down her arms as she turned her head to look at me over her shoulder. I could see the desire in her eyes, heaver and more potent than before, but the slight frown between her eyebrows showed she was still hesitant.

Leaning in, I pressed a gentle kiss to the corner of her mouth. "It's okay, Penelope," I said softly, meaning so much more than I was capable of saying at the moment. "I've got you."

She was still for a moment, processing my words and their meaning. Then, coming to a decision, her face softened, and she raised one hand, reaching behind us to place it on the back of my neck. When she spoke, it was barely a whisper. "Okay."

Like a switch had been flipped, our mouths crashed together, the hot, wet kiss full of more passion than any I had ever experienced. My hands roamed over Penelope, trying to touch every part of her I could reach. My palm was flat against her toned stomach, my thigh moved of his own accord to rub against hers in the water, like my body was desperate for any bit of friction I could get.

For her part, Penelope moved like a wave, up and down as our kiss progressed, her fingers tight in my hair. Suddenly, she stood, breaking all contact as the water rushed off of her body like a waterfall. I froze, not sure if I had overstepped at some point, but before I could say anything, Penelope surprised me by settling herself on my lap, her legs spread wide over mine. She wound her hands around my neck and pressed back in, kissing me with just as much intensity as before.

I groaned into her mouth when I felt her breasts press against my chest, all her beautiful soft against my muscular hard. We were the perfect complement to each other, the living embodiment of 'opposites attract' and I couldn't get enough of her.

Wrapping my own arms around her, one hand sinking into her hair below her messy bun, the other landing firmly on her ass, squeezing the plump cheek repeatedly, I groaned into the kiss, moving my tongue against hers, tasting the crispness of the wine we had been drinking. Penelope pressed herself to me, moving against me, seeking pressure where she needed it. She moaned again as her core rubbed against my cock, hard as steel in my swim shorts. I dug my fingers into her ass even harder, pressing against her everywhere I could, wanting to consume her fully.

We kissed like that for ages, writhing together, sharing space and breath, until I pulled back, grasping her by both hips to still her movement. Penelope blinked her eyes open, looking dazed and flush and absolutely gorgeous. Keeping hold of her hips, I stood, causing a shocked gasp to escape her, as I spun us both and placed her ass on the tiled edge of the hot tub. Stepping between her knees, I ran my hands up and down her thighs, loving the way her skin felt, so smooth and silky beneath my own work-roughened hands. I leaned in for a kiss, this time just a quick press of our lips before I moved down, kissing against her neck, then to her collar bone, and across the incredible curve of her breasts, open mouthed kisses, my tongue darting out to sample her skin where ever I could reach.

Penelope's hands curled around the edge of the tub, her knuckles white as she leaned back slightly and let me taste her. And taste her I would.

Everywhere.

My hands made their way to the tops of her thighs as my mouth reached her navel, my tongue tracing around the rim of her belly button, feeling the muscles of her stomach contract as I did. Pulling away, I glanced up from where I was, kneeling on the bench between her legs, to find her staring at me, her lips parted, breath coming in heavy pants. Her eyes tracked my movement as my hands moved farther up her legs, over her hips, finally landing on the draw string bows of the bikini bottoms. Moving slowly, watching her face for any negative reactions, I found the ends of the strings and pulled. As the bows came undone, Penelope sank her teeth into her full bottom lip, swollen from our kisses, and simply stared at me. I waited, my thumbs tracing gentle circles on her hip bones, while she considered what I was offering. When she again didn't seem to be able to make the choice on her own, I raised my hand and used my thumb to pull her lip out from between her teeth.

"Penelope," I said, sucking her battered lower

lip into my mouth and laving the dents her teeth had made with my own tongue. "I want to taste you," I said, watching her pupils dilate at my words. "I *need* to taste you. Will you let me?"

For a moment, I thought she might have stopped breathing. But then she exhaled a shaky breath, swallowed heavily, and looked me dead in the eye as she said, "Yes, please."

CHAPTER SIXTEEN
Penelope

It felt like my heart was going to explode in my chest. Like my lungs were in a vice and my brain was completely gone.

Staring down at Stone, his intense gaze on mine, I couldn't remember having ever felt this way. Like I was burning up and shaking apart all at the same time. My whole body felt hot, and as his gaze roamed over me, I swore I could feel it like a physical touch, electric and alive everywhere he looked.

I never wanted it to end.

Stone moved between my legs, his broad chest pushing my knees farther apart, the delicate skin of my inner thighs dragging over his ribs, and a tingle of electricity settled in my core. I could feel my inner muscles clench in anticipation as his hands slowly peeled away my bathing suit bottom, exposing my hot flesh to the cool air of the desert night.

As Stone ducked his head, his tongue again slowly dragging down my stomach and I held my breath, afraid that any noise I made might shatter this moment before it started. I watched as he bypassed my sex, moving his mouth to my inner thigh where he pressed soft kisses and light nips, increasing my anticipation as he worked his way north again. He switched sides to my other thigh, repeating the process and driving me out of my mind.

"Stone," I breathed, desperate for him to touch me where it counted. He paused his kisses, his fingers digging into the flesh of my legs as he looked up at me from under his dark lashes. He met my eyes, gave me a grin that set my insides alight, then descended on me with a hunger I had never experienced.

Stone pressed his mouth against me, his tongue darting in and circling my clit with rapid licks. Pushing my legs even further apart, he flattened his tongue and dragged a long, slow sweep from bottom to top, moaning when he reached my entrance and pressed his tongue inside. He continued this way, alternating the quick flicks with the slow licks, until my head started to spin. Finally, my arms couldn't hold me up any longer, and I leaned back, resting on my elbows on the cold tiles. From this angle, I could see everything, watching as Stone's fingers squeezed indents into my skin, knowing that tomorrow, light purple bruises would remain as evidence of everything he was giving me right now.

I relished the thought.

As I continued to climb higher, my muscles shaking more the closer I got, Stone moved one hand off my thigh and slowly slid one thick finger inside me. My inner muscles clenched around him, and he groaned into me. Involuntarily, my hips began to rock, thrusting up against his face, desperate for that little bit that would push me over the edge.

I whined in protest when Stone withdrew his finger, but gasped when he replaced it with two, curling them upward as he did, pressing against my upper wall in the most delicious way.

The sounds coming out of my mouth were desperate and needy and I couldn't even think to be embarrassed about them. I needed this, and I needed Stone to give it to me. All the tension that had built between us over the last month had created a powder keg within me, the pressure reaching dangerous levels, and this was most definitely the best way to release it.

As I watched him work, his dark hair stark against the pale skin of my abdomen, he lifted his eyes and met my gaze. The heat and desire I saw there floored me.

"Penelope," he ground out, barely moving his mouth far enough away from my body to get the words out. "You taste so fuckin' good." I gasped again as he replaced his lips around my clit and began to thrust his fingers in earnest. "Come on, Blondie. Give it to me."

I lay there, spread out on the tile, Stone's eyes boring into mine, but I couldn't quite get there. I was close, so close. I just needed…something. My breaths were coming in shallow pants, my swollen lips parted and my eyes wide. Finally, when it seemed I would never reach the peak, I reached up, supporting my weight on one elbow, and yanked down the top of my pink bikini, exposing my breasts.

Stone's eyebrows shot up, but he never stopped

his ministrations, continuing to pump his fingers in and out while his tongue danced circles around my clit. Keeping my eyes on his, I took one of my nipples between my finger and thumb and squeezed, twisting and pulling hard.

The quick shock of pain was exactly what I needed, finally flying high into the climax I had chased after. As I soared, my vision an explosion of colors, I heard Stone's voice, as though from a great distance, as he exclaimed, "Fuckin' hell."

After what seemed like hours, but was likely only a matter of moments, I blinked to clear my vision, seeing Stone staring at me, his fingers still inside me, but his head up high, mouth open as he looked at me.

"Holy shit, Penelope," he said in awe. "That was hot as fuck." I blushed, averting my eyes and replacing my bikini top, feeling a bit insecure now that the moment was over. "No," he said sliding his fingers gently out of me and resting his hands on the tile on either side of my hips. "Don't you do that. Don't be embarrassed, because that was the sexiest thing I have ever seen." He leaned over me and pressed a kiss to my mouth, his warm skin dragging across my sensitive nipples, causing them to stiffen all over again. I moaned softly as his tongue met mine, realizing he tasted of chlorine and wine and me. It was dirty and erotic and I couldn't get enough.

Dragging my hands up his back, I threaded my fingers into Stone's hair, holding him against me as I eagerly met his kiss. My mind was a mess, overcome with the multitude of sensations assailing me; the fire of

Stone's kiss, the warmth of the hot tub still bubbling away over my calves, the cool tile against my skin, and the sizzling electricity of his touch as his hands roamed over my body, exploring like he had all the time in the world. He was all I could feel and see and smell and taste. He was everywhere, and I loved it.

Suddenly, Stone stood, leaving my heated body bereft of his weight and warmth. Sliding his hands down my arms, he grasped my hands and pulled me back to sitting, his hooded eyes on mine the whole time.

"We should go inside," he said quietly, releasing my hands and heading for the hot tub's stairs. I dipped down below the water line, hiding my naked bottom half in the darkened water. I watched, wide eyed, as Stone moved to the lounge chair and retrieved my robe. Holding it out to me, he waited patiently for me to exit the tub, then continued to hold it while I inserted my arms and drew the soft fabric closed around me. Tying the knot again, I stood awkwardly while he gathered the wine glasses and turned off the tub. I tried not to let my mind get away from me, but I couldn't help it. What now? What was he thinking? More importantly, what was I thinking?

Stone was my boss, and the son of the owner of the company. The last thing I wanted was to be seen as that girl, the one who tries to sleep her way to the top. Never mind the fact that we lived on opposite sides of the country. How could this possibly work?

Telling myself to take a breath, I tried to reel in my chaotic thoughts. It was too soon to be thinking about any of that. I needed to remind myself to take this for what it was: a short-lived fling. I could keep this casual, and remember that emotions were unnecessary. They were certainly unwanted. Regardless of how tender he had been on our date, making me feel special and desired, or how he made me come alive when he touched me, I could not let myself get in over my head with Stone Pennington.

"Penelope?"

I snapped my attention away from my deranged thoughts and back to Stone, who stood by the door waiting to go inside. Flashing what I hoped was a convincing smile, I moved quickly past him, noting once again how incredible he looked without a shirt. I had known he was fit, but seeing his muscles on display, the golden tanned skin still damp and the water running down his carved chest in little tempting rivers, just proved that my imagination had been woefully inadequate when it came Stone.

We moved through the kitchen, Stone depositing the glasses in the sink as he passed, then headed for the stairs. Side by side, we made our way to the second floor, where he would normally go right and I would go left. This time, we both paused, uncertain and slightly awkward, as we considered our options. Taking my lip between my teeth once more, I looked at Stone, seeing again the way his eyes simmered with desire. He reached up, and, using his thumb, plucked my lip out from between my teeth with a soft smile. My heart raced as he stepped back, afraid of what it meant if this was where we ended things.

Afraid of what it meant if we didn't.

Without saying a word, Stone held out his hand to me, a silent invitation for me to choose.

I thought about everything we had been through in the last month, all the tension and stress, and finally the simple beauty of the last two days. How Stone had shown me a side of himself that I thought very few people ever got to see. I considered the consequences if this went badly; my career could be damaged, but if I wasn't careful, my heart would be in danger as well.

All my adult life, I had worked hard to remove feelings from any interactions I had with people. It was simpler that way. People couldn't let you down if you expected nothing from them. And they certainly couldn't leave you.

But since coming to Las Vegas, I had made that mistake not once, but twice. Both Stone and Daphne were working their way into my heart – for very different reasons, but the result was still going to be the same. When these next three months were over, we would all go our separate ways and I would be alone again.

Did that mean that the inevitable outcome was not worth the experience? My mother had told me to keep my eyes and my heart open. Perhaps it was time I followed her advice, regardless of the pain I might be facing when it was all over.

Taking a breath, I met Stone's eyes and placed my hand in his.

I could see the relief in his face and posture, and he wasted no time in closing his fingers around mine and pulling me to him, wrapping me in his arms and delivering another scorching kiss. I clung to him, breathing in his delicious scent, wanting to cover myself in it and be sure that I remembered what this moment was like with every sense I possessed. How his arms banded around me tightly, how each sound he made walked the line between agony and ecstasy, and how I would forever associate the smell of clean pool water with how Stone was making me feel right now.

Pulling away slowly, Stone guided me down the hall behind him, drawing me into his room and closing the door. I had just a moment to take in the space, with its huge bed and dark wood furniture, before Stone was on me again, pressing me back against the closed door and kissing me, his forearms bracketing me with one on either side of my head, his chest pressed against mine, holding me in place. Starting at his shoulders, I ran my hands over Stone's chest, finally feeling for myself all the strong planes of his body. I drug my fingers down the sides of his ribs, feeling every delectable indent, then moved around to his back, sliding back up again, splaying my palms against him and pulling him against me.

"Penelope," Stone ground out, his hands going to the knot of my robe, his mouth moving to my neck where he once again found the spot that made my knees go weak. I moaned loudly, my hands pressing against the door as I tried to hold myself up. Stone pulled the cotton robe off my shoulders, leaving it puddled on the floor, then ran his hands down my back and under my butt. I squealed when he bent and hauled me against him, my arms flying to his shoulders and my legs going around his waist without thought.

"Stone, I-" but he cut me off with another kiss. I didn't realize we had moved until my back hit the bed, the cool sheets a shock against my heated skin. Stepping back, he flicked on the bedside lamp and I watched as his hands dropped to his waistband, pulling the swim shorts off quickly and revealing himself to me. I couldn't help but stare, seeing him naked and hard before me, knowing that, at this moment at least, he was all mine. Meeting his eyes once more, I smiled as I reached behind my neck to untie the bikini top, pulling it off and tossing it across the room. Stone ran his gaze all over me, his hands clenching and un-clenching by his sides, as if it took everything he had not to touch me.

But that was exactly what I wanted. Moving myself farther up the bed and settling onto the mountain of pillows there, I bit my lip and motioned him to me. Stepping to the bed, Stone gently placed the tips of his fingers on my ankle, slowly dragging his fingers up my leg. The familiar electric sensation was back, shooting through me from where he touched my skin, raising goosebumps and all the little hairs along my body.

"So soft," he muttered as his gaze followed his fingers. I tried to hold still, but the sensations he caused made me want to move, to squirm and wiggle and arch against his touch like a contented cat. When Stone reached my breast, he spread his fingers wide, engulfing as much as he could in his palm and

226

squeezing. We both hissed out a breath at the same time, loving what we were doing to each other.

Stone released my breast, leaning down to the night stand and withdrawing a foil packet. He tossed it on to the bed beside me, then placed his knee on the mattress and climbed up, straddling my body at my hips. Leaning forward, fists pressed into the pillows beside my head, Stone kissed me again, and this time there was no mistaking the possession he was communicating. He didn't just kiss me, he conquered me, and the press of his lips and the thrust of his tongue left no doubt as to who I belonged to in that moment.

Arching up into his kiss, I slid my hand down between us, taking him by surprise when I wrapped my hand around his solid length and squeezed gently. Stone released a groan into my mouth, thrusting his hips slowly against my palm, allowing me to work him at my own pace, learning the feel of him, the heat in my hand and the heat of his body against mine stirring something deep inside me.

We continued like that, just enjoying the feel of each other, until suddenly Stone pulled away, moving backwards and kneeling between my open thighs. Not taking my eyes off of his heaving chest, I reached beside me for the condom, tearing it open and sitting up. Looking to him for permission, I held the condom between us, waiting for his nod before placing it over his tip and slowly rolling it down.

Once we were protected, I lay back down on the pillows, my mind a chaotic storm of lust as Stone hovered over me. "You are so beautiful, Penelope," he whispered reverently. I looked into his gorgeous hazel eyes, seeing so much in their depths, and placed my hand on his cheek, leaned up and kissed him. Stone sank into the kiss, pressing the entire length of his body against mine, as one hand traveled down my side, caressing each curve as he went.

When he reached my hip, he squeezed, then slid his hand under my thigh and tugged, drawing my knee up against his ribs and opening me wide for him. When I felt him at my entrance, I arched my head back, moaning again as Stone trailed his lips down my neck and placed gentle bites along my collar bone. I felt his breath hot against my throat as he pressed in slowly, my muscles giving way to his steady pressure, the slight twinge of pain testament to how long it had been for me. But Stone went slow, giving my body time to adjust to him, and when he finally pressed his hips tight against mine, we both paused, our eyes meeting as we took in the moment. Stone gazed at me, his mouth open as his eyes roamed my face. Finally, I couldn't wait anymore.

"Stone," I said breathlessly, drawing his eyes back to mine. "Please," I said, wiggling my hips in a vain attempt to gain some friction. "Please, move."

He began slowly, drawing out almost all the way, then thrusting back in, bottoming out with a grunt. Stone gradually increased his pace, holding my leg tightly against him and running his lips over my body wherever he could reach - my chest, my neck, even up to my ear where the sound of his harsh breathing only increased my enjoyment.

Kneeling up, Stone released my knee, instead drawing both my legs around his waist and placing his hands on the mattress on either side of my chest, allowing him to continue to pump steadily while also having access to my breasts, where he ran his tongue around each nipple in turn and caused my entire body to light up with sensation. Digging my fingers into his dark hair, I held him tight against me, wanting more of his warm mouth as he worked us with a steady rhythm. When Stone took my nipple between his teeth and bit down, I was surprised by the orgasm that hit me seemingly out of nowhere, crying out his name and clenching down on him tightly. His responding curse only heightened my own pleasure, knowing that I was the reason he was swearing.

Stone was moving rapidly, his previously smooth motions seeming frantic as he chased his own release. Finally, he pressed against me, buried deep within me, shuddering out my name as he came. For a while, neither of us moved, content to just stay where we were, our sweaty chests pressed together, hearts pounding against each other. After a few moments, Stone pressed a tender kiss to my forehead and held the condom in place as he withdrew. I felt strangely empty inside as I watched him walk to the attached bathroom, and I was unsure of what to do next. Was this the part where I left? Headed back to my own room and back to our roles as roommates and coworkers?

I was saved from my wandering thoughts when Stone reappeared, a lazy smile on his face. He didn't hesitate as he turned the lamp off and climbed back into bed, moving close to me and pulling me against him, my head nestled on his chest while his arm wrapped around my shoulders. I was glad for the darkness, knowing my face was likely etched with disbelief. I huffed out a shocked laugh before I could think better of it.

"What is it, Blondie?" he asked, his voice muffled with sleep.

"I just can't believe it. Stone Pennington is a cuddler."

"Yeah," he said, his chest moving with his silent laughter. "Don't tell anyone, it might ruin my rep."

"It's okay," I said, my jaw cracking with a yawn. "Your secret is safe with me."

He ran his fingertips lightly up and down my back, the touch now more emotional than sexual, but the feeling of electricity that I got whenever he touched me persisted.

"Good night, Penelope," he said softly.

"Good night, Stone." It was the last thing I remembered before sleep took us both.

CHAPTER SEVENTEEN

Stone

Walking through the hotel grounds, I couldn't shake the feeling of pride that was building in my chest. The exterior work was almost complete, and the limestone bricks that made up the façade reminded me so much of home, their warm creme tones identical to those on the actual Alamo mission in San Antonio, that I couldn't contain my excitement. Even the date on the keystone above the main door, 1758, was identical. The walkways were poured concrete in a taupe color, reminiscent of the deserts of Texas, and the landscaping was done in an array of various cacti and other hardy shrubs and palms surrounding intricate water features and stone sculptures. The entire scene presented as a beautiful and welcoming oasis. I loved it.

Moving through the main doors, I entered the reception area and the casino proper. Staff moved around like bees in a hive, everyone trying to get as much done as they could in as little time as possible, and I did my best to engage with as many of them as I could with a quick word or a nod of acknowledgment. The space smelled of fresh paint and wood varnish, as the gaming tables and bar areas were getting their final touches. Once the exterior was well on its way, the secret theme was out. Penelope had done an incredible job with the reveal, and her social media campaign was a hit. Reservations were coming in fast and hot, with the hotel already nearly fully booked between now and Christmas. We were ten weeks from the Grand Opening, but only six from the Soft Launch and there was still so much to do before we could even think of calling ourselves ready.

Thinking of Penelope and the Grand Opening at the same time brought me up short. I stopped, realizing that as soon as our project here was done, our time together would be finished as well.

Two weeks had passed since that incredible night in the hot tub, and things had only gotten better. I expected awkwardness the next morning, but there really was none. We just seemed to slide into this comfortable routine. Every day, we came to the hotel, worked hard and kept it professional, then headed back to the house, where we spent time together. Sure, some of that time was spent on sex - awesome, mind-blowing sex - but a good portion of it was spent just getting to known each other, and the more time I spent with her, the more I liked her. We cooked together, watched TV, talked about our families, our childhoods, even the awkward teen years that no one really likes to discuss. Penelope and I talked about everything.

Except what would happen when these next few months ended.

Shaking my head to dispel the thought of her going back to New York and how that made my heart clench in ways I wasn't prepared to examine, I continued through the main casino and toward the center of the property. Along the way, I glanced at the displays stationed at the main intersections and thoroughfares. Harold had gone to a lot of effort to find and secure western memorabilia during the last year or so. The boxes had not stopped coming to my office, and I eventually had to assign a team to deal with them.

They had been working hard, and now as I traveled the property, moving from the gaming area and into the high-end shopping district, there were displays of items everywhere you looked. Some were historical pieces, things like clothing, tools, and even documents from the American Frontier. There were photographs and other artwork that depicted this quintessential period of American history which spanned from the tail end of the Civil War to the end of World War I. The men and women of the Wild West had shaped a great portion of this country, including my beloved Texas, and it was important to me that our future guests were able to appreciate the part they had played in making America the great nation that it became.

Just before I exited the building to the interior courtyard and pool area, I paused again to look at the most recent display case. A mannequin stood inside a tall glass rectangle wearing none other than Clint Eastwood's poncho from the film *"A Fist Full of*

Dollars".

I didn't know how Harold had accomplished it, but I couldn't help but smile as I looked at it, the brown and beige poncho that was so iconic to western film, fringe and all. He had asked me about my favorite Spaghetti Western movie, then gone out and acquired the damn thing. It was a really...*fatherly* thing to do.

There went my chest again. Shit.

Maybe I was having a heart attack. I should probably see someone about that.

When I had called to thank him for it, he had sounded so pleased, so genuinely happy to be talking to me about something that made me happy, that I couldn't help but smile as he went on and on about other film and TV items he hoped to get a lead on. Apparently, Harold had a thing for *Bonanza,* and was in negotiations to get his hands on the leather vest Lorne Green wore in the opening credits. After we ended the call, I spent hours on my laptop searching for other items available from the show. I didn't understand it, but I really wanted to do something nice for him in return.

Nope, I didn't understand that one bit.

Walking through the automatic doors that led outside from the shopping area with its giant air conditioning unit in the vestibule working hard in the afternoon heat, I headed outside to The Oasis, the giant spread of pools and lounge chairs that made up the outdoor space of the hotel. The different pools were spaced around the area, with cactus gardens and palm trees throughout, and the bars and eateries were made of the same pale limestone as the rest of the building. The place still carried the western feel, with the cabana beds made to look like chuck wagons, their arched canvas covers in place to protect our guests from the relentless desert sun. There were tables made out of barrels and wagon wheels were assembled side by side to take the place of fences. Some people might say that the aesthetic was over the top, but, hey, what in Las Vegas wasn't?

Making my way past the pools, I followed the meandering pathway to the farthest back corner of the property, directly opposite from where the business offices were kept, to the corrals. Carson Young had done an exceptional job with his team, and the place looked straight out of the movies, with split rail fences and a beautiful classic looking barn to house the animals. He and I had debated which animals would be kept on the property and had finally settled on only a couple horses and some goats. The maintenance was low, and we could rotate them out regularly to the property that was owned by the company out in the hills so that the animals wouldn't get over exposed to the people coming and going around the hotel.

That property also afforded us another option for our guests to experience the Old West, and that came in the form of trail rides, an option I would be taking Carson up on today.

"Good afternoon, Mr. Montgomery," Carson greeted me as I approached the barn. Just the smell of the old wood and hay had me missing home like crazy. What I wouldn't give to pick up a pitch fork and jump to work. Nothing like shifting a few hundred bales to really clear your mind.

"Afternoon," I said gruffly. Less gruffly than I normally would have said it, but give me a break; I was still me. "Is everything ready?"

"Absolutely," he said, handing me an envelope. "Inside are directions to the property and the standard information packet that all guests using the Trail Ride Experience will be receiving. I talked to Smitty out at the ranch and he said the place is yours for the day. They've got everything you asked for ready to go," he added with a knowing smile. I wasn't going to let him make me second guess myself.

"Excellent. Appreciate it, Young."

He shook my hand and headed back to the hotel proper. Tucking the envelope in the back pocket of my jeans, I wandered over to the fence, leaning my elbows on the top rail and watching the pretty mare as she explored her new digs. With just a few weeks until guests would be arriving, Carson and Smitty, the ranch manager, had suggested that we begin rotating the animals in now, allowing them to warm up to the sights and sounds of the hotel. By exposing them to the place now, and having them present as it ramped up, we all hoped it would ease their transition into being part of our facility here. If anyone could appreciate the amount of effort that went into properly working with animals, it was me, so Carson and I went to great lengths to ensure we had the best care team in place, including a dedicated veterinarian and health center at the ranch.

I heard Penelope's footsteps coming up behind me, quiet and quick, and turned slowly to take her in. Her blonde hair, in its typical bun, glowed in the afternoon light. Her eyes were bright as she smiled at me, causing them to crinkle a bit at the corners. She wore jeans and a long-sleeved top, as I'd requested, and she looked beautiful, her happiness and curiosity shining through.

"Mr. Montgomery," she said, her mischievous smile giving away that she still wanted to keep things as professional as possible at work, but that she remembered that outside this property, she called me Stone. Loudly. And often.

"Afternoon, Miss Lund," I said, tipping my hat. I had been wearing my regular clothes more and more these last two weeks. Today I wore worn jeans, a long-sleeved button-down shirt, my boots, and my black Stetson. "I see you've almost dressed to the specifications of the memo I sent you yesterday."

Penelope frowned, glancing down at her attire. "What have I missed, Mr. Montgomery?"

I smirked at her, then nodded to her feet. "Don't you own a pair of boots, Blondie?"

"You know I don't, Cowboy." She relaxed her formalities seeing as we were the only people around this part of the property. "I wore flats. That's the best I could do."

"They'll do just fine, Penelope. You ready?"

"I don't know," she sassed, placing her hands on her hips. "You won't tell me where we're going, so I can't say if I'm ready to go there."

I laughed, which was something else I was getting used to. Laughing. Relaxing. These weren't typically things that I did, at least not with anyone other than Silas and my mom. But Penelope seemed to be able to get me to drop some walls, at least a little. Being around her just made everything seem lighter.

Glancing around quickly to be sure there were no other staff members around, I reached down and grabbed her hand to start towing her to the parking lot. Penelope gave a soft giggle, then hurried to follow me. When we reached the truck, I tugged her close, pulling the keys from the pocket of my jeans.

"Do you want to drive?" I had spent the last two weeks getting her comfortable behind the wheel again, having her drive around the quiet residential streets of Summerlin and gradually working her way to busier and busier streets. She was hesitant with the truck at first, but I hoped to get her driving it confidently before I moved her to the standard transmission Mustang.

Eyes wide, Penelope shook her head. "On a real road? I don't think so, Stone. I'm not ready."

"Sure you are. You've been doing great."

Penelope bit her lip, working the flesh between her teeth, her face scrunched up in concentration as she stared at the big truck, and I give her the time to think it over. I watched her quietly as she looked from my face to the keys, leaning back like they might bite her. Finally, I saw her eyes change, going from wide and frightened to narrowed with determination. Reaching out, she snatched the keys from my fingers and clicked the button, unlocking the big truck with a beep.

I smiled at her, opening the driver's side door and helping her up. Penelope was not short, standing about five and half feet tall, but the truck was huge, and, besides, I liked finding excuses to touch her.

By the time I was in my own seat, Penelope had the truck started and the air on; even that early in the year, the sun made parked cars unbearable in a very short amount of time. She turned the satellite radio to the alternative rock station we both liked, then smiled up at me. "So, where to, Cowboy?"

"I'm still not gonna tell you," I teased, plugging the address into the built in GPS on the dash board. The computer did its thing, and the snooty voiced chick came over the speakers, directing Penelope on her first turn. Putting the truck in reverse, she slowly backed us out of the parking stall and then headed out of the lot and onto the busy Las Vegas streets.

She was quiet, only occasionally asking for direction or confirmation in her actions, but I was glad because it gave me an excuse to just look at her. She was so different at work than she was around the house. At the office, she was all buttoned up; from her tight bun to her pencil skirts, Penelope was always the epitome of professional chic. But once we got to the house, she transformed, letting her hair down in both a literal and metaphorical sense. She had a lightness about her that was both addictive and contagious. Her smile was always genuine, and when you talked to her, you could see that she was really listening. She cared about the things I told her, and I found myself wanting to tell her more.   Like my relationship with Harold, or how I always felt like I had to protect my mother, even if she didn't really need it.

Penelope took in what I had to say, and she made me believe that I mattered, like my thoughts and my feelings were just as important to her as they were to me.

And that terrified me a little, because with every interaction we had, no matter how much she seemed to be working her way inside my fortified walls, there was still an expiration date for her and I.

I was finding that I hated that.

The GPS lady had guided us through town and out, the traffic dwindling as we went.   When we passed the first sign for the Hoover Dam, Penelope's eyes lit up.

"You ever been to the Dam, Blondie?"

"Stone," she scoffed.   "I've never been anywhere.   Heck, that day we collided at the airport was my first time on a plane."   She shook her head. "It was memorable, that's for sure."

I laughed lightly, letting the matter drop, but as we turned off the interstate, which had only caused her to mildly hyperventilate when she realized I expected her to actually drive on it, I started thinking that I'd like to show her Hoover Dam one day.   I'd like to show her the beaches of the Gulf Coast at Galveston, where I'd gone for weekends away with my mom.   I'd like to take her to San Antonio and show her the real Alamo. I'd like to take her to San Diego and watch her eyes light up as she explored the zoo.

The list went on, but one fact was evident through all my thoughts: I wanted to keep Penelope Lund.

I just had to figure out how to do it.

As we cruised down the small two-lane road that was State Highway 165, Penelope pulled me from my daydreams about her when she sighed.

"I just can't believe all this space," she said, gesturing to the miles and miles of Nevada desert that surrounded us. "I've never seen anything like it. There is just...nothing. It looks like it goes on forever."

"I guess it's pretty different from what you're used to."

"It's the complete opposite from what I'm used to. In New York, even out in Queens, there's nowhere you can look that you can't see another person. Maybe they're walking past you on the street, or maybe they're sitting on their balcony four stories up, but there is always someone near by, living their life right alongside you. It's comforting, in a way, to know that you aren't alone. But there is an element of suffocation that I feel sometimes, knowing that there is always someone near, for good or for ill.

"But out here," she paused, looking around again at the low hills with their brick red coloring and the smattering of low brush. "Out here it's just you and the desert." The look on her face was pensive, like she was discovering something she'd never imagined. As I stared at her beautiful face, so lost in thought, I tried to picture what seeing something like this for the first time would feel like, but I couldn't seem to put myself in her place. "Out here," she went on after a time, seeming to have come to a conclusion about how it all felt. "I've never felt so...*free*."

I had no response to that, and she didn't seem to expect one, so we continued on in silence as the hills crept closer to the highway, penning us in as we continued along our computer guided route. When the thing finally announced we had arrived at our destination, I could hear Penelope's quick inhale.

"A ranch?" she asked excitedly as we parked and climbed out of the truck. "You brought me to a ranch?"

"Not just any ranch. This is Pennington Ranch."

"Oh," she said, eyes going wide. "Carson told me about this place. It's where the animals are kept for the hotel."

"Exactly. I thought you might like to check it out, maybe get some photos for your socials of the Trail Ride Experience we will be offering."

"Stone, this is such a great idea." Her smile was brilliant, lighting up her entire face. "I would love to get some shots of the property, the animals, and the staff. Maybe I could get some statements, as well, for the website." I watched her as her mind went a million miles an hour, creating and sorting ideas for how to use this opportunity to the best benefit of Pennington Hotels. She truly did love the company, and everything she did was to help it succeed. Looked like my dad was right about her.

Shit. *My dad*? Did I really just think of Harold

that way?

So much was changing so quickly. I couldn't keep up.

Shaking that off, I turned back to Penelope, who was staring at the property with her hands on her hips, muttering under her breath about lighting and hashtags. It was adorable.

"There's one more thing you need to do, Blondie."

She turned, eyebrows high. "What's that?"

"Experience the trail ride, of course."

The look of shock on her face was totally worth it.

CHAPTER EIGHTEEN
Penelope

"You can't be serious!"

"As a heart attack, Blondie," he laughed, the smug look on his face made me want to sock him.

"There is no possible way I can get on a horse, Stone." I would not tell him that my heart was racing, both with fear and at the prospect that I might actually do it. Growing up, I had dreamed of riding horses, like most little girls, I expect. But while most girls may have been imagining castles and knights, I was dreaming of something a little different.

"Sure there is," Stone replied, moving around me and heading to the barn. I stared after him for a second, then scrambled to catch up.

"No, Stone. You don't understand. I can't."

"What do you mean?" he asked, looking at me with genuine concern. "Are you allergic to them or something?"

"No," I laughed. "At least, not that I know of. I haven't been around horses since I was little. But my dad used to take me to see his friends in the Mounted Unit in Midtown once in a while." It was always so incredible, seeing the police horses of the NYPD. We didn't go often, but when we were able to, it was always like magic. Horses, in the middle of Manhattan. "I haven't been on a horse since the last time we went. I think I was six." The memory, as always, brought both sadness and joy. I missed my father every day, but remembering him always made me smile.

"Well, then it's time to get back in the saddle, Blondie." Stone held out his hand, his usual scowl now replaced by a half smile that was so sexy I could hardly stand it.

Taking my hand in his, he drew me into his chest, wrapping his other arm around my shoulders and holding me close. Suddenly, I didn't care much about horses or photos or anything besides the enticing smell of his spicy cologne and the way his arms felt wrapped around me. Memories of the last two weeks assaulted me and my cheeks heated, remembering the way Stone and I had shared so many nights of explosive passion. I had never experienced sex that good. Just the thought of all those nights, nights spent in Stone's bed, had my stomach muscles clenching. The man was very, very talented.

I was startled from my sexy memories by the sound of approaching footsteps. Turning, I saw a man coming from the barn. He was older, maybe early fifties, with a barrel chest and arms that looked like they'd been worked hard all his life. He had on jeans and a western style shirt, pearl buttons and all, and a classic beige cowboy hat; he was the epitome of every western movie I'd ever seen, right down to his grizzled graying beard.

"Mr. Montgomery," the man said, extending his hand. Stone took it, shaking it with a nod.

"Smitty. Good to see you. This is Miss Penelope Lund, our marketing director."

"Ma'am." Smitty touched the brim of his hat, and I couldn't help but smile. "Glad you could make it out today. I have everything if you'd like to follow me."

As we moved to the barn, I looked around the property a bit more. There were several buildings and fenced areas, and a good-sized shed, open on one side, which housed a few tractors and off-road vehicles. Across from the barn stood a classic looking farm house, with the giant wrap around porch and all, painted cream with dark green shutters. It was quaint and tidy and I loved it. A woman stood on the porch, also dressed in jeans, and she waved when she saw me looking. I raised my hand back with a smile.

Bringing my attention back to where I was headed, I squinted as we entered the barn through the broad double doors, the sudden loss of daylight making the interior of the building look pitch black for a few moments. As my eyes adjusted, I could see that it was a huge space, with stalls for horses on one side and a storage system on the other side that reminded me of a locker room, the kind you see on TV when they interview athletes after a game. Open sided stalls lined the wall, each with several items hanging in them. There was a long leather looking jacket, as well as what

I assumed were chaps and a cowboy hat at each place.

"This is the main barn, Miss Lund," Smitty began explaining, having noticed my curious stares. "When guests come to the ranch, this will be where they are assessed for appropriate dress. If anyone needs something, like long pants or what not, we will do our best to accommodate." He gestured to the locker closest to him, and I noticed they were all labeled with sizes, allowing the person to choose what worked best for them. It was really pretty brilliant, and I would have to tell Carson how much I loved it.

Remembering that I had a job to do, I pulled out my company phone and began snapping some photos of the barn and the horse stalls, trying to frame the shots in an artful way, using the app on the fancy phone that I had been provided. After I had gotten a few that I thought would look great, even with a bit of editing, I turned back to see both men watching me, Smitty with a cheeky grin, likely at my city-slicker wonder at finding myself in a real barn for the first time, and Stone with a look that was filled with both happiness and heat. Just seeing the way his eyes were hooded had my tummy fluttering again and moisture flooding my panties. Darn him. He was going to make this trail ride even more difficult than I had originally thought.

"Right," I said, clearing my throat and my dirty thoughts. "Tell me what to do next."

After a bit of debate about my foot wear, Smitty and Stone both agreed that because this would be a slow and gentle ride on a clearly marked trail, I wouldn't need boots, but that I should probably bring some for next time.

Like there would be a next time.

I frowned at the disappointment that thought brought with it, knowing that riding a horse with Stone would only be a one-time experience. This entire *thing* that we had, whatever you would choose to call it, was destined to be short lived. There was no way around it. There was nothing about Stone and me that could equal end game, no matter how much that thought made my heart hurt.

Feelings were not an option in this situation. I had to remember that. It had never been a problem for me to remain emotionally disconnected in the past. Why then, when there was no future possible, was I finding it more and more difficult to stay that way?

I stood back as Stone and Smitty discussed things I had no idea about, like girth straps and saddle horns, and before long we were back out in the sunshine, with two fully saddled horses idly swinging their tails back and forth. My heart began to hammer in my chest again as I watched the huge animals approach. One was tall and had a beautiful deep brown coat that looked to have red highlights in the afternoon sun. The second was a lighter brown, with patches of cream-colored spots on its rump. That was the one that turned its head toward me, reaching for me with its mouth, startling me into taking a hasty step back.

"Oh, that's Annie. She's a good girl, she won't hurt ya none," said Smitty, chuckling lightly at my unease. "She's just tryin' to smell ya, is all."

"Oh," I said, smiling a bit as I approached the horse. "Well, hello, Annie." I lifted my hand to her, allowing her to brush her nose across the back of it. "It's nice to meet you." She moved her velvety soft muzzle across my knuckles, tickling me with her thin whiskers, then abruptly pulled her head back and sneezed all over me.

I gasped as Stone snorted out a laugh at my expense.

"That just means she likes, ya, don't ya, Annie girl?" Smitty said, rubbing his hand up and down her strong neck vigorously.

"Well," I said, tossing a glare at Stone. "Thank you, Annie, but consider yourself lucky that I don't return the gesture, hey?"

That caused Smitty to bark out a laugh which turned into a hacking cough. Once he'd thumped himself on the chest a few times, he turned his water eyes to me. "Well, Miss Lund, I think you and Annie are gonna get along just fine." He moved toward me, and I fought the urge to back up again. As I watched Smitty and Annie pass me and head for the nearest fence, Stone came up on my other side, his own horse in tow.

"You're gonna be fine, Blondie," he said quietly, his large warm hand coming to rest on the back of my neck, his fingers gently massaging the tension away. "I'll be with you the whole time. Smitty said Annie is as gentle as a baby duck. She'll give you no problems." I turned and looked at him, his hazel eyes warm and his crooked smile making my heart clench.

I allowed myself a moment to enjoy the feeling, before I shook it off, remembering all the reasons why feelings were not permissible.

Stone followed Smitty and Annie toward the fence. I trailed behind, partly because I was unsure what to do next, and partly because I was enjoying looking at Stone's ass in his jeans. He had been wearing more and more relaxed clothing to work these last few weeks, ditching the suits piece by piece until he was wearing worn jeans and button-down shirts; he even wore his boots and that big shiny belt buckle. If I didn't know better, I'd think he was tired of pretending. I could totally relate to that. He was pretending he was more than the illegitimate son of a hotel tycoon who grew up on a ranch, and I was pretending I was more than the working-class girl from Queens, fumbling her way around Manhattan in shoes she couldn't afford.

If he was as exhausted by the whole charade as I was, I wouldn't blame him one bit.

Stone's voice brought me out of my musings when he called me over. "Come on, Blondie. Climb on up."

He gestured to a wooden stool with stairs on one side, and a flat face on the other. Smitty had pulled Annie up beside it, and the stool was designed to help me reach the saddle. I ascended slowly, not wanting to spook my horse, no matter how docile they told me she was. Stone tied his own mount to the fence and then came to stand beside me at the stairs.

"Okay, Penelope. Nice and easy, now. You're

gonna place your foot in the stirrup, grab on to the saddle horn here, and pull." He reached out and grasped the item in question, giving it a firm shake which caused Annie to toss her head, whipping her mane around like she was in a Beyoncé video. I jumped back with a squeak, forgetting that I was standing on the top step of the stairs. Just as I started to fall backward, Stone grabbed me by the hips, preventing me from landing on my behind in the dirt. "Whoa. Whoa, now girl," he soothed, and for a moment, I didn't know if he was talking to me or the horse.

"I got it," I said with a laugh, squaring my shoulders and gripping the saddle horn with one hand. I placed the other on the back of the saddle while Stone held tight to what I knew was the bridle. I placed one foot in the stirrup, took a breath, and jumped, swinging my leg over and seating myself in the saddle. Annie shuffled around a little as my weight settled on her back, but very soon we were both comfortable with each other.

Smitty came over and adjusted my stirrups, then passed me the reins. I took them hesitantly, afraid that this would end horribly, but at the same time ridiculously excited. I had never even been on a horse before, but this didn't seem so bad.

"There's one more thing you need, Miss Lund," Smitty said with a grin, his eyes nearly disappearing beneath the wrinkles on his tanned cheeks. He shuffled to the barn, reappearing a moment later with a cowboy hat in his hand. It was a regular looking tan straw hat with a black band and a turquoise stone set on to one side. "This here belongs to my Darlene," he stated, tilting his head toward the ranch house where the woman, Darlene I assumed, was still standing. "But she won't mind none. You'll need it out there under the desert sun."

"Thank you." I smiled as I took the hat, putting it on and adjusting it around my bun. I looked toward the house and Darlene smiled, giving me a thumbs up.

Stone and Smitty talked a bit more while Annie and I got acquainted, her big brown eyes blinking slowly as she looked around with an uninterested stare. I watched as Stone mounted his own horse with a grace and ease that had me jealous. He was beyond comfortable on the big animal, looking for all the world as if he had been born on horseback. Stone moved over to where Annie and I waited, a smile on his face bigger than any I had ever seen him wear. He absolutely radiated happiness. True, bone deep happiness, and looking at him, I realized that Stone Pennington would never live a life that didn't involve riding horses. He shouldn't. Watching him there, looking every bit the Texas rancher he was raised as, I knew it was something that would never change, no matter how much my foolish heart may have pictured him in New York.

It was a silly hope, one conjured by my subconscious during the nights I had recently spent sleeping curled against him in his bed. But a person couldn't control their dreams any more than they could control their heart. And it seemed that, with every day

I spent getting closer to Stone, both my dreams and my heart were getting away from me.

"Are you ready to ride, Blondie?" Stone asked with a wink as he moved ahead of me and headed for the trail that led east from the ranch and into the valley that was nestled between the low hills. Annie swung her head, watching as the other horse moved at Stone's confident instruction of clicks, nudges, and gentle words, and she slowly plodded after them.

I was tense, sitting stiffly in the saddle, one hand on the reins and one clutching the saddle horn, waiting for the moment when Annie would take off like in the movies and I would go flying. But after a while we both relaxed into the ride, her following slowly, and me learning how to move with her, the rolling of her back much like a wave, moving in a steady rhythm, and soon I was able to enjoy the scenery. The desert landscape was gorgeous, the huge blue sky contrasting against the tans and reds of the sand and the deep browns and grays of the low hills and rocks. Stone kept up a running commentary about the plants and animals that he knew, listing off things like the yucca plant and the rabbitbrush, as well as pointing out a red-tailed hawk and an honest to goodness roadrunner, a quirky looking bird with long tail feathers and a fluffy little hair-do that was to die for.

It didn't take long and the sandy planes began to fill up with bigger shrubs and even a tree or two, the varying shades of green popping up along the trail as we meandered our way along.

"You make a pretty great cowgirl, Penelope,"

Stone tossed back over his shoulder as we passed through a narrowing of the trail. "Minus the boots, of course."

"Why thank you, candy corn," I teased, pulling my very best Dolly impression. Stone caught on right away, tossing his head back with a laugh. "Annie and I are becoming the best of friends, you know. Oh," I dropped the accent, sitting up straighter. "I didn't ask what your horses' name was."

"This is Big Jake."

"Really? Like the John Wayne movie?"

Stone spun in the saddle to look at me, his eyes wide. "You know John Wayne?"

I laughed. "Yes, Stone. I grew up in New York, not on the moon. Who doesn't know The Duke? My dad was obsessed. We'd watch the movies over and over. He had a whole collection of them on VHS. When I was younger, we even had a cat named Hondo."

At that his mouth opened wide. "No way! My horse in Texas is named McNally!"

"Well," I giggled. "What better way to name a pet than after a classic John Wayne character?"

He shook his head back and forth. "I can't believe it. A John Wayne fan. I think I may have underestimated you, Miss Lund."

"Well, people tend to do that, Mr. Pennington." He almost hid the flinch when I used his fathers name.

"So, tell me," he proceeded, moving the conversation along. "What was your favorite movie?"

"Oh, that's a tough one."

"No, it isn't. The answer is *The Alamo*. That's the clear winner in this discussion, darlin'." I had noticed that as our afternoon progressed, Stone's accent thickened. Most days I hardly noticed it, but it appeared that being on horse back was drawing it out, and his Texas drawl was doing things to my lady parts that I would never have though possible from mere words. "I mean, come on. A true story about American heroes? There is no other option."

I laughed again, trying to put a lid on my lust. A difficult task, to be sure. "That's a valid point, although I hesitate to point out your personal bias, being from Texas and all."

"Alright, then, smarty pants. What's the best?"

"You didn't say best, you said favorite. Those are two very different answers. However, for the sake of this discussion, I will concede that my personal favorite *is* the best, and that would be *True Grit*."

"Ah. Of course. You pick the one with the strong-willed young woman who takes no shit from anyone."

My smile was small, the discussion bringing up memories I hadn't waded through for years. "True, Mattie Ross is a spitfire, but the real reason I love that movie is more personal than that." I took a breath, gasping a little as our horses crested the rise and the Colorado River came into view, its broad flat surface looking like cold iron in the harsh afternoon light. "It is so peaceful here," I said quietly. Annie and Big Jake moved to the edge of the water, obviously being familiar enough with this route that our interference was not required; we were just along for the ride.

Taking another breath, letting the quiet of the day fill me up for a moment, I sat on my horse and just looked.

I looked at a landscape I had never in my whole life expected to be near, appreciating every nuanced level of its harsh beauty.

I looked at the empty tract of land and water, wondering if we would see even one other person for the rest of our ride, and trying to remember if I had ever felt so...liberated in my entire life. So free from the day to day constraints of life and the pressures of society in general.

And I looked at Stone, waiting patiently for me to have my moment, not a care in the world beyond what I would say next.

That was a powerful feeling in and of itself. I didn't know what to do with it.

"No," I said quietly, not taking my eyes off the water. "The reason I love *True Grit* the most is because Rooster Cogburn is a flawed man. He's the law, being the U.S. Marshall, and so he's held to a standard above most folks, even though he's just as human as they are. But, even with all his flaws, he's still a man of honor and integrity and he wakes up every day and does what's right. No matter the cost."

I closed my eyes against the sting of tears that surfaced as memories of my dad assaulted me from all sides. How much he loved being a police officer, and how, sometimes, people hated him for doing his job.

And what that job had ultimately cost him, cost

us, as a family.   As a city.

As a nation.

It was a price many of us were still paying.

When I opened my eyes, I found Stone staring at me intently, the look on his face one I couldn't quite read.   After a moment he smiled, one side of his mouth curving up.   "Yeah," he agreed.   "That just might be the best after all."

CHAPTER NINETEEN
Penelope

"Our new hire targets are behind in regards to our casino floor staff and dealers right now," Gideon Langford, Gaming Manager for *The Alamo* stated flatly, looking only mildly annoyed by this fact. "The staff that we do have is scheduled to start their training in two weeks, but we are doing another wave of interviews before then, so I am hopeful that the remainder of the positions will be filled in time to join them."

Those of us seated around the table nodded as I looked at each of them in turn. I had been here in Las Vegas for almost two months, and those weekly executive meetings had gotten more and more tense as the date of the Soft Launch crept up on us. There was just so much left to do, and time was running out. Gideon was not the only one behind on his hires, as all departments seemed to be scrambling for staff. Geoff Yates, the food and beverage manager, had complained that two of his sous-chefs had quit this week, leaving for other opportunities, and his server and bartender teams were not complete either. Operations manager,

Curtis Jones, was still looking for appropriate people to fill the shift managers positions in both guest services and housekeeping, and Silas, who was head of hotel security, was in the process of doing background checks on everyone who applied for any position, but close to completing his own team of security staff.

All in all, things were behind schedule and heading toward being over budget, and the scowl on Stone's face only supported what everyone in the room was feeling; stress.

"Let me know if you need to branch out as far as where you are looking for potential hires," Stone said gruffly. "I want these positions filled as soon as possible. Our staff should all be well trained for our Soft Launch in six weeks, so that every guest has the Pennington Hotels Experience, no matter how new this hotel is."

Gideon nodded, his face showing no indication of how he felt regarding Stone's statement. I had found that that was just Gideon, though. He was stoic, rarely showing anything beyond and eyebrow raise or a nod. Where Stone was a grouch, at least to most people, his face usually set in an expression of annoyance tinged with a dash of anger, Gideon was carefully blank. His features always looked carved out of marble, his dark skin and deep brown eyes barely moving as he surveyed the room around him. He was intimidating, that was for sure. Where Stone's moods had raised a fire in me, prompting me to dish out his own crankiness right back at him, Gideon caused me to hesitate, never sure how to approach him or how any interaction would be received.

It was for all those reasons that I hesitated before I spoke now. "If you'd like, Mr. Langford," I started, going for polite and respectful. "I could post on our social media accounts. Since we have started here, our follows have increased significantly. I'm sure, between our own followers and any corresponding shares, we could reach a few million people by the end of the day."

Every head at the table turned my way, but I didn't take my eyes off Gideon, willing myself not to falter under his intense gaze. His eyes roamed over my face, seemingly searching for something. After a moment, he pursed his lips and nodded. "That may be beneficial. Thank you."

I shot him a full smile, pleased to have gotten a positive response. I really just liked being helpful, but getting a nod from Gideon seemed like an extra win.

"Thank you, Miss Lund," Stone said, sending a smile of his own my way. "That's an excellent idea."

His comment received a derisive snort from Toby, and I turned see him glaring at me coldly.

"Is there a problem, Mr. Reynolds?" Stone asked, as the tension in the room rose another notch. I shifted uncomfortably in my chair. I had a feeling I knew what was bothering Toby, but there was no way I wanted it discussed at the table.

"Nope," Toby replied, popping the "P" and leaning back in his chair and crossing his arms. "No problem. I'm being totally professional, right Penelope?"

In reality, he was being totally disrespectful, both to Stone and me, and to the others attending this meeting. I glanced around, seeing confusion on the faces of the others, except for Gideon, who was looking at Toby with that same impassive expression, even if his eyes were narrowed slightly.

Everyone was quiet, watching as Stone and Toby squared off across the conference table. I could see Stone's jaw muscles clenching, knowing he was doing everything he could to refrain from exploding at Toby. I had asked Stone when we first got together to please be discreet at work. Everyone knew what happened to a woman's career when she slept with the boss. I couldn't imagine that situation got any better when the Human Resources Manager considered himself the spurned party. Stone was sticking to my request, even though I could see it was hard for him. I had to step in before things went from bad to worse.

"Of course, Mr. Reynolds is being professional. He has always been above reproach, and I am sure we all appreciate him for it."

Toby rolled his eyes, clearly insulted by my comments. Stone stood up from his place at the head of the table and for a second I thought he was going to get physical. But he simply gathered his things, then leveled Toby with his best intimidating look and said, "I think we are finished here for today. If anyone has anything further they'd like to say, I'll be available."

Everyone took that as their cue to hightail it back to their respective offices, with Toby leading the way, slamming the door open in a huff.

Damn. That was becoming a serious problem.

Soon Stone and I were the only ones left in the room. He held his rigid posture until the door closed behind the last person, then exhaled a huge breath of air, leaning back in the chair and dragging his hand over his face in exasperation.

"Shit," he breathed.

"Yeah," was all I could think of to say in return.

"I gotta say, I didn't expect that from him."

"Neither did I, to be honest." I chewed on my lower lip, nervously running through different scenarios in my mind. All of them ended up with me losing my job in disgrace. "Do you think he'll say anything? About... us." I hedged, wondering if there was an 'us' to be mentioning. Stone and I hadn't had discussed what we were, both of us content to just enjoy the time we had together. But now that the end was closer than the beginning, it seemed like talking about it was inevitable.

I'd still rather not, though. Ignorance was bliss, as they said.

Stone grunted. "I doubt it. His pride is wounded, so I don't think he'll want the whole world knowing he lost."

"Lost?"

He turned to me, one side of his mouth lifting in a playful smirk. "Yeah, Blondie. I got the girl."

I blushed, but said nothing. We still had to have that talk, after all. No matter how close Stone and I had gotten, there were still a lot of things standing between us, and about seventeen hundred miles.

Gathering my things, I headed back to my office and started drawing up the ads for our needed staff members. Normally, I would contact Toby to get lists of job requirements and qualifications for each position, but I figured that now would not be a good time. Instead I sent off an email to his assistant, and had several great posts created in short order.

I was just finishing the last post when Stone knocked on my open door. Glancing at the clock, I realized it was later than usual.

"Sorry," I said. "Am I holding you up? I am almost finished for the night."

Stone entered my office and closed the door behind him, twisting the lock before strolling toward me. "Good, because we are the last ones here right now," he said, his voice low and husky. Watching him stalk across the room and around my desk sent adrenaline coursing through my system. He moved slowly, coming to stand behind my chair, leaning over as he had before. Only this time, he pressed his lips to my neck while trailing his fingers up and down my arms. I shivered, my body coming alive at his touch. "So, I was thinking," he whispered, his mouth right by my ear, causing desire to pool low in my belly. "That maybe we could take advantage of this situation."

"Oh," I said, my mouth suddenly dry. "And what, exactly, did you have in mind, Mr. Montgomery?" I used his preferred name this time, not wanting to do anything that might make him change his plans for me.

"First," he said, turning my chair sideways and

standing before me. "I was thinking that I would start by kissing you." With that he pressed a kiss to my lips, warm and tender. He continued, deepening the kiss, placing his hands on either side of my face, cradling me.

I kissed him back fiercely, the fire in my belly growing, becoming an inferno. It was like that every time Stone touched me. He created a storm inside me, one that only he could put out.

Pulling back from his kiss, I leaned back in the chair, watching as he stood straight. When he released me, I smiled at him, then slid from the chair and to my knees in front of him. I could see the realization in his eyes when he caught on to my intentions, and then watched as his gaze filled with heat and lust.

Turning to the task at hand, I ran one hand over his hard length, caressing it through his jeans. I could hear the slow and deep intake of breath as I did, and it made my heart swell with pride that I could do this to him. That I could make him feel good, the same way he did for me.

Continuing to stroke him with one hand, I used the other to open his belt, pulling the large buckle out and releasing the strap of leather. I glanced up at Stone again as I used both hands to pop the button on his jeans, watching him watch me as I slowly drew the zipper down, revealing the large bulge behind a pair of black boxer briefs. Working the jeans off his hips and butt, I let them drop as I once again began stroking him, one hand working his erection, the other trailing slowly up and down his muscular thigh, feeling him flex every time I changed direction, trying to keep him guessing as to my next move.

Releasing him, I placed both hands on his hips, sliding my fingers under the waist band of his underwear, pausing a moment as I leaned in, dragging my nose up his length from base to dip, inhaling the rich, musky scent that was delicious and purely Stone.

Stone groaned, and I smiled again as I slowly began to roll his boxer briefs down his legs, revealing him to me in all his hot, hard glory. Once he was clear of his shorts, I grasped him at the base, giving one slow pump before extending my tongue, circling the tip once, twice, then wrapping my lips around the head. His taste melted against my tongue, the light salty flavor filling my mouth and sending liquid heat through my system. I began to move, pulling him deep, then retreating, working my tongue in tandem with my hand, the rhythm building to a steady pace. I could hear Stone's breathing increase, his low grunts letting me know when I'd done something particularly enjoyable, and he placed one hand on my head, not forcing, but gently guiding me to the things he liked best. He released a strangled moan when I brought my other hand up to cup his balls, rolling them lightly in my palm before giving a gentle tug.

Suddenly, Stone pulled away, grasping my wrist and pulling me to my feet. He slammed his mouth down against mine, his tongue pressing in forcefully as he wrapped his arms around me.

"Fuck, Penelope," he grated out, his forehead resting against mine as he caught his breath. After a moment, he kissed me again, quick and hard, then turned and shoved all the things on my desk to one side, my papers flying off on to the floor, the laptop turned sideways and balanced precariously close to the edge.

It was so hot.

I let out a squeak when Stone grasped the hem of my pencil skirt, hiking it up high over my hips, then pulled my thong down to my knees. On his way back up, he lifted me, placing my behind on the desk where my computer was just sitting, and dragging my underwear all the way off my feet, tossing them behind him in a casual move, his cocky grin making my nipples tighten and throb under my shirt.

I looked at him with wide eyes as he drew a condom out of his wallet, rolling it on and then grasping my thighs and slowly drawing them apart, his eyes trained on my wet core, his smirk fully in place. Rocking my hips in a needy dance, I reached for him, wrapping my arms around his shoulders and pressing kisses to his neck, the days' stubble tickling my lips.

"Please," I begged softly, wanting him inside me. *Needing* him inside me.

"I'd like to fuck you on your desk, Miss Lund," Stone growled, the blunt head of his dick poised at my entrance enticingly. "Would that be alright with you?"

"Yes," I gasped, trying to shift my hips forward and guide him inside, but he pulled away, teasing me, as his one hand trailed down my collar bone and over by breast, massaging gently. "Oh, God, yes."

"That's my girl," he breathed against my neck, the words sending a thrill through my chest. I tried not to let them send my mind places it shouldn't go, focusing instead on the feel of him entering me, stretching me slowly as he pressed inside. Every inch he gained caused my hands to clutch at him tighter, my fingers digging into his shoulders as I reveled in the feel of his possession. When he was pressed against me as tight as he could go, Stone paused, staring at me, his eyes filled with fire and something else I still couldn't name.

Or maybe I just didn't want to.

I closed my eyes as he kissed me again and started to move, his hips picking up what was becoming a familiar rhythm, both of us falling smoothly into each other. I kept one hand on his shoulder, the other I stretched behind me, leaning back on the desk to be able to move with him. Stone tugged the sides of my wrap blouse open, revealing my creamy lace bra, and bent forward, his mouth working my nipple through the pale fabric, sending a shock wave directly to my clit. I moaned, leaning my head back, as Stone drove us both closer and closer.

My breathing became ragged, and Stone released my breast and dropped his hand between us, his thumb pressing firm circles on my sensitive bundle of nerves. "Yes, Penelope," he said harshly, his teeth gritted as he held himself back to wait for me. It only took two more strokes and I exploded, my mouth falling open in a silent scream as my muscles clamped down and wave after wave of bliss surged through my body.

I felt Stone pick up his pace, his rhythmic

strokes faltering as he chased his own release. When he reached it, he wrapped his hand around the back of my neck and drew me into another soul-stealing kiss. We stayed like that, joined in every way possible, until both of us had calmed our breathing, Stone trailing his finger tips lightly up and down the back of my neck.

Neither of us said anything, content to just be, until the sound of Stone's phone ringing forced us back to reality. I winced slightly as he pulled out, my delicate parts tender from all the activity they had seen in the last few weeks. Stone quickly disposed of the condom, then grabbed his phone from his pocket and answered as he pulled his pants up.

"Yeah," he said, his gruff personality firmly back in place. I smiled and shook my head, slipping off the desk and searching out my panties. "What do you mean, they're wrong?" Stone barked. I stood, panties back in place, and met his eyes, noticing he was frowning in my direction. "I'm sure it was just a mistake. I'll look into it and have it corrected right away. Thanks for letting me know." He hung up without saying goodbye. Such a guy thing to do.

"What is it?" I asked, a sense of dread already replacing my bliss from the very excellent desk sex.

"That was Gideon," Stone said carefully. "He said that your new job postings are garnering a ton of interest." I smiled wide before he continued. "It's most likely because the hourly wages are all wrong."

"What?" I gasped, bliss now completely forgotten as I pushed Stone away from my desk and retrieved my computer. "That's not possible. I got all the information from the Assistant Human Resources manager just today. Everything should be accurate." I quickly opened the first post I had made, seeing the amount of likes and comments was through the roof, but that Stone and Gideon were both correct; the listed hourly wage for the position was double what it should be. "What the hell? That is *not* what I posted," I insisted, switching to the email program and looking again at the information I had received that contained the correct numbers.

I bounced over to the other job postings, all of them now wildly inaccurate and drawing way too much attention because of it. "Shit, Stone. I have to fix this. Now." I sat heavily in my chair, working as fast as I could to repair the damage.

Once I had corrected all the job postings, I had to draw up a retraction, apologizing for the mistake. So much for feeling proud of my suggestion from earlier. Now I looked like a complete screw up. Again.

I finished up, double and then triple checking everything. Stone had sat patiently in my office chair, working on his own things and answering texts and emails on his phone. When I closed the laptop with a sigh, he looked up, a frown puckering between his eyebrows. "You alright, Blondie?"

I shook my head slowly and glanced at the closed computer, feeling tears pricking at the corners of my eyes, but refusing to let them fall. "I know those posts were right, Stone. I know it."

"Hey," he said quietly, drawing my attention

back to him. "I know you are good at your job, Penelope. I have seen you in action. Whatever happened today, it's over. You fixed it. Don't let it get to you."

I nodded, but I didn't say anything. His words were kind, but still hinted at the fact that he thought this mistake was mine.

It wasn't. I knew it wasn't. But how in the world was I going to prove it?

CHAPTER TWENTY
Penelope

The theater was empty except for Carson and me, but the stage was lit up like the fourth of July. I couldn't stop smiling as Dolly and her crew ran through their dress rehearsal. There were only three weeks remaining until the Soft Launch, and the show was looking fantastic. I watched, entranced, as the performers pranced and paraded around, the impersonations shockingly good, while the comedy was sharp and the dance numbers were full of the glitz and glamour that you expected form a Las Vegas show.

In short, it was a freaking hit.

"Penelope," Carson whispered, leaning in to speak close to my ear. "This is gonna blow the roof off this town! I can't wait for the Soft Launch. We have already sold out for that night, and the Grand Opening as well. I can't thank you enough for finding these ladies."

"I didn't do anything, really, Carson. Just introduced you to a friend."

When the final act ended and the lights came up, I offered a standing ovation of one. Dolly smiled at me from her place at center stage, waving her arms and blowing kisses. I was waving frantically back at her when I caught movement out of the corner of my eye. Turning, I saw Stone standing at the end of the row of chairs, hands on his hips as he surveyed the stage. I couldn't help the thrill that ran through my system at seeing him, dressed in jeans and boots, looking every inch the sexy cowboy I had found him to be. I gave myself a moment to get my hormones in check before walking toward him and nudging him in the ribs with my elbow, bringing his attention back to me.

"What did you think, Cowboy?"

"I think we have a hit on our hands. The shareholders will be pleased."

"Well, as long as we can please the shareholders, our jobs are complete, right?" I mumbled, only half joking.

"Unfortunate, but true, I'm afraid," he replied, a frustrated frown on his face. I guess he would know, dealing with much more of that part of the business than I ever had. If - no, when - I got promoted, I was going to have to get much more acquainted with those aspects of Pennington Hotels.

Sounds delightful.

"Listen, Penelope," he said awkwardly, crossing and uncrossing his arms, looking so uncomfortable that I frowned. Stone had a lot of different moods, but for the most part they were all born of a place of confidence. If he was looking nervous and uncomfortable, I suspected something big was troubling him. "I was hoping you would come to lunch with me. There's something I need to discuss with you."

I swallowed the rapidly forming lump in my throat and forced a strained smile. "Of course," I ground out. "Just let me finish up and I'll be right with you."

I turned away before he could respond, afraid of what he might have to say. I scurried over to where Dolly and Carson were going over some notes, my mind racing to come up with what Stone could want to discuss, but the only thing I could imagine would result in his level of discomfort was us. Not that there was an *us*, per se, but it would make sense that he would want to talk about whatever it was we had going on. I mean, I had spent the last month and a half sleeping with him.

And not just sleeping with him, but actually *sleeping* with him - in his bed. Waking up next to him, sharing coffee and showers and breakfast and everything. It was all so domestic. And it had been ridiculously easy and comfortable, as long as I didn't look too far into the future. Because sitting together on the couch and squabbling over what to watch on Netflix was fine, hell, it was great, but it often took everything I had in me to remember that it was all going to end.

To remember to keep my heart out of things.

And I was terrified that I hadn't succeeded.

That was why the prospect of whatever Stone wanted to talk about was so daunting. Part of me was afraid that he was going to tell me it was over, whatever we had. That he was done and we were through.

But another part of me was terrified that he would tell me we weren't.

I wasn't sure which prospect scared me more.

Plastering a smile back on my face, I approached Carson and Dolly, her chipper laughter lightening my heart effortlessly.

"Well, hey there, butter tart," Dolly gushed, wrapping one arm around my shoulders. "How'd you like the show?"

"Spectacular, as always."

"Well, thank you, darlin', but you know we couldn't have done it without you. You're like my very own good luck charm."

I chuckled, watching as Carson nodded his agreement. "I think you're plenty charming all on your own, Dolly. If you two don't need me, I'm going to head out."

Dolly looked over my shoulder, then smiled slyly. "Why, if I had that hunk of man waiting on me, I'd be getting my behind outta here just as quick as my stilettos could carry me." She looked down at my feet, once again encased in my black flats. "Oh, honey bear, we have got to get you some real shoes!"

"I've been telling her that for weeks," Stone interjected, any trace of his discomfort gone as he moved to talk to Carson quietly, before looking back at me. "Are you ready to head out?"

"She sure as heck is!" Dolly answered for me. "Now, get, you two, and don't come back here for the rest of today. Dolly's orders!"

"Yes, ma'am," Stone replied with a wink in her

direction then motioned me ahead of him as we headed for the parking lot.

The silence was uncomfortable as we drove to the restaurant Stone chose for lunch. I was so distracted that I didn't even notice which one it was. We made our way though most of our meal making half hearted attempts at small talk, neither one of us seemingly interested in broaching the subject that brought us here today.

Finally, after the waiter removed our plates and dropped off some coffee, Stone cleared his throat.

"Thank you for coming with me today, Penelope."

I smiled, but couldn't say anything, my mouth dry and my stomach clenching.

"I want you to know that these last few weeks have been...well, I've never spent as much time with a woman as I have with you."

I could feel my smile slipping as he talked, wondering what he was getting at. Was he trying to tell me he was a womanizer? I didn't particularly need to hear about the women who came before me.

Stone must have seen something in my face, because he quickly changed direction.

"I'm not saying this right," he huffed, frowning and shaking his head. "What I mean is, I really enjoy spending time with you." My pulse slowed as he made a recovery, turning the conversation to something less likely to make me vomit. "It's become so much more than just sex. I'm not a relationship guy."

And he blew it again.

But really, what did I want him to say? I wasn't a relationship girl. This was exactly what I had been telling myself since Stone and I started this...whatever it was. I was sending myself mixed messages, so I couldn't imagine what Stone was thinking. I decided to cut the guy a break.

"Stone, I get it."

"You do?"

"Yes," I said, steeling myself for what I had to say next. I wanted this to be as easy as possible. On both of us. "I understand, and it's okay. I never expected anything to come out of this. I mean, we live on opposite sides of the country. Don't worry. You don't owe me anything." I finished with a smile, even thought my heart hurt more and more with every word I uttered.

So much for keeping my feelings out of it. I should have known.

Never trust your heart. It sneaks up on you every time.

"Penelope," he grumbled, causing my eyes to snap to his from where they were focused on my clenched fingers. "That's not it. That's not it at all."

I tipped my head and stared at him, completely confused. "It's not?"

"No, Penelope. I'm not trying to break up with you."

"You're... you're not?" I was totally lost.

"No. I'm asking you if you'd come to Austin. To be with me."

I froze, my mouth falling open. There was no

way this was real. No way he could be seriously asking me to go with him to Texas. My mind could not seem to latch on to one of the many thoughts swirling around like a cyclone long enough to respond.

Finally, I found my voice. "Texas? You want me to go to Texas?"

"Yes, Penelope," he smiled, still looking unsure. "I think that what we have is worth pursuing. I think you are incredible and smart, driven, kind, and absolutely beautiful. I'm asking if you think enough of me to give us a shot."

"Stone," I said, still in shock, but recovering enough to contemplate some of the implications of what he was asking. "I can't just move to Texas."

"Why not?" He seemed to genuinely not understand.

"For one, I have a life in New York. My mother is there. My job."

"You can get a marketing job in Austin, Penelope. Hell, you could probably do your current job there. I'd talk to Harold and he could-"

"No, Stone."

He froze, frowning again. "No?"

"No, I don't want you to talk to your father about getting me a job." I couldn't help the anger that was welling up inside me. "That is exactly the type of thing I have been trying to avoid. The nepotism. That's the type of crap that Constance and Toddrick are trying to pull. I want to make my way on my own merit, not because of who I'm sleeping with!" I whispered the last part, looking around franticly to make sure no one heard.

"Penelope, it wouldn't be that way."

"Stone, it would be exactly that way. You, of all people, should understand not wanting to have your success tied to someone else." I could tell by the way his shoulders hunched he did understand. "And what about my mother? My life in New York? I'm going to be getting promoted to VP of Marketing, and that means I am going to be in New York."

"You might not get it," he said, trying to be helpful but only pissing me off more.

"Well, thank you for the stellar vote of confidence."

"Damn it, Penelope. That's not what I meant. Fuck," Stone ran his hands through his hair in frustration. "I'm tryin' to tell you that I wanna be with you. Doesn't that mean anythin' to ya'?" His accent was in full force as he let the one emotion he was comfortable with surface. His anger. This was the Stone I had met all those months ago.

Well, I was not the same meek little flower to be trampled all over. Not anymore.

"Yes, Stone, it does. It means a great deal. But wanting to be with me doesn't mean that you get to uproot my entire life and have me make all the sacrifices. Relationships are supposed to be give and take."

"Penelope, you know why I can't live in New York," he ground out.

"Yes, Stone. I know. Because you blame the entire city of New York for the fact that your parents aren't together. Well, guess what? At least you still have both parents. At least you have a father who is still doing everything he can to try and earn your love. Some of us no longer have that option, and it gets pretty aggravating watching you throw a temper tantrum every time his name is mentioned, *Mr. Montgomery*."

Stone looked like I had slapped him, jerking back in his chair and staring at me. I paused, my chest heaving from my rant. How had things turned so bad so quickly?

"Look," I said when I had regained some of my composure. "I think we both have some things to consider. I think I'll walk back to the office." Tossing my napkin on the table, I stood, Stone rising at the same time like the good southern gentleman he was raised to be. Damn him and his charming manners.

"Penelope, wait. Just - just let me drive you back. We can talk on the way." He reached for my arm as I stepped away from the table, but I moved out of his reach.

"No, thank you. I prefer to walk. I need to be alone for a bit." Shouldering my bag, I moved to the exit. "Thank you for lunch." I left him standing in the middle of the restaurant and didn't look back.

I stomped my way up the street, headed back toward the office, and tried to replay the conversation we had just had. What a disaster. But surely he had to see that a relationship couldn't involve one person making all the sacrifices and the other making none. I couldn't just pack up my life and move to Austin...could I? I considered the possibility as I chewed frantically on my lip.

I mean, what was really keeping me in New York? My work? Stone was probably right; no matter what I did, Toddrick was likely going to get the VP position. So, really, why couldn't I work in Texas? The weather alone was a bonus, seeing as East Coast winters had never been my favorite.

And my mom, well, she was hoping to retire sometime. Why not sooner rather than later? She could come with me, or find a place somewhere else, like Florida, maybe, where she could spend her days looking after herself for a change. And the bills would follow us wherever we went, so that wasn't an issue either.

I moved down Las Vegas Boulevard, my heart stuttering when I passed the Eiffel Tower, remembering the magic of our first date and everything that had followed. Stone had been nothing but sweet and considerate the entire time, to me at least, and every day we spent together I saw more and more of the kind and generous person he was under all his gruff and grouchy.

How could I have let my temper get away from me like I did? Stone put himself on the line, and I threw it back in his face. As I walked up the long drive that led to *The Alamo*, I resolved to apologize as soon as he returned to the office. Maybe I would arrange dinner to be delivered to the Summerlin house tonight. We could sit on the back deck, looking over the hills, and I would tell him that I had thought it over and, while I wasn't sure what I was going to do, we could at least discuss it like the civil adults we were.

God, I was so embarrassed. My behavior had been terrible, immature and puerile. He deserved better from me, and I planned on giving it to him.

I made my way through the property and to the business offices, waving at the call center girls on my way by. Once I was on the third floor, I headed straight to my office, leaving the door wide open so that I wouldn't miss Stone when he got back. I sat at the desk and opened my email, only to stand again in shock at what was waiting in my inbox.

Photos.

Horrible, intrusive photos. Of me. And Stone. Right here in this office.

My blood ran cold as I scrolled through the email, my eyes skipping the text and immediately honing in on the photographs that would ruin my life if they got out.

I remembered the exact moment three weeks ago, me on my knees at my desk, Stone's hand on my head, guiding me. There it was, in all its full color glory, splashed across my laptop screen like some amateur porn site. Who the hell had taken these photos and what did they want?

The pictures moved from me on my knees, Stone's dick buried to the hilt in my throat, to me on the desk, my head thrown back, tits out, looking for all the world like a complete and total hussy. Our faces were both clearly visible and there was no mistaking the location.

My hand shaking and my lunch threatening to

make a reappearance, I scrolled back up to the top of the email to read the attached letter.

Hello whore;

I'm sure by now you know that there is no hope for you to have any kind of future with Pennington Hotels. However, if you don't want these photos released and your reputation ruined forever, then you will do exactly what I say.

First, you will hand in your resignation to head office by midnight tonight.

Second, you will never again set foot on a Pennington Hotels property.

Third, you will delete this email and never speak of it again. To anyone.

If you refuse to follow any of these instructions, these pictures will be released, and everyone in the industry will know that Penelope Lund gets what she wants the old-fashioned way… on her knees.

Remember. Midnight tonight.

There was no signature, and I didn't recognize the address as it came from one of those free to use email companies. This was ridiculous. Who would do such a thing?

Who would be so offended by Stone and I being together that they would go to such extreme lengths? My mind flashed back to Toby and the disgusted look on his face at the last meeting. He had certainly changed from the kind and caring person he had been on my first day here in Las Vegas.

But why would Toby want me to quit my job? Stop seeing Stone, sure. But leave the company? I didn't see how that would benefit him in any way.

But then it hit me. Like a baseball bat to the face, and I knew. I had been so stupid. So naive to think that my effort, my drive and desire to succeed would mean anything in the long run. Because I had gone up against a giant, assuming I could beat her.

Constance Pennington-Grover.

That cowardly bitch. Was she that afraid of losing? Of not getting something she thought was hers by sheer desire alone?

Looked like she was.

I was standing, staring at the laptop and fuming, planning to pick up the phone and call Harold Pennington myself to let him know just what was happening, when my email pinged with another incoming message. I hesitated to open it when I saw that it was from the same mystery address, but my morbid curiosity won out, and I clicked on it.

And was promptly sick in the garbage can next to my desk.

It was a video. Of the entire encounter. Our flirtatious banter. Me dropping to my knees. Stone tearing down my thong. The whole sordid affair.

Because that's what it looked like. Not the intense and deep connection that Stone and I had been building over the last two months. No, this looked like a stereotypical office tryst, with the gold-digging tramp trying to work her way up the corporate ladder one blow job at a time.

The person who sent this was right; my career would never recover from something like this. I would be labeled a slut and ruined for life. Scarlet fucking letter style.

There was no way I could let that happen. Sure, Stone and I had something, something that I had decided was worth pursuing. But what if it didn't work out? What if our relationship fizzled out and I had to go back to New York? I couldn't do that if I was branded a tramp.

Either no one would hire me, or they would, but they would expect me to behave like these photos insinuated I did.

Stone would survive any fall out. Men always did.

They seemed to come out of these type of situations with both their reputation and their dignity firmly intact.

Sad but true.

No, I had no choice. I had to take the option that protected me, even if I destroyed my heart to do it.

It was the only way forward.

I couldn't stop the tears as I opened a new email, composing a hastily worded resignation letter and hitting send before I could think better of it. Deleting the two emails that had just imploded my entire life, I slammed the lid of the laptop down. Pushing away from the computer like it had burned me, because it sort of had, I gathered anything personal I had in the office and headed for the elevator. I had to get to the house and get packed before Stone showed up. If he caught me, either here or there, there would be no way to hide what was happening. I couldn't let him get involved. He was just beginning to re-establish a relationship with his family. If he asked his father to choose, Constance or me, he'd likely be devastated when I lost, ruining the connection he was forging with Harold all over again. I couldn't put him in that position, not for me.

As I entered the lobby, I could see Moira coming back from her own lunch. One look at my tear stained face and she was headed my way.

"Penelope, what happened?" she said, her eyes showing her genuine concern as she reached for me. "Are you alright?"

"Yes," I said, trying my best to control the waver in my voice. "I will be. If I could ask you, Moira, to please book me the earliest flight out to New York. I will be leaving immediately."

"Leaving? But I thought..." She didn't finish, but I could see the confusion in her face. Yeah, I knew what she thought.

"I'm sorry, Moira. I have to go. Please, just book me the flight. You won't be able to reach me. I left my company phone on the desk upstairs." I moved past her, dislodging her hands as I made for the exit. "Thank you. Really, Moira. Thank you for everything." She just stared at me in open-mouthed shock as I left.

I was in a cab and back at the house before I realized it, my brain feeling like fog as I dashed inside, gathering everything I had brought with me and stuffing it into my ratty old suitcase as fast as I could. I barely looked around, not wanting to see the places in the house that held some of the best memories of my life.

I couldn't bear it.

I managed to keep that focus, gritting my teeth and just moving, until I was on the plane, my first-class seat not expected, but very much appreciated.

As soon as we were in the air, I curled up in the extra wide chair and sobbed, watching the city I had come to love fade behind me, and Stone Pennington with it, leaving my heart as barren as the desert sands below me.

CHAPTER TWENTY-ONE
Stone

I drove for hours, meandering around outside the city and tearing down dirt roads, leaving red clouds of dust in my wake. I was too wound up to go to the office, afraid of what I'd say when I saw her again if I didn't get my fucking temper under control first.

What the fuck was her problem?

This is what you got for taking a chance. I spent my whole life avoiding emotions to prevent situations exactly like this one. I watched my mom as she wallowed in her broken heart, never quite recovering from the loss of my father's love. I swore to myself that I would never let that be me. Never let someone have that much power over me, and sure enough, the first time I dared to let someone in, she stomped all over my heart the moment I offered it to her.

Penelope Lund. Who woulda thought? Of all the girls I could have fallen for, I had to pick the prim New Yorker full of fire and sass.

To be honest, that's what drew me to her in the first place. The fact that she was one of the few people

287

who knew I was Stone Pennington, and she didn't care. She wanted nothing from me. Not fancy gifts or jewelry like so many other women I 'dated', nor did she want me to use my connections to get her ahead in her career. She only wanted my time. At least I thought she had.

Now I wasn't sure about anything.

I guess it was selfish of me to just assume that she'd pack up and move. I should have discussed options with her, letting her know she had choices, even if I knew which I wanted her to make. She wasn't the kind of girl who wanted to be told what to do. I knew that about her and I still let my mouth dig me a hole I wasn't sure I would be getting out of. But if there was one thing I could count on, it's that Penelope Lund was strong. Every time I threw my attitude at her, she stepped up and threw it right back.

This time would be no different, and I couldn't wait.

With that thought in mind, I turned my truck back to Las Vegas, following the setting sun as I made my way to *The Alamo*.

Getting off the elevator, I went directly to Penelope's office, only to find it empty. Her laptop was closed, but her phone was on the desk, so she must still be in the building. I wandered over to Moira's desk, seeing her ending the phone call she was on.

She hung up the phone and jumped when she saw me, startled that I was so close to the desk. "Mr. Montgomery," she said. I was really going to have to sort out this name thing, and probably sooner rather than later. "What can I do for you, sir?"

"Moira, I was hoping you could find me some dinner reservations for tonight. Nothing too fancy, but relatively soon, if possible. I am just going to find Miss Lund and then we'll be heading out."

Moira tilted her head and stared at me, confused. "Miss Lund?"

I sighed. Moira knew that we were both living at the Summerlin house, so even if she didn't suspect the extent of our relationship, there was no reason for her to act like me taking Penelope out was a strange request.

"Yes, Moira. As soon as she returns to her desk, I'd like to leave, so if you would find us a place, that would be great," I finished, turning to go to my office.

"But, sir," Moira was practically shouting how, her eyes wide and, maybe a little afraid. "Miss Lund. She's gone, sir."

I stopped and turned, narrowing my eyes, not quite sure I'd heard her correctly. "Gone? Gone where?"

"New York, sir. I booked her flight this afternoon. She'll have left by now."

"She did what?" There was no way she'd have left. Even if she was that pissed at me, the Penelope that I knew, *my* Penelope, wouldn't just leave town. She'd confront me. She'd sass me, tell me all the reasons I was wrong.

She wouldn't just leave...would she?

Was it possible she had headed for New York

and left me, the same way my father had all those years ago?

There was a strange sensation building in my stomach, churning and boiling, and emotion I didn't have a name for, because anger was too damn tame.

Moira opened her mouth to continue, but the elevator dinged open at that moment, spilling a frantic-looking Silas on to the third floor, his eyes widening when he saw me.

"Stone! I'm glad I caught you," he said, holding up his phone and waving the screen in my direction. "We need to talk, man."

"Not right now, Si. I have a problem I need to handle." I turned back to Moira, ready to demand more information, but Silas grabbed my arm, spinning me around.

"Seriously, man. We have to talk. Now."

"Silas, I mean it. I don't have time so whatever it is will have to-" I cut off as my own phone began to ring. I glanced at the screen, my heart jumping with hope it was going to be Penelope, even though I'd seen her phone on her desk not two minutes ago. Instead I saw Harold's name lighting up my screen. I felt bad just sending him to voice mail these days - damn Penelope, making me feel all sorts of things lately - so I answered the call.

"Harold, listen, I can't-"

"Stone, do you want to tell me why I received Penelope Lund's resignation letter in my inbox this afternoon?"

Suddenly, I was paying all kinds of attention.

"She did what?"

"You heard me. She emailed in her letter of resignation this afternoon. What the hell is going on out there, Stone? I thought you had this project under control. Do I need to head out there again?"

"It's not the project, at least, I don't think it is." I watched as Silas began shaking his head, gesturing again to his phone. "Listen, I have to look into this. Don't do anything until I call you back, alright?"

"Alright, son. If you're sure. But, call me if you need anything. I want this resolved as much as you do, I suspect."

"Of course. I'll call you back. Thanks, Dad."

I had hung up the phone before it even registered to me that I'd called him dad. Silas looked at me, one eyebrow raised, but I just shook my head.

"Penelope quit her job today. She's headed back to New York."

"I know, man," Silas said, turning his phone so we could both see the screen. "That's what I need to talk to you about. My buddy out in California, Hack? The one in the Motorcycle Club? He's been digging into the information we sent him. He's sure there is more to these mistakes than it appeared on the surface."

"What mistakes? Penelope's?"

"Yeah, man. The screwed-up emails, the misinformation to the high roller clients, even the job postings that were in error. Hack thinks they are all related." He scrolled up on his phone, pages and pages of data flying by, computer code pointing out what, to this Hack guy was probably obvious, but I couldn't make sense of any of it. I frowned at the screen, shaking my head.

"What does all this mean? Are you saying someone was sabotaging Penelope?"

"We think so, but we have no actual proof. Just some, let's say, less than legal investigative work done by Hack. He'd have looked deeper, but there are a few things standing in his way. First of all, he was not exactly invited to this little party, and secondly, something about him working across state lines, he needs your permission to dig deeper."

If this could help me sort out what had gone on with Penelope today, then I was all for it. "Tell me what he needs me to do."

A short time later, both Silas and I were sitting in front of Penelope's laptop as Silas's mysterious friend Hack worked on it remotely, the screen jumping from window to window as he dug around in areas of a computer only a true savant could find.

"It's pretty obvious, once you get inside," Hack said, his voice sounding tinny from where it came out of the speaker phone beside the laptop. "There is a pretty clear breach, where someone uploaded a Trojan to this device, and it granted them remote access. They have basically been playing around in here for weeks."

"Can you tell what they were doing? Has the company been compromised?" If this was corporate espionage, it could bring Pennington Hotels to its knees. The legal fees to fight something like this alone would be astronomical, never mind the damage to consumer confidence if there was a data breach of personal information. Customers trusted us to guard their identities when the booked on line and gave us credit card info. If that had been compromised, we'd need to go to the press immediately.

This could be a fucking disaster.

I was saved from my negativity spiral when Hack spoke up again. "It doesn't look like there was anything nefarious happening." He paused, and there was the distinct sound of a deep inhalation, followed by a groan on the exhale. I looked at Silas.

"Hack," Silas questioned. "Are you getting high right now?"

"Relax, Hedge," Hack responded, referring to Silas by the nick name his Army buddies used. I wasn't sure how he'd gotten it, but he didn't use it out side his military circle. I was pretty sure that Hack and his MC buddies all used their military nicknames regularly, but I wasn't clear on the details. "I can do this shit blindfolded. A little weed is only good for my process."

"If we could please get back to the future of my father's multibillion-dollar company," I ground out, having no patience for the guys' laid-back California attitude.

"Right," Hack continued. "Like I was saying, it doesn't look like they dug anywhere too deep. In fact, outside tampering with the email and social media posts, the only other thing this person accessed was... oh, shit."

"What," I said, my blood pressure rising with every stalled moment. The screen was still flashing,

Hack's cursor and keystrokes going faster than my eyes could even follow, swirling lines of code that made no sense to me at all. "What are we looking at?"

"I was about to tell you that the only other thing accessed was the laptop's camera. It seemed innocuous, until I checked the email trash bin. Dudes, you're not gonna like this at all."

Finally, the rapid-fire motions on the laptop screen stalled as Hack brought up a single window. I recognized it as our company email server. But my heart fucking stopped when I saw what he was showing me.

Someone had been watching us, filming us. The violation I felt was instant, and my stomach revolted at the thought of some sick son of a bitch having access to private moments I shared with Penelope. If I thought I was mad before, I had never felt anger like I felt at that moment, and as I ground my molars until my jaw ached, I vowed to do what ever I had to do to find this pervert and make them pay.

"Stone," Silas said, pulling my focus away from the photos. He better not have looked more than a glance, or we'd be having words. "Man, did you read this?"

I hadn't even noticed the text in the email, too enraged by the photos to even consider that there was more to what I was looking at, but as I read the words now, I wanted to punch something.

"Motherfucker!" I roared, my fury a living thing inside my chest. "Can you find out who did this? I want to end them. They will rue the day they thought they could mess with my woman."

Silas whipped his head to me, but I didn't have it in me to address all the things that had changed recently. He hadn't been staying at the house, our disagreement over Daphne had pushed a wedge between us, but he was here for me now, and I would make it right. But first, I had to take care of Penelope.

"The person doing the accessing is using a VPN and proxy servers all over the map. I could track it down but it would take time."

"I don't have time. I have to fix the before these photos get released. They would ruin Penelope, and I can't let that happen to her." And if I ever had any hope of working things out between us, then I had to ensure that these photos never saw the light of day. She'd never forgive me if people found out; I wouldn't expect her to.

"Well, I'll work on it, but in the mean time, I might be able to get something more immediate. I can tell you the exact moment the virus was uploaded to this computer. If you have security footage from that day, you could see if it was someone you knew."

"That will do, Hack. What do you have?"

Hack provided the date and time, and Silas used his own tablet to access the security footage. We both sat there in shock as we watched my half-sister Constance enter Penelope's office on the day her and Harold came to Las Vegas.

"That bitch!" I shouted, and Hack chuckled over the phone.

"I guess you know who you're looking at."

"You bet your pot-smokin' California ass we do," I growled. "I know enough to move forward on my end, Hack, but I'd appreciate it if you could keep looking. I want this to be air tight and as legal as possible so that I can wrap this up in every way. I don't want Constance to wiggle her way out of trouble this time. She has gone too far." If Constance thought she could play dirty and win, she had another think coming. Her and her moron of a husband were about to learn that you don't mess with Texas.

"You got it, guys. Hedge, I'll get really dirty here and find everything I can for you. Give me three days and I'll have it all wrapped up for you in a nice red bow."

"Thanks, Hack. Appreciate ya, brother. *Hooah*!"

Hack responded in kind, and then we ended the call. Silas turned to me, his face displaying nothing as he waited for me to say something.

I took a deep breath, trying to get a handle on all that had happened since Penelope and I had lunch today. I was shocked when I found out she'd left Las Vegas. Shocked and pissed. I hadn't taken her for a runner. But this information changed everything. She didn't run from me. She ran to protect herself, and there was no way I could blame her for that. I wished she had come to me, so that we could face this together. But Penelope was used to taking care of herself, and I hadn't exactly given her reason to think that I would be there for her, not after the way I had spoken to her at the restaurant, giving orders and only worrying about my own interests.

Penelope didn't need me rushing in to save her; she had already saved herself and taken care of the situation in the best way she could with the options available to her. But I sure as shit wasn't going to sit back and watch Constance and Toddrick take something from Penelope that she had earned fair and square. Penelope had worked too damn hard to have a conniving witch like Constance and her limp-dick husband take that job from her by force.

Penelope had done what she thought was best, to protect her future when she was offered an impossible choice. Now I had to do what I thought was best, and that meant only one thing.

"Moira!" I shouted, and the woman was in the office so fast, I could only assume she had been standing right outside the door. I knew she and Penelope had gotten close over the months, so her concern was warranted. And I had been doing a lot of shouting in this office tonight, even for me.

"Yes, sir?"

"I need a flight to New York as soon as possible," I barked, my usual gruff manner now even more pronounced.

Moira didn't seem to mind, if the smile that split her face was any indication. "Yes, sir!"

"Wait," Silas said, causing both Moira and I to turn to him. "Make it two." Moira nodded and hurried away.

Silas looked at me, not speaking, but expressing more than words could ever say all the same. Silas was my best friend, we had stood with each other through everything, and I had fucked it up with my stubborn attitude. It was time I made amends, for real, not just the bullshit non-apology I gave him earlier.

"Silas, man, I...I'm sorry. I was such an asshole." At that he snorted, some humor entering his gaze. "I know you'd never do wrong by Daphne. I know she'd never meet someone who would treat her better or with more respect than you would. I'll keep my nose out of your business from now on. I promise."

He stared at me for a bit, then shook his head. "Thanks for that, Stone, but I am afraid that ship has sailed."

"What do you mean?"

"When I broke it off at Daphne at your request, she got pissed. She accused me of being a coward and not fighting for what I wanted, and she was right. Best friend or not, I shoulda' knocked your ass out over her. But I didn't, and she deserves better than that. She deserves a man who would fight for her. Like I should have."

He was sad, I could hear it in his voice, but like me, his pride got in the way. I placed my hand on his shoulder and squeezed, not saying anything, but conveying everything I could in that one gesture. When he smiled at me and punched me in the arm, I knew we were gonna be okay.

"Alright, jackass," he said, shaking me off. "Enough of this emotional shit. At least one of us has to get the girl in this story, and it looks like it's gonna be you.   Let's get our asses to New York."

CHAPTER TWENTY-TWO
Stone

"I just can't believe she would do such a thing." Harold paced in front of the fireplace, his face contorted in a frown. I scoffed and he looked up, meeting my eyes, then he sighed. "Alright. I can. I can totally believe it. But I just don't understand *why*. I gave her anything she ever wanted."

"You couldn't give her this." I was sitting in one of the wing-back chairs my father kept in his study, enjoying a bourbon and the fireplace as well. It may be the end of April, but it was definitely not warm in New York. "Not if you wanted to keep the company alive. Toddrick is an idiot. Having him as VP of Marketing would have been a disaster and the board would have had your head."

Three days had passed since Penelope had resigned from Pennington Hotels, and Harold was still struggling to come to terms with Constance's treachery. Hack had come through, delivering all the information we needed to nail Constance for a litany of cyber crimes, as well as a few real-world ones, like blackmail and sexual harassment, just to name a few.

The problem was, I wasn't sure that was the best choice anymore. If we went public with her crimes, people would need to know details, and I wasn't willing to put Penelope in a position to have to deal with all that public scrutiny. More often than not, it didn't matter how innocent a woman was in a situation like this; people thought the worst of her, regardless. I didn't want that for Penelope.

If there was a chance that Constance could be made to pay, without having to involve the police, and, by necessity, the press, that would be ideal.

And I really wanted her to pay.

I had been having fantasies of my father completely disinheriting her, forcing her and Toddrick out onto the street, and making her have to actually get a freaking job for once in her life. She wouldn't be so stuck up if she had to put in a forty-hour week like the rest of the world.

I thought of Penelope's parents, hardworking everyday people who, while they had admittedly struggled, had probably been happier than Constance had ever been a day in her life. My own mother, though she was often lonely and maybe even a little sad, was still full of light and joy more often than not.

Then there was Penelope. Through hard work and dedication, she had earned a scholarship, a prestigious position, and, according to Harold, the VP promotion as well.

"Shit," Harold cursed, slamming his fist on the mantle as he made another pass. I'd never seen him this agitated; kind of reminded me of my own temper.

As I watched his face, scowl firmly in place, it occurred to me that I was more like Harold than I knew. Our mannerisms, our actions, even our facial expressions, all so similar. I hadn't spent as much time around him growing up as he'd wanted, and that was on me, but even with our interactions being minimal, I'd turned out to be just like him in so many ways.

I guess blood really was thicker than water.

"How do you want to handle this?" I questioned, knowing that as CEO he had a lot riding on this situation and how it was handled. Harold turned to me, his face scrunched in concentration, and I noticed, really, for the first time how old my father was. How much time I had let slip by and all the opportunities we'd missed to be, well, a family. I set my glass down and stood, moving to him and waiting for him to decide the fate of Constance and Toddrick. Once I knew what he wanted to do, then I would go talk to Penelope. I would tell her that she was getting justice and her job back.

What she wanted to do about us would be another conversation all together. Because as far as I was concerned, there sure as shit was an 'us', and I wasn't her giving up without a fight.

Finally, Harold seemed to come to a decision. "Give me a few days. Is your friend in California available for a little additional contract work? I think we will need his assistance."

"I'm not sure he does the kind of work you're looking for," I replied. Truth be told, I wasn't sure what kind of work he did, but I knew it was likely not the same sort of stuff Harold was used to dealing with.

"You let me worry about that. Just get in touch with him and let him know I will make it worth his while. I will compensate him handsomely for both his speed and discretion."

A grin split my face as I watched Harold, seeing the wheels turning in his head. "You devious old man," I chuckled. "I didn't know you had it in you."

He smiled wide at me for a moment, then his face fell. "I think there is a lot we don't know about each other, Stone."

I blew out a breath, feeling my chest constrict at the direction this conversation was going, but, if being with Penelope had taught me anything, it was that there was no time like the present. You never knew when your whole world would change, and I had wasted enough time trying to prove a point that didn't need proving.

My father loved me, regardless of how his relationship with my mother turned out. As a son, I had come to realize that that was enough.

It was time I told him so.

"Harold, I owe you an apology."

"No, you don't Stone," he started, but I raised my hand.

"Yes, I do. I never gave you a chance. What happened between you and mom, that should have stayed between you and her. You never did anything but right by me, and I turned my back on you every time. I am so sorry for that."

Harold stared at me in open-mouthed shock as I

spoke, and by the time I had finished, his face had crumpled, eyes wet as he fought back tears. He took a deep breath, and then another, before he responded.

"I loved your mother. I truly did. When I had to leave Austin, I asked her to come with me, but she refused. She told me she didn't want to tie her life to a man and not have anything for herself. That she wanted to be someone before she became someone's other half. I should have respected her for it. Instead, all I saw was a person who wouldn't do what I wanted, what I thought was best. So, I left, and I left her behind. I thought that my loving her should have been enough for her. It was foolish and impulsive and I have regretted it every day since.

"I thought about her so many times," he said, his voice catching. "I wanted to see how she was, what she was doing. But I didn't want to look weak, so I intentionally stayed away. Actively refused anything to do with the Austin location, until I couldn't make any more excuses. I returned to Austin, and there you were." His eyes shone with love as he took me in, reaching out to grasp my shoulders, and I took a deep breath of my own.

"I swear to you, Stone, if I had known, I would have been there in a heartbeat. You are everything I could have hoped for in a son, and I could not be prouder to call you mine." With those words, something inside me shifted, clicking into place where previously there had only been a void, a black hole filled with anger and resentment.

He was proud of me, proud that I was his son.

I wasn't a mistake.

He wanted me.

I closed my eyes against the tide of emotion battering against my insides, feeling whole and complete in a way I hadn't realized I needed. When I opened them again, I looked at my father and for the first time, I felt nothing but love. There was none of the resentment, none of the pain that I had spent a lifetime collecting, using it as a shield to hide the broken kid I was.

The broken kid that I made myself into by refusing to accept that what my father's actions weren't intended to hurt me. That he had done the best he could, the best I had allowed him to do.

I lifted my hands, shaking slightly with the energy flowing through me, and placed them on Harold's shoulders, imitating the way he held me. I couldn't remember a time when we had touched like this, affectionately, and the longer I held on to him, my fingers clawing at his shoulders, the more I realized I had been missing it.

Suddenly, like neither of us could wait a second longer, we wrapped our arms around each other. I stood there, grasping him like a lifeline in a turbulent ocean, and at that moment, there was nothing in the world that could make me let go of him.

My dad.

* * * *

It was the first time I had been to the Pennington Hotel corporate headquarters, and frankly, it was underwhelming. The hotel, the flagship building in the Pennington Empire, was impressive, of course. It was old-world class, the epitome of uptown style and sophistication. Over one hundred years old, the build looked like something out of a fairy-tale, all white and shining in the middle of the typical Manhattan gray. Designed in the French Renaissance style, with gorgeous Corinthian columns lining the entire frontage, each column standing almost three stories tall. The grand limestone steps at the center of the building opened in a sweeping arc to the street, and as a result the entire thing looked like it had been picked up from the French countryside and dropped into the Upper East Side. Taking up an entire city block, it contained thirty floors of rooms and suites. Some of the most expensive suites were owned and used like apartments, the occupants taking full advantage of all the amenities of staying at a hotel, but with the ability to put their clothes in the closet permanently.

The top of the building was done in a series of castle-like turrets, topped with domed and faceted roofs of hammered copper, now showing their green patina after so long exposed to the elements. The windows were all of repetitive size and shape, with the top floor showcasing incredible Palladian styled windows, arching dramatically toward the sky.

It was through one of these monster windows that I now watched as the traffic below crawled along, no one looking particularly excited to be going wherever it was they were headed. Couldn't say I blamed them; with every block looking just like the next, this place truly was a concrete jungle. If it wasn't for the gorgeous spread of Central Park in front of me, I might start feeling a little claustrophobic. As it was, I couldn't wait to get the hell out of this town. I'd never thought I would miss Las Vegas, but having spent almost a week in the eternal fog that was Manhattan, I was ready for the bright lights of Sin City to welcome me back into their lively embrace.

Turning my back on the view, I faced the boardroom housed on the top floor. Technically, this was more like a mezzanine floor, as the guests were told their penthouse suites were on the top, but this was a taller, and smaller floor, that you couldn't see from the ground, caged as it was behind the towers with their copper roofs. It provided the executive staff with a nice view, but didn't take away from the pomp and circumstance of the penthouse guests, because, lord forbid they not feel like they were at the top of the world. All told, the head office area was probably smaller than the building we had been working from at the back of *The Alamo* property for the last few months. But space was always at a premium here in The Big Apple, so the residents didn't tend to bemoan their small digs the way people in the rest of the country might.

The table in the conference room held a dozen men and woman, with room for more. The board of directors for Pennington Hotels, they were the ones dad called when he needed to make big moves. He may have been the CEO, but the board of directors was in charge of the purse strings, so to speak, and anything that affected the bottom line had to be put to them first.

I'd gotten well acquainted with them over the last four days, to say the least.

Things had happened so quickly I could hardly believe it myself. Personally, I wanted to march right up to Constance and tell her exactly what I thought of her bullshit behavior, but dad had reasoned with me. In order for this to work, things had to be done correctly, and that meant following protocol. I hated it, because all I wanted to do was get to Penelope, but in order to protect her, protect both of us, this had to be done right.

I was still standing with my back to the window when the door opened again and Constance breezed in, looking for all the world like she owned the place, even though she never would.

And that thought made me inordinately happy.

I had never wished her ill, not really. Sure, I laughed that time she fell in the mud, but come on, that was what siblings did, but I had never actively interfered in her life. This time she had crossed a line when she messed with Penelope, and I was about to show her what that meant in the way that would hurt her the most.

Her pocketbook.

The haughty look on her face fell for a moment when she saw me standing there, but she was quick to replace it again, moving toward our father and pressing an air kiss to his cheek before turning her narrowed eyes on me. We just stared at each other, neither giving anything away, until Toddrick slumped into the room, his red-rimmed eyes staring down at his phone.

"Thank you for coming, Constance," Harold started, completely ignoring Toddrick as he flopped down into the nearest chair. I watched as Constance's nostrils flared as she saw him rubbing at his nose, but she kept her perfect socialite mask in place and took a seat closest to the action.

"Of course, Daddy," she simpered. Shit, she was really laying it on thick. "You said it was important. I knew you wouldn't have pulled Toddrick from the Atlantic City project for the day for nothing."

"You're right. It is important." Harold cleared his throat, his eyes going to me. I knew this was hard for him. Having just gained a relationship with me, he was now risking what he had with Constance, because there was no way she was going to take this lying down. I didn't push him, just sat quietly and let him come to terms with what he was about to say.

"As you know, I have been thinking about the future of Pennington Hotels for a long time. It was always important to me that the company be kept in the family. I built this empire for my children, and I wanted to be able to pass it down to them when the time was right." He paused, and I could see Constance's pupils dilate as he talked. I knew the woman liked money, but she was actually turned on at the idea of taking over. As if dad would pass the reins to either her or Toddrick. Constance had never done anything in her life more difficult than choosing a plastic surgeon, and Toddrick, well, he'd never really done anything. If it weren't for the fact that his own family was absolutely rolling in money, Constance would never had looked twice at the lazy lout. But Constance being what she was, she didn't choose her husband for his shining personality; she chose him because he was in line to inherit a significant fortune from his father, who ran some sort of investment company.

"With this in mind, and with the unanimous approval of the board, I would like to announce that the new Chief Executive Officer of Pennington Hotels will be my son, Stone Pennington," Harold finished with a smile and a gesture to me. The board members gave a light round of applause, and I nodded my head politely.

I could have done without that, to be honest.

But the whole time I never took my eyes off of Constance. Her face, usually so bland and expressionless, was now morphing into a look of pure rage. Her lips curled back, showing her overly bleached teeth, and her cheeks burned an angry red under her expensive foundation.

"What?" she shrieked, drawing the attention of everyone in the room. Except, Toddrick, of course, who appeared for all the world as if she hadn't spoken. "Father! This is preposterous. Stone can't be CEO. He's not even a real Pennington!" she growled the last part as if the fact that we shared any blood at all was fundamentally offensive to her.

I guess, in a way, it always had been.

"Constance, he is every bit as much my child as you are. And, as the board agreed, his education and experience with Pennington Hotels make him an excellent choice to be my successor." The words caused those strange warm feelings to flow through me again. I bit my cheek to keep from smiling, which was just not something I was used to.

Constance swung her angry gaze to me, her polite society façade now completely gone. "I won't stand for this, Stone," she snarled, rising from her chair and pointing a long manicured finger at me. "There is no way I am going to let you just waltz in here and take what should rightfully be mine." She paused, her eyes widening as much as her Botox would allow. "This is about that little tramp, isn't it?" Constance's eyes were wild, glazed in her fury. "That piece of trash thinks she can come in here and-"

"Enough!" I cut her off, speaking for the first time. I had anticipated her rage, but for myself. I wouldn't listen to her talk shit about Penelope like that.

Constance froze, then cackled like the witch she was. "You think you're in love with her, don't you?" She threw her head back and howled like a loon. I was afraid she might be losing it completely. "You think that feelings and hearts and flowers are gonna make everything okay for you, Stone? That coming in here and taking the position that should be mine will prove that you are more than just a bastard? That you aren't just some fucking mistake?"

"Constance, that's enough!" Harold was fuming now, finished with this whole scene. "Let's not speak of mistakes unless you are willing to face your own."

This had her regaining some of her composure. She settled back into her chair, smoothing her sleek black bob around her face. "I'm sure I don't know what you're talking about, father," she stated smoothly.

"Unfortunately, you do." Harold sighed, then opened the file before him. "I have here proof, Constance. Proof that you used illegal Trojan software to infiltrate a Pennington Hotels computer, after which you proceeded to access company documents-"

"I am a Pennington, those documents are just as much mine as they are yours," she insisted.

"You may be a Pennington, Constance," Harold said, his voice tinged with sadness. "But you are not an official employee of the company. That makes what you did a crime."

"And," interjected Walter Castenberg, the chairman of the board for the company. "That's before we even get to your little blackmail scheme." Constance's face paled at the mention of the biggest of her crimes. "You'll be expected to hand over all the materials you obtained illegally, including the photos and videos." This earned him another scowl. "You're lucky your father talked us out of pressing charges, little girl. I doubt you'd survive long in prison," he sneered, clearly disgusted that she was going to get away with it. But Harold had advocated hard for her to stay out of jail, and I agreed with him. I would do anything to keep the pictures and video of Penelope out of the public eye.

Constance was quiet, her eyes darting back and

forth between Harold and me as she tried to keep her anger in check. Toddrick still hadn't said a word, but at least he was paying attention now.

"Fine," said Constance as she stood, her posture every bit the American Royalty she saw herself as. "I guess if there is nothing further to say, then we will be leaving. Toddrick," she actually snapped her fingers at him, like she would a dog. Poor fucker went to stand, too.

"Not so fast," Walter pipped up again. "Toddrick Grover," Walter said, and waited while Toddrick swung his head to look at him, mouth open, blinking like a dazed cow. "It has come to our attention that, while acting as an employee and representative of Pennington Hotels, you have been seen engaging in illegal activities, including, but not limited to, solicitation and the use of cocaine, a Schedule II controlled substance, though I'm sure you knew that already."

I watched as Toddrick swallowed heavily, his fleshy throat dancing above his too-tight collar. Constance was glowering at her husband. Then she whipped her eyes back to scowl at Walter. "You have no proof, and I won't stand here and allow you to hurl unfounded accusations at my husband."

I had to give her credit; she was quick on her feet. Unfortunately for Constance, Hack was better.

In a matter of a day and a half, he had provided Harold with enough ammunition to make sure that Toddrick went down for trafficking, not just possession. Ammunition, in the form of photographs, that Walter now casually threw across the table toward Constance. I watched her grit her teeth as the folder of photographs spilled out on the conference table, pictures of Toddrick with his face buried in a mountain of cocaine, or another, with him and a few other guys snorting lines off some woman's naked backside. I learned, through Harold, that both sets of photos had been taken from the security system at the Atlantic City hotel he was supposed to be marketing. I guess good old Todd figured that if the hotel wasn't open, the cameras wouldn't be on. Unfortunately for him, he was wrong.

"Nothing to say about that, Mr. Grover?" Walter questioned dryly. Toddrick merely shrugged. Knowing how things generally worked in this type of situation, even if the company did press charges, Toddrick's rich daddy would have him bailed out and his name cleared in no time. It wouldn't even be a blip in the Society Pages. "Well, if that is all, then consider this your notice of termination. You will have your things cleared out by the end of the day. Security will escort you out. And going forward, you are *both* banned from any Pennington Hotel property world wide." And with that, Walter motioned for the huge man in a suit, who had entered without anyone noticing, to come forward. He placed one hand on Toddrick's arm, and the other he used to grasp Constance, who jerked out of his hold.

"Don't touch me, you filthy animal!" she shrieked. Taking a step toward me, her teeth bared and her breath sawing out of her like she'd run a marathon, she hissed, "This isn't over, Stone. You and that little bitch will pay for this. You are nothing! You aren't even a Pennington!"

I looked at her sadly, stunned at the fact that she had such hatred for me simply because my father had loved my mother before he had met hers. Constance never could handle sharing anything, even her father's love.

"Yes, I am, Constance," I said, loudly enough for Harold to hear me as well. "I absolutely am a Pennington. I always have been. Even when I was trying not to be."

As the security guard grabbed her again, she continued to shriek the whole way out of the room. "I'll make you pay for this, Stone! You and your little blonde whore!"

When they were gone and the room was quiet, I turned to Harold. The sadness in his eyes cut me deeply. I had never wanted to come between him and his daughters, but Constance made her own choices, and Harold had no option but to do what he had done for the sake of the entire company.

"I don't know what I could have done differently with her," he said quietly, shaking his head.

"You helped her as best you could, Dad," I replied, watching as the board of directors made their way out of the room, now that the drama was over and the future of their company was headed in a direction they were comfortable with. "She didn't exactly give you much choice."

"I know, son. I know." He was quiet for a few moments, turning to look out over the city, and I let him stew. Sometimes, quiet was the best thing for a person. Standing beside him and just taking in the view, I tried to come to terms with my own recent choices.

Finally, Harold blew out a big breath and shook his head, turning to me. "Well, now that that's settled, what are your plans?"

I smiled grimly. "Give a guy a chance to get his head around it first, yeah? Shit," I cursed as I placed my hands on my hips. "I can't believe I'm moving to New York. Silas is gonna bust my ass over this."

"Oh, son. I wasn't talking about that. We'll deal with company stuff later. I have a plan for your transition I think you may be quite pleased with." He winked conspiratorially at me, his eyes sparking with glee. I didn't know if I should be excited or nervous about what he was thinking. "I was asking what are your plans for Miss Lund? It's not a happy ending unless the hero gets the girl."

Chuckling, I shook my head. "I don't think I'm anyone's hero, Dad."

"Nonsense, son. Everyone is someone's hero. The trick is to find the one that thinks so. Now, do you have any ideas on how to woo your lady?"

"Actually," I said cautiously. "I do have one, but I might need some help."

"If it's something I can make happen for you, son, you can consider it done."

I had been giving this a lot of thought. I hadn't wanted to go see Penelope until this was settled, until I could promise her that Constance wouldn't be able to hurt her. I could do that now, and my heart rate picked up at the prospect of seeing Penelope again. "Well, Dad, I don't suppose you have any friends in the NYPD do you."

To that, my father burst out laughing. "Oh, Stone. I like your style."

CHAPTER TWENTY-THREE
Penelope

A week had gone by. An entire week and I hadn't heard from Stone.

Not that I blamed him. After all, I had left out of the blue, with zero explanation. And I hadn't exactly tried to call him either.

The truth was, I was afraid. I was afraid that the reason he hadn't reached out to me was because he didn't want to.

Didn't want me.

When I left that restaurant, I was so angry. Angry that he'd just decided my life for me. Angry that he'd just assumed that I'd follow him wherever he wanted to go, with no questions, like some docile little sheep.

I felt that I had to take a stand. So I had.

I just hadn't expected it to be this permanent. I had fully intended to talk to him, to discuss the possibilities for us. If he wanted there to be an us, I was ready to sacrifice to be with him. But I wanted to be asked, not told. I wanted my opinions and feelings on the matter to be considered.

And then disaster struck.

When I opened that email, my whole life changed. Seeing myself like that, seeing a beautiful and passionate moment, a *private* moment, turned into something that looked dirty and degrading, it broke me a little.

But getting on the plane knowing that my time in Las Vegas, my career with Pennington Hotels, and my relationship with Stone were all over?

That broke me a lot.

I had spent the last week moping and feeling sorry for myself.

Oh, and job hunting. Because there was no way I could mope for long. Not when the bills needed to be paid.

So I sat there at the little table in our kitchen, looking through the want ads on my phone and wishing for the first time in my life that I wasn't in New York.

Right at that moment, I would have given just about anything to be back in Nevada. I missed Las Vegas for so many reasons, not the least of which were the friends I had made there. I would miss my lunches with Daphne and my talks with Dolly that always dissolved into fits of giggles. I would miss Moira and the girls from the call center, and Silas and the way he always knew just what to say that would embarrass Stone in the best way possible.

And I missed the hell out of Stone.

His gruff demeanor and the way he worked so hard to prove himself, especially when he didn't have to. How he always wanted what was best for the people around him, even if he tried to do it anonymously. I loved watching him interact with Daphne, being the big brother he was always meant to be, and the way he was with Silas, solid and reliable and the type of person you knew you could count on when you needed them.

I missed the way he looked at me, like I was a puzzle he couldn't quite figure out, but he enjoyed trying all the same. I missed how his hands felt against my skin, his rough calluses causing shivers as they roamed my body, mapping every plane and curve. And the way his warm heat reached all the way to my bones.

I missed his kisses, the slow and passionate ones that felt like they could go on forever, as well as the rough and frenzied ones that told me that he couldn't wait another minute to be with me, touching me, inside me.

And I missed the way he held me, late at night, when he was asleep, his face finally releasing the stress and angst he carried around. I would lay next to him and watch as a kind of peace settled over him, but the whole time, he never let me go, his body always reaching across the bed for mine as though even his subconscious had to know where I was at any given moment.

That was what made the fact that I hadn't heard from him hurt the way it did. I didn't know how I could have felt so much, could ache for him this way, and yet he seemed to feel nothing at all.

I looked up from my phone when I heard the key in the lock. My mom came in, her peacock blue scrubs bright in the late afternoon sun. She had worked the early shift today, so I told her I would cook dinner, which meant I picked up a frozen lasagna and tossed it in the oven.

She turned to me, her eyes concerned even though there was a smile on her face. "Hey, there Penny Lane." I smiled at the use of my childhood nickname. She hadn't called me that for a long time. I was typically my dad's thing, being that he was the Beatles fan in the house, but mom tended to bring it out when I needed a bit of a boost.

Apparently, she thought that was today. And I was grateful.

"Hi, Mom. How was your shift?"

"Oh, not too bad today, actually. The girls say hi. They want you to come by, when you can."

"I will." Just the thought of all the ladies my mom worked with made me smile. They had been so kind, gifting me those beautiful pink shoes before I left, their faith in me never wavering. I kind of felt like I had let them down, and I wasn't ready to face them yet.

I was too ashamed.

Shoving that thought to the back of my mind, I took a breath. "I went to see Dad today."

My mom looked at me from where she was hanging her jacket in the closet. "Oh," she said solemnly. "And how was that."

It was hard, actually, but needed. I knew that if he were here, dad would be telling me to fight, not just what Constance had done to me, but for Stone, too. I think my father would have liked Stone, once he got past the grumpy parts. They both had that thing inside them that made them care, that made them want to look out for those that couldn't look out for themselves. In my mind, I could see them sitting together, watching a western, while mom and I cooked a meal. It was an image that made my heart clench, and I held on to it for a few moments before answering my mom.

"Good, I think. We talked." I talked, he listened. "It felt good to be back there. But," I paused, wondering how she'd take the next thing I was going to say. "I don't think I'm gonna go back for a while, you know? I think dad would want me, want us, to move forward a bit." I watched as my mom smiled, her eyes filling with tears as she reached for me.

"I think you're right, baby." I could see she meant it, even if it hurt a bit to say. "I think it's time. Your dad will always be with us, but we can't stay still anymore." She pulled me into a hug, squeezing me so tight I felt some of my jagged edges coming back together. "I am so proud of you, Penelope."

I buried my face in her shoulder to hide my tears, loving the smells I always associated with my mom; her shampoo, warm coffee, and the disinfectant the hospital used. They felt so familiar, so needed right now, when everything seemed so different. "How can you be proud of me, Mom? I lost. And I-I..."

I had told my mother, in as little detail as

possible, about the photos and the blackmail. I was so ashamed I couldn't say it again.

"Penelope, don't you feel bad about it for one damn second." She pushed me back, her hand sweeping my lank hair out of my eyes. "You did nothing wrong. It was your privacy that got invaded, and that makes you the victim," she spat, her anger over my lack of desire to pursue charges was real, but she understood the risks that meant for me as well, so left the choice up to me. "You are a grown woman, and if you want to," she paused, wiggling her eyebrows at me. "Get it on in your office, then that's your choice."

I burst out laughing, my tears still there, but knowing she didn't think less of me because of my behavior was a weight off my shoulders. "Thanks Mom. But, please. Never say that again, alright?"

She smiled at me, and this time it reached her eyes. "I make no promises. Now, I'll finish dinner while you go take a shower. I love you, my girl. But, man, do you stink."

Great, now I was embarrassed again. "Deal."

Twenty minutes later I re-entered the kitchen, fresh as a daisy in clean yoga pants and a long-sleeved shirt. My freshly washed hair was up in a messy bun and I had on thick woolly socks. It may have been spring, but the Mojave Desert this wasn't, and a chill hung in the air. I seriously hated cold feet.

Mom was just pulling the lasagna out of the oven and I was setting the table when the sound of sirens made us both look up. It was kind of a habit for families of police officers, and one we couldn't seem to kick. It was just two short bursts, not the whole siren wail, so we didn't think much of it. But when it happened again a few seconds later, and then again, we decided to check it out.

Opening the front door, I could hardly believe the sight that greeted me. There were half a dozen police cruisers parked on our street, lights flashing like a carnival. Neighbors were starting to pour out of their homes looking as curious as we were as to what was going on. When the officers started to get out of their vehicles, I realized I still recognized a few of them from dad's time on the force. They waved at us, the smiles on their faces telling me something was up.

I was about to approach someone to ask for details when a sound reached me coming from around the corner. I may have only been riding once in my life, but the sound of hooves was unmistakable. Looking to the end of my street, I was shocked when I saw a horse.

And then another.

My smile was instant when I realized that there were six horses from the Mounted Unit coming toward us. In Queens, that wasn't a common sight, at least not in this neighborhood. The six horses marched toward us steadily, their riders sitting tall and proud in their helmets and aviator sunglasses as people waved and cheered.

When they reached our house, they stopped, each horse pausing in formation, except the final horse, who continued to move, passing all the others as it

324

approached. I stared in confusion as the rider began to unbuckle his helmet, but I gasped in shock when I recognized that dark head of hair.

Stone sat atop the horse, his smile wide as he removed the sunglasses and hung them on his shirt pocket as if he did it every day. I stood frozen, unable to truly process what I was seeing, until he swung his leg over the horse and dismounted. Stone strolled up my sidewalk like the sexy cowboy he was, his rolling gait making every move look smooth and confident. When he reached the bottom of the stairs, he smirked up at me. "Hey there, Blondie."

The laugh that burst out of me was full of joy. "Hey yourself, Cowboy."

As he stood there looking up at me with so much emotion in his eyes, I couldn't help the tear that escaped, rolling silently down my cheek, regardless of how hard I was smiling.

Being near Stone just filled me with so much emotion, I couldn't help but let it out, even if that meant tears.

"I gotta say, you sure are a sight for sore eyes."

"You too, Stone," I replied quietly, feeling suddenly vulnerable. "I was worried when you didn't call. I mean, you didn't even question my leaving."

"Oh, I questioned it, Blondie. I questioned the hell out of it. But that's why it took me so long to get here. I had to take care of some business first."

My eyebrows went up at that. "You mean..."

"Yeah, I sure do." I watched as emotion flashed across his face, once again showing me so much in his eyes. Where before they had only expressed anger and annoyance, now I was seeing a whole range of things he would have normally kept inside. I had a feeling that Stone was done hiding from me.

And I was damn glad about that.

"You won't be having any more problems with my sister or her husband. Everything is taken care of, Penelope." He looked deeply into my eyes, his promise there for me to see. "It's over."

The relief I felt was astronomical. I had been living in fear of waking up to see myself splashed over a tabloid, disgraced and shamed for what was truly an act of love.

Because I did love Stone. I knew that now.

And I was ready to do what it took to be with him.

"Thank you, Stone," I said, wrapping my arms around his neck, my entire body trembling with the relief of having him here with me. "Thank you so much."

"Anything, Penelope. You know that."

I smiled and nodded. When I heard a sniff behind me, I remembered my mother was there, along with a squad or two of police officers and almost all our neighbors. Good grief, how had I forgotten?

Stepping back, I glanced again at Stone's handsome face.

Oh, yeah. That's how.

"Stone, I'd like to introduce you to my mother, Sonja Lund."

Stone came forward, hand extended. "Stone

Pennington, ma'am."

"Pennington, now, is it?" I questioned, watching as he shook my mother's hand and she practically swooned. Good grief. There was no way I was ever taking Stone to meet the ladies at the hospital. He'd never make it out again.

"Yeah, Blondie. Pennington forever."

"Damn right!" came a shout from behind him. I looked past Stone's broad shoulder to see what I had missed before. One of the mounted riders waved and smiled, grinning like a loon from atop his horse.

"Mr. Pennington?" I laughed. The man looked like a kid in a candy store, he was so happy.

"Hello, Miss Lund. Pleasure to see you again. I'll expect you to be reporting back to work as soon as possible. We still have a hotel to launch, and I need my new Vice President of Marketing working hard to make sure it goes off without a hitch."

I had thought I couldn't be any more shocked, but apparently I was mistaken. "But, I resigned," I stammered, not truly understanding. "I emailed you my resignation."

The old man smiled at me, looking for all the world like a jolly old grandpa. "I am truly sorry, Miss Lund, but I received no such email. Looks like you still have your job, whether you like it or not."

I turned back to Stone. "Is this for real? I'm the new VP?"

"As real as it gets, I'm afraid." I stared for a beat longer, then I erupted in a squeal that was half shock and half laughter. I spun around and hugged my mother furiously, then turned back to see Stone smiling at me, pride shining in his eyes, and something else I was hesitant to name.

He looked at me seriously for a moment. "You okay? Honestly?"

I reached for him, letting my hands trail up his arms and come to rest on his shoulders, drawing him closer to me. "Did you come here for me?" I asked, looking into his gorgeous hazel eyes.

"You bet I did. You're never getting rid of me."

"Then, yes, I am honestly okay," I said, ready to take a chance. Ready to be vulnerable in a way I hadn't ever been before. "I'm better than okay. I'm in love."

I waited with baited breath as he froze, and the part of me that always doubted myself was afraid I'd just ruined everything. But it wasn't long before his smile broke free, the biggest one he'd ever shown me. I laughed as a dimple popped on one cheek, knowing I'd do anything I could to make sure I saw it as often as possible in the future.

"Well, that's damn good news, Blondie. Because I love you, too."

With that, he leaned down and pressed his lips to mine, wrapping his arms around me and hauling me against him tightly. My feet left the ground as I clung to him, feeling as if I might burst with joy. All my worry and sorrow melted away as I felt my heart pound in triumph.

The crowd that had gathered around us started to clap, and I threw my head back with a laugh, having forgotten for the second time that they were even there. All I saw, all I felt, was Stone. His arms around me, his lips on my neck, and his heart beating wildly against mine.

This was perfection. And I never wanted it to end.

"Now, how 'bout you go grab some shoes and get back out here?"

"Where are we going?" I asked, giddy at the prospect of doing anything, as long as it was with him.

"Well, later tonight, we have a flight to catch."

"We do?"

"Of course we do. You have a hotel to market, and there are only ten days left until your Soft Launch. I'm sure you have a ton of work to do."

My mouth dropped wide open. "Holy smokes! I do! I have so many things to finish. Oh, man. I just left everyone hanging. I have to get in touch with the vendors and check on the guest performers for the evening. I was expecting to meet with the videographer last week. And I missed the appointment with the printing company, so I'll have to-"

"Breathe, Blondie. Just breathe. Moira has been handling everything. She managed your calendar and spreadsheets just like you planned. The whole thing is still on schedule."

I exhaled in relief. "That's amazing. Oh, man. You are gonna have to give that woman a raise."

"So she's been telling me," he grumbled, rolling his eyes. "Now, come on. Get your shoes. We don't have all night."

"What are we doing?"

"Penelope," he looked at me, shaking his head from side to side. "What kind of cowboy would I be if I didn't take the girl and ride off into the sunset?"

This man.

I threw my arms around his neck, crushing him to me once more. "I do love you, Stone Pennington."

"Glad to hear it, Blondie." He squeezed me once more, then spun me toward the house and swatted my butt. "Now, get. These fine officers have work to do."

As I returned to the sidewalk, shoes and hoodie firmly in place, I waved at the officers I knew. "How did you manage to arrange all this anyway?" I asked as we stood next to the horse Stone had ridden, a beautiful bay with a gorgeous black mane and tail.

"It pays to have a dad who knows everyone in town," he said with a wink.

I looked at him in shock. "Dad? Not just Harold."

Stone looked at his father, laughing and chatting with some of the police officers near him, and the love that shone in his eyes made me so happy. "Yeah," he said quietly. "My dad."

I squeezed his hand, conveying all my pride and love for him into that touch. "Seems like a few things have changed for you this week."

Stone slung his arm around my shoulders, drawing me into him, and I breathed in his scent, the spicy cologne that I had missed so much while we were apart. "Penelope," he said quietly, his lips pressed to the top of my head. "Everything has changed. Absolutely everything. And I'll tell you all about it. But first," he stepped away from me, placed his foot in the stirrup and mounted the horse like it was his job. I grinned as he reached for me.

"I don't' know if I can do it without Smitty's stairs, Cowboy."

"Sure you can. Just put your foot in the stirrup and hold on to me."

I did as he instructed, and was soon snuggled against his warm broad back, my arms wrapped around his waist as he sat astride the horse, when I had a sudden thought

"Stone? What's this horse's name?"

Stone laughed out loud. "Penelope, you're not gonna believe it when I tell you."

"What?"

"This horse's name is Crockett."

I was stunned. "You're joking!"

"I am not. When I saw it on the stall, I knew he was the one I had to ride today."

It was serendipitous, to be sure, because John Wayne had played Davy Crockett in the movie *The Alamo*.

And if that wasn't an appropriate horse for us to be riding, then I didn't know what was.

I turned my head to see my mother smiling at me as tears slipped down her face. I waved as she blew me a kiss.

When everyone was mounted again, the police

cars bleeped their sirens one more time and then Stone coaxed our horse into motion and I held on to the man I loved as he turned us west into the setting sun.

CHAPTER TWENTY-FOUR
Stone

The casino floor was buzzing, the sound of happy chatter a low rumble that hung over the louder noises of slot machines and roulette tables. I stood near the bar, a glass of bourbon in my hand, and surveyed the room, that feeling of pride swelling in my chest again as I did.

The Alamo was incredible and I loved every square inch of it. From the rounded cream-colored corners of the external façade, to the wooden finish on the bar tops and the tin lantern style lights that hung throughout the cavernous space, I felt like my heart and soul were in every aspect of this hotel. It spoke to me on a visceral level, breathing life into me as I wandered the halls, drinking it in.

The sound of laughter drew my attention, laughter that I was very familiar with. I turned my head to see Penelope looking incredible in a floor-length black gown, her hair falling in golden waves down her back, the daringly high slit in the side of the dress parting as she moved to reveal her sexy pink high heels.

As if she could feel my stare, Penelope turned my way, a slow smile spreading across her face as she took me in, uncomfortable as fuck in my tuxedo, but playing my role for the evening. With the amount of press and celebrities here, it was important that all the Pennington staff looked the part, even, and maybe most especially, me.

Earlier today, Harold had held a press conference officially announcing me as the new CEO of Pennington Hotels, and the subsequent media frenzy had left me exhausted. I was glad for the quiet time with my bourbon. In all my wildest dreams, I couldn't have imagined ever ending up here; it all just seemed so surreal. Standing in a hotel that I had a hand in launching, practically from the ground up, as the CEO of my father's company was completely surreal. Hell, even just being on cordial terms with my father would have been beyond belief as little as six months ago.

But so much had changed, and it all came down to that bombshell in the pink heels. Penelope had opened my eyes to so many things, and I could never thank her enough for it. She had shown me that it was okay for people to make mistakes, okay to forgive them, and that vulnerability is not necessarily a bad thing. Because being vulnerable to Penelope? Opening my heart and letting her in, even knowing the wreckage she'd leave behind if she left? That was worth every ounce of risk. Just to get to hold her, to spend my days in her presence and my nights in her arms, made all the rest bearable.

Penelope was light and goodness and laughter

and all the things I was missing in my life due to my own stubborn pride.

And, God, how I loved her for it.

I was drawn from my mushy thoughts, and from admiring Penelope's incredible legs in that dress, when Harold approached me, his own tuxedo looking sharp and with a sparkle in his eye I hadn't seen before. The man looked happy. I guess the prospect of retirement after over fifty years of hard work would make anyone happy.

"Stone, my boy. Great work earlier. The vultures sure did love you. Those camera jockeys were eating up your pretty face, weren't they? I bet they're glad to see the backside of this old man, don't you think?"

I smiled into my glass, shaking my head. "Oh, I'm sure they'll be sick of me in no time. After all, a pretty face, maybe, but a pretty personality? Not a chance." Penelope may have softened me in some aspects of my life, but I was still the same grouchy asshole in others, in business most of all. I was determined to continue my father's legacy in a way that would make him proud, and I couldn't do that by being a pushover.

"Just remember, son. You catch more flies with honey, yes? It's a balance. You can be the smiling face they want to see, but don't ever let them forget that that smile belongs to a shark."

There was the fiery businessman that had built a billion-dollar empire; I could learn a lot from him. I felt a pang of sadness in my chest as I realized all the time I had missed with my unnecessary obstinance. All the wasted years I could never get back.

As if he could sense my thoughts, my dad turned serious. "Hey," he said, drawing my gaze to his eyes, so like my own. "None of that. We're here now. That's all that matters."

I nodded, not trusting myself to speak. I could only move forward, and that's exactly what I intended to do.

Harold and I stood in silence for a while, just watching the party flow around us. Occasionally, someone would approach us, talking about the leadership change, the hotel, or some other aspect of the event that they felt was important enough to discuss. I had to give it to them, the food was outstanding, and I would have to remember to thank Geoff Yates and his team in my speech later. Christ. I hated public speaking, but that was just one more thing I was going to have to work through. Because I wanted this. I wanted to succeed at this, and I hadn't even known it until it was offered to me.

I spied Gideon Langford across the casino, his shrewd eyes watching every move people made when they sat at his tables. The former FBI agent was intimidating as hell, but there wasn't a better man around for reading people, and Gideon could spot a liar or a con artist from a mile away. He tried to explain it to me once, something about micro expressions versus macro expressions. I didn't follow, but I knew that there was no one on the planet more suited to be the Pit Boss of *The Alamo*. As they said, the house always wins. And with Gideon in charge of the casino floor, I knew that would always be true.

Casting my glance around again, I saw that Penelope was now standing on the far side of the room laughing with Dolly and Carson Young. The show had been the astounding success that we knew it would be, and *The Queens of The Alamo* was already splayed across the internet as a must-see Las Vegas attraction. That was all down to Penelope. I was so proud of her. She had such drive and ambition, such a keen sense of the business and the market, not to mention she ruled on social media, as well. She was a total asset to the company, and I was thrilled she was my Vice President of Marketing.

As I watched her interacting with her peers and coworkers, I noticed Carson darting his eyes to Dolly repeatedly, following every move she made as she worked the crowd like the entertainment professional she was. No matter where she went or who she was interacting with, Carson was at her side, a silent shadow that couldn't seem to take his eyes off of her.

It wasn't until I saw her return one of his looks that it clicked for me.

Interesting. Good for them.

Penelope excused herself from the conversation, gliding across the floor as she made her way to where I stood with my dad. She smiled slyly as she approached. "Gentlemen, how are you enjoying the event?"

"It's spectacular, Penelope," Harold gushed before I could even respond. I did, however, slide my arm around her, drawing her to me as I trailed my fingers over the exposed skin at the low back of her dress. I smirked when I felt her shiver at my touch and she leaned farther into my chest. "I could not have asked for a more wonderful party."

Penelope blushed at his praise. "Thank you, Mr. Pennington."

"Harold, please."

Her blush deepened. "Harold." She turned and looked at her success. "I can't believe how many famous people are here. I mean, it's like the freaking Oscars or something!" She was giddy, but trying desperately to hide it. I could relate to her excitement, though. Harold may have been used to fancy red carpet events, but it was all new territory for Penelope and me. And as I saw the star from the latest Hollywood action blockbuster slide up to the bar next to the hottest female singer in country music and make small talk, it occurred to me again just how different my life was going to be from here on out. Growing up in Austin, I had spent time around musicians, but nothing of this scale. It was a little overwhelming if I stopped to think about it.

So I tried not to.

"So, tell me, Penelope," Harold went on, as if two of the most famous faces in the world weren't sipping gin and tonics not ten feet away. "How did you enjoy your time in Las Vegas?"

Penelope smiled. "Well, it was eventful, that's for sure." She tossed me a cheeky wink that had me chuckling, then she went on. "But, honestly? I love this town. I didn't think I would, but I do. I love everything about it. It's so vibrant and alive, busy, but in a completely different way than in New York. There is a pulse to this city, a heartbeat all its own." She sighed, her eyes going glassy as she spoke of the town we both fell in love with.

Fell in love in.

Blinking away the wetness that was gathering on her lashes, she smiled broadly at my dad. "I'm really going to miss it."

Harold looked to me and I nodded. We had discussed this at length and I wanted him to present it to her, see how receptive she would be. "What if I told you that you didn't have to miss it?"

Penelope frowned gently, the little furrow appearing between her eyebrows. "What do you mean?" She looked to me, but I just smiled.

"I'm talking about big changes for Pennington Hotels, Penelope. I'm talking about relocating our executive offices to Nevada." Penelope gasped, her mouth dropping open in shock.

"Are you serious?" she questioned, her eyes widening as the spark of hope appeared there.

"Absolutely I am." Harold looked around the casino again, taking it all in. "This casino was my dream. My passion project, if you will. Where else but in Las Vegas can you let your childhood fantasies become a reality?" We all nodded, watching as the servers dressed as old west saloon girls wandered between the tables, their fishnet stockings and tight corsets marking them as part of the team. There were themed rooms and wagon wheels, old photographs and historical items everywhere we looked. "For a little boy who wanted to be a cowboy when he grew up, this was my chance to make it happen.

"It also happens to be something very close to my son's heart as well. When we started construction, I had the business center built big enough to accommodate the executive offices if that was the direction I decided to go. Before I knew Stone would be willing to take over as CEO, I had intended to move here myself. I'm getting far too old for those New York winters."

We all laughed at that. No one liked January in New York. No one.

"But now, I think that this might be the right place for you and Stone, for a lot of reasons. The first being that you already have an excellent team established here. And now the disaster that is the Atlantic City project will require a delay and a marketing overhaul." He grimaced at the thought of the mess Toddrick had left behind. Constance hadn't spoken to any of her family since that day, but I had a feeling she was not just going to let sleeping dogs lie. "We are going to need our best people on that, and you, my dear, are our best."

"Thank you, sir. I mean, thank you Harold. I won't let you down."

I turned to her, looking into her beautiful blue eyes, so expressive and open. "Penelope, I know before I talked about Texas, and I made decisions about us without discussing it with you, not giving you the opportunity to make your own choices. So, with that in mind, I'm asking you now." Her quickly drawn breath was the only hint at her shock. "Penelope Lund, would you like to move to Las Vegas and run a hotel empire with me?"

Her laughter rang out around the room, drawing looks from the people nearest to us, including Mr. Hollywood at the bar, who ran his eyes over her in a way that had me scowling at him when Penelope couldn't see. He raised his hands and turned back around, smiling like the smarmy ass he probably was.

Drawing my attention back to Penelope, I saw her nodding furiously, her smile brighter than the desert sunshine. "Yes," she gasped, throwing her arms around my neck, squeezing me tight. I never wanted her to let go. "Yes, I most certainly will. Thank you!"

She released me, much to my displeasure, and turned to Harold. "And thank you, so much. This opportunity is just beyond anything I could have imagined."

"Well, you certainly deserve it," he replied, draining the last of his glass and setting it on the bar behind him. "Both of you. Truly. Now, if you'll excuse me, it's time for one last time around the gauntlet. This may well be my last opportunity to schmooze with these fancy folks. After this, it's all on you, son." He laughed at my groan, slapping me on the back as he walked away.

Penelope wrapped her arm around my waist, snuggling in against my chest, and I couldn't help the smile that appeared on my face. I loved that we had gotten to this place, that she was comfortable enough to just stand here like this, wrapped around me, and just be. It was important to her that she wasn't judged for our relationship, and I completely agreed. For the most part, people had been very receptive, not caring one bit that we were an official couple. I did still catch the occasional dirty look from Toby, but we'd had a chat about that and I didn't think he would be a problem anymore.

At least he'd better not be.

"I can't believe this is real," Penelope breathed, and I squeezed her close.

"Believe it, Blondie. It's you and me against the world now." I placed my finger under her chin, drawing her eyes to mine. "Forever."

Her lips parted at the implication of my words, but instead of looking panicked, as she might have, her pupils expanded and she smiled wide again, showing me her perfect teeth and that gorgeous lip she liked to chew on. "You bet your ass it is, Cowboy."

Taking her hand, I led her as we made our own circuit around the party, stopping at all the tables and glad-handing as many people as I could. Ava Carlisle was looking fierce and predatory in a blood red dress that didn't hide a single thing, her long black hair pulled tightly back from her face. She introduced us to her highest of high rollers, a group of Japanese business men who could not say enough about our *Queens of the Alamo.* God love Japan.

"I can't believe the entertainment line up," Penelope whispered as another famous band made their way past us from one gaming table to the next. I watched as the lead singer settled at a blackjack table, while the other band members were a bit more interested in the women scattered around the place. "The entire first year is a different band every month. That arena space is gonna be packed every night."

"That's the idea. I have to admit, Carson lining up twelve different acts in the first year was a miracle. Most places struggle to convince one big name to commit at all."

"I think it was the short-term contracts that did it. Everyone could come down and have fun, without having to give up other things, like tours or recording time. Carson is a genius."

"He is," I agreed. "But I'm working on something for next year that I think will be a perfect fit."

"Oh?"

"Yeah. Do you know The Gun Show?"

"Know them?" she exclaimed, her eyes going huge. "I freaking love them! God, their last album was a masterpiece. Lyrics that would break your heart. Wait." She turned and stepped in front of me, halting our movement with a palm on my chest. "Stone, are you telling me you have The Gun Show lined up for *The Alamo*'s arena?"

"Hey, now," I admonished, looking around to see if anyone had over heard. "I *may* have The Gun Show lined up. May have, Blondie. Don't get your autograph book out just yet."

"Stone, if you only knew! I tried to get tickets

last time they played Madison Square Garden, but the price was way outside my price range. Hang on," she said, her brain finally catching up the fangirl raging around inside her head. "Isn't the lead singer in rehab?"

I grimaced. "Yeah," I said. "Rem's a good guy. He's just been through some serious shit in his life. The last two or three years were really hard on him. I've talked to him a few times since he went in, and-"

"Holy shit!" her mouth gaped open and she pressed her hand to her own chest now. "Wait just a minute. Are you seriously telling me you know Remington Ford? Like, *the* Remington Ford? Lead singer of the hottest country rock band on the freaking planet?"

"Yes," I said cautiously. "We used to hang back when I frequented Dirty Sixth." I had known Remington since he was just a snot-nosed kid with a busted guitar and a leather jacket. But, damn, did that boy have talent. Life sure kicked him in the ass, though. I was hopeful that a steady gig at *The Alamo*, and maybe my steady presence, could help him get back to the life he deserved. Because that guy deserved the world.

"Oh, my God, Stone! You have to introduce me. Please. Oh, please." She looked like she was about to pass out.

"Well, I'm not sure I want to now. You might run away with him. Don't girls have a thing for bad boy rock stars?"

She laughed, linking her arm with mine as we started walking again. "Not this girl. I'm more of a grumpy cowboy fan, myself."

As we moved from the casino and out to the pool area, the place looking spectacular, all lit up against the darkness with decorative lighting, Penelope and I found ourselves wandering hand in hand back to the corral. We hadn't been on horseback since that day in New York; there had just been way too much to do, but I planned on getting her out to the ranch again real soon. The Grand Opening was four weeks away; I was sure we could fit in a ride or two somewhere along the way.

Penelope leaned her elbows back against the fence rail, tipping her head up to look at the sky. The lights of the city took away some of the stars we had grown used to seeing in the desert sky, but I knew it was still an impressive sight. I, however, couldn't take my eyes off her. Out here, we were alone, away from the crowds of the party, and the glow of the garden lights made her creamy skin shine like gold. Unable to help myself, I reached for her, leaning down and running my mouth over the delicate curve of her throat, feeling her pulse increase against my lips. After a few tender kisses I pulled back to look at her, taking in her flushed cheeks and parted lips. I'd have given anything to be able to have her, here and now, but I knew that was not the right move, for either of us.

Didn't stop me from thinking about it, though. Adjusting the tent that was forming in my pants, I backed off, hoping a bit of distance would make me presentable enough to re-enter the party soon. I didn't stop touching her, though. I couldn't, and so I kept one arm around her back, running my fingers over her neck and shoulders in a wispy pattern.

"Are you certain you're okay with this, Blondie?" I asked, wanting to be absolutely sure this was her decision. "I know how much New York means to you."

Penelope smiled at me, her gaze so full of love it completely blew me away. The fact that this woman, this sweet, kind, hardworking woman, felt that way about me was beyond comprehension. There was no way I was ever letting her go.

"Stone," she said, her voice low in the dark. "Those days we spent apart, when I didn't know if I would ever even talk to you again, they were the loneliest days of my life. I was home, in the city I grew up in, with my mom by my side, but I had never felt more alone." Penelope leaned against me, pressing her full body against mine, her head on my chest, as if she could hear my heart calling for her. "The only place I want to be, Stone, is wherever you are."

My heart took off at a gallop, racing toward a future with Penelope that I could never have even imagined for myself, but one that I was looking forward to starting right this minute.

"I love you, Blondie. So much." I placed a chaste kiss to her full lips, savoring her taste.

"I love you, too, Cowboy," she replied, threading our fingers together as she drew me back to the party. "Forever."

Epilogue
Stone

Eighteen Months Later

The evening sun was still hot, making the suit feel like an oven as I stood there trying not to panic. There were more flowers than I'd ever seen in one place, the deck of the pool at *The Alamo* looking more like a tropical garden than the desert oasis it was designed as, but it was what Penelope wanted. There was no way I was gonna tell her no.

I looked around the pool deck, cleared out and emptied for the day's big event, my eye never really able to turn work off as I scanned the hotel grounds for things that may need attending to. There was nothing, of course. We ran a tight ship with a great team. I still kept my eyes open whenever I was on site, which wasn't as often as I'd like these days.

Being CEO was great, more fulfilling than I could have ever thought. But I sure did travel a lot. When my dad had suggested moving the base of operations here to Las Vegas, I thought it would be the perfect way to be able to spend time with Penelope in a location we both didn't hate.

When he then suggested we take over the Summerlin house together, I was elated. Penelope was not.

According to her, she didn't want to just jump into living together. She was worried that it would put a strain on our new relationship. When I pointed out that we had lived together for months, strain and all, and still ended up falling in love, she gave a little. She moved in with me, but insisted she keep her stuff in the guest room like she had before, saying she wanted to 'maintain some boundaries'.

That lasted all of two nights. Then I hauled her into my bed and kept her there, where I made her make those sexy noises that I loved so much, until she relented.

Was it bad of me to use sex as a weapon to get what I wanted? Maybe.

Did I care? Not one bit.

That woman was mine, and there was no way even something as simple as a hallway was ever gonna be between us again.

Unfortunately, life didn't always work out the way you planned. I had to travel so much in the first several months of my new appointment as CEO that it seemed like I was hardly in Las Vegas at all. I'd hired an operations manager for *The Alamo*, a woman named Alexis Vaughn, who was doing great work, but I sure missed this place when I was gone, and was always glad to be back in Sin City.

Back home.

Casting my gaze around the pool area again, I noticed that there were only a few dozen people there, which was more than I would have liked, but the choice wasn't mine alone to make. The white chairs were laid out in neat rows, with the aisle in the middle, and the back of each chair was tied with some sort of gauzy navy-blue fabric. I wasn't really sure what it was called; all I knew was Penelope and Daphne gushed over magazines and websites for months, choosing colors and flowers and dresses. There was a lot of laughing and a lot of wine and I loved listening to them as they tossed out words like 'tablescape' and 'décolletage' and I just left them to it. The happiness and sheer joy that Penelope often exuded was still something I wasn't used to, something I cherished every day. I never wanted to take her laughter for granted.

Music started playing softly, and I turned, seeing my friend Remington Ford sitting off to the side, one knee propped up on the rungs of his stool as he strummed his acoustic guitar. I caught his eye and gave him a head nod. He tipped his chin up at me then returned his focus to his playing, something soft and instrumental that he wrote just for today. Penelope cried when he told her he was doing it. Over the last six months, they'd gotten close. Not in a way that I was concerned about, but in a way that Rem really needed. The kid was so starved for family, he had become like a little brother to us both, and we loved watching him grow.

As I made my way to the make-shift alter that had been assembled next to the pool, Silas stepped up and took his place beside me, his face revealing nothing, but

I knew this was going to be hard on him. This would be the first time he laid eyes on Daphne since she moved back to New York. Neither of them will discuss the other, and that alone tells me that they aren't quite finished yet, but I had more than learned my lesson about meddling. Those two needed to figure it out on their own.

My attention was drawn to the end of the aisle, where my baby sister appeared, standing in a beautiful navy-blue dress, holding a bright bouquet of flowers with a huge smile on her face. They told me the dress was 'tea length' but hell if I knew what that meant. All I knew was she looked beautiful and I hoped she knew it.

As she began to move toward the front of the aisle, I chanced a glance at Silas. If I didn't know him so well, I'd have never seen it, but the longing in his eyes kind of broke my heart.

Daphne neared the end of the aisle, but paused and leaned down to press a kiss to Harold's cheek where he sat in the front row. I smiled, noticing he was wearing the gift I had given him last night. That damned Lorne Green *Bonanza* vest. He loved the thing, and seeing the camel colored leather peeking out from under his suit jacket made me proud that I had managed to find it for him.

Seated next to Harold was my mother, Eleanor, holding his hand as she beamed a smile my way.

When Harold had said he was tired of New York winters, I expected him to join us in Las Vegas. But he declined, instead taking himself back to Austin, and he hadn't left since.

I guessed it was true what they said; it was never too late.

My attention was stolen from my parents when the guests, the people who were here today out of love for Penelope and me, all stood to attention, their heads turning to the far end of the aisle.

My throat was dry, my chest tight, as I stood there waiting for her. Waiting for the moment that I got to say before all our friends and family how much she meant to me. How much I adored her, and cherished her, and would never, ever let her go.

My heart raced as I waited, but when Penelope rounded the corner, it stopped all together.

She was so damn beautiful it hurt.

Her dress was gorgeous; made out of a shiny material, it fell over her body like a champagne waterfall, hugging every last curve. It draped in the front, hinting at her fabulous cleavage, then flowed down around her to puddle on the ground at her feet, making it look like she was gliding when she walked. In her hands she was carrying a huge bouquet made of white and navy flowers, though for the life of me, I couldn't tell you which ones.

Because I couldn't seem to take my eyes off of her face. Her smile was wide, her cheeks pink, and her eyes sparkled as she looked at me with all the love I felt for her. Everything we had been through, everything we had overcome in the last two years, had all been leading to this.

We were going to tie ourselves together so that no

matter what, we would always have the other to lean on. To always be there for each other, like they say, in good times and in bad.

And I was all in.

Her walk down the aisle took far too long while also somehow taking no time at all, and all too soon she was standing there, ready to cross over to the alter to stand by my side.

At last, after all the times I had to watch her walk away, she was finally walking toward me.

Penelope paused, smiling at me like she had a secret, and I raised one eyebrow at her. I heard Daphne let out a quiet giggle behind me and I knew this was something Penelope had cooked up just for me.

While I watched her closely, she winked at me as she released one hand from her bouquet, reaching down to grasp her dress near her knees. I watched, transfixed, as she slowly, so slowly drew the glossy fabric up from the floor. Suddenly, Penelope cocked one hip and darted her foot out to the front.

Showing off a brand-new pair of hot pink cowboy boots. I tossed my head back and laughed, my heart so light I felt like I could fly away.

Oh, yeah. This woman was mine for sure.

THE END

Acknowledgements

They say it takes a village, and I think that applies to all things in life.

Along every step of this journey, I had people with me, encouraging me and guiding me, and sometimes holding my hand. I didn't realize how needy I could be until it came down to the wire, so thanks for sticking it out. I want to promise the next one will come with less emotional baggage, but I wouldn't want to lie.

With that in mind, there are some people that I need to thank for helping me get through this, because I absolutely could not have done it alone.

Eve R. Hart, you are a gem and a guardian angel all in one. I could not have completed this to the standard that I did if it weren't for your patience. You popped my author cherry, girl! I adore you forever, and I am your biggest fan.

Jessica Gadziala, you are an inspiration. Watching you work and grow and handle everything that this Indie life throws at you has shown me that it can be done with grace. You are what I strive to be. Your kindness shines right from your beautiful soul.

Emily Emery, my friend, my bestie, my sounding board, and sometimes therapist. Where would I be without you? I love you forever, girl.

My husband, Steve, who offered support, even when he maybe didn't want to. I could not have asked for a better man to stand with me. I promise you, Celeste is coming.

My boy, Grayson, who endured all my computer time and still loved me after everything, even if dinner was late.

Mom and Dad, thank you for supporting me through everything, always, no matter what.

The Girls Club for cheering me on from the sidelines. You ladies are divine and I appreciate all you do.

My Sister Wives. I just can't express how lucky I was to find you two ladies. My life was made better because of one random Mardi Gras encounter, and I cannot wait for our next ride!

Shawn and Sandy, your adorable love made this book possible. Hold on to her tight, Cowboy.

And lastly, to the Inner Circle. You guys know who you are, and what you mean to me. First In, Last Out.

Thanks, everyone.

DCK

About The Author

Dove Cavanaugh King is a long-time reader who devours books like they are oxygen.

She will ready anything - *literally anything* - as long as the snark is strong and the sex is hot.

Her first reading love was fantasy novels, the kind with dragons and mages and lots of swords.

Reading romance is a recent switch, but once she caught the bug she never looked back.

The sexy biker books were hard to shake.

When not doing all things book related, she likes to watch disaster movies, the more far-fetched the better (I'm looking at you, San Andreas). Star Wars and musicals and Dancing with the Stars are what fill in the gaps.

Oh, and sometimes she goes outside.

Dove currently lives on the west coast of Canada with her husband and son and one elderly dog.

Socials

Come hang out with us on Facebook...we have all the memes!

www.facebook.com/DoveCavanaughKingAuthor

Other Works

Stay tuned for these upcoming titles

The Opposites Attract Series

Book One - The Cowboy and The Bombshell

Book Two - The Soldier and The Princess

Book Three - The Pit Boss and The Card Shark

The Gun Show

Rock Star Series

The War Dogs

MC Series

Made in the USA
Columbia, SC
01 July 2020

12777145R00214